REA

ACPL ITEM
DISCARDED

cherries in the snow

MAR 1 1 2005

P9-DTL-570

ALSO BY EMMA FORREST

Namedropper
Thin Skin

MAR 1 1 2005

cherries
in the
snow

A NOVEL OF

LUST,

LOVE,

LOSS, AND

LIPSTICK

emma forrest

 THREE RIVERS PRESS • NEW YORK

Copyright © 2005 by Emma Forrest

This is a work of fiction. Names, characters, places, and incidents
either are the product of the author's imagination or are used
fictitiously. Any resemblance to actual persons, living or dead, events,
or locales is entirely coincidental.

All rights reserved.

Published in the United States by Three Rivers Press, an imprint
of the Crown Publishing Group, a division of Random House, Inc., New York.
www.crownpublishing.com

THREE RIVERS PRESS and the Tugboat design are registered trademarks of
Random House, Inc.

Library of Congress Cataloging-in-Publication Data
Forrest, Emma.
    Cherries in the snow : a novel of lust, love, loss, and lipstick /
Emma Forrest.—1st ed.
        p. cm.
    1. Cosmetics industry—Fiction. 2. Loss (Psychology)—Fiction. 3. Female
friendship—Fiction. 4. Lipstick—Fiction. I. Title.
    PR6056.O6836C48 2005
    823'.914—dc22
2004018180

ISBN 1-4000-5365-X

Printed in the United States of America

Design by Debbie Glasserman

10 9 8 7 6 5 4 3 2 1

First Edition

for barbara and amy

Acknowledgments

Many thanks to Carrie Thornton at Crown and Chiki Sarkar at Bloomsbury; to my longtime friend and London agent, Felicity Rubinstein, and to my New York agent and new friend, Emma Parry; to Elinor Burns at Casarotto Ramsey, who read this book at least fifty times; and to Lisa Forrest, who read it forty-eight.

Special thanks to Bonnie Thornton and Suzette Pilgrim for allowing me to poke around their psychological makeup bags, to Sarah Jones and Steve Colman for their Sunday-night wisdom, and to Jennifer Belle, in whose writing workshop this novel was born. I owe so much of the good cheer in these pages to Perry and Junior, Dr. Shannon O'Kelly, Cliff Curtis, Nikkie Eager, Sassica Francis-Bruce, Jeffreys "F" and "R," and the one-and-only, incredible Judy. Without Sarah Bennett and her techie genius, the manuscript would have been lost forever.

Late in the year, the New York chapter of the National Organization for Women (NOW) instigates a letter and phone call appeal demanding that he stop referring to women as "little girls" in his music. A spokeswoman in Springsteen's office defends his use of "little girl," calling it a "rock and roll term." She is quoted in Rolling Stone *magazine as saying that no calls or letters had been received, except from NOW members wishing to disassociate themselves from the project.*

—JIM CULLEN, *Born in the USA: Bruce Springsteen and the American Tradition*

Contents

cherries in the snow

1 DUTCH COURAGE

WHEN I COME INTO the office, Holly is clutching the morning paper, pointing to a headline and leaping up and down. This being a dream, they are real leaps that hold her midair as if she has a propeller attached to her raspberry beret. "Have you seen the paper? They voted you number one!" I look at the paper, which is pink, a few shades lighter than her hat—puce, let's say—and though I can remember no such periodical, there is a nice picture of me, a little too pouty, at the top of the page. "The top one hundred," screams Ivy, materializing beside her lover at the conference table. "They voted you number one!" She is bouncing up and down with excitement, her gargantuan breasts spanking her double chins in slow motion. "Oh, my God!" squeals Vicki. "Oh, my God," I squeal back, although I am pretty sure the doe-eyed farm girl and I are talking about different Gods. I am at number one. "The top one hundred under thirty"—and then I read the rest of the sentence: "worst writers in the world."

I wake to see that the light on my Apple laptop is blinking

saucily at me like "Yeah, baby, you were great last night." Ugh. I regret it, that chapter I pounded out after dinner, two glasses of merlot to the wind, banging the keyboard without mercy. Go away, Apple laptop, your plastic curves don't look so hot in the morning light. There is lipstick smeared across my cheek. I always put on a bright red mouth before I sit down to write. It gives me a kind of Dutch courage.

Before brushing my teeth, my usual habit is to check for e-mail from my father. Today I delete the chapter, shove the computer into my messenger bag, wash my face, and head for work. I take the bus—the better to think straight. I am on deadline to come up with the names for the Grrrl cosmetics summer line. This is my job. I am good at it. The fact that I am good at it makes me nervous. I have a little test tube of sparkling blue-black eye powder in my purse that I keep spilling everywhere. "Dark Night of the Soul," I scribble in my little green notepad. "Demonlover." It's procrastination, this makeup naming. I am supposed to be writing my great novel. There is no deadline. There is no great novel, not even an average one. Just one deleted chapter after another, and that's when I actually get something on the page. No one knows about it except Isaac and he's long gone.

Naming the makeup at Grrrl is the first job I've been good at. I was a lazy librarian. A slothful gym receptionist. A really lousy salesgirl. I lasted a week at my favorite shoe store and now I can't go back. Feet are transfixingly ugly. The wealthier the person, and therefore the more likely I was to get a good commission, the uglier her feet. I couldn't do it.

No one is reading the paper when I get to work. Vicki has an issue of *Allure* on her desk. Ivy is eating a bagel with cream cheese and jelly. Holly is painting herself a fifties' eye in gunmetal gray with a long angled brush.

"When I was a little girl," says Holly, "I would take my

mother's blusher brush"—and right there you might think she's about to reminisce in *Anne of Green Gables* tones about her golden childhood—"I would take my mother's blusher brush and shove it up my ass." She pauses. "No," she says delicately, "not shove. I would insert it in my ass."

I was about to eat the fruit I'd bought at the corner stand for breakfast, a mango—or is it a papaya? Instead I put it back in its brown paper bag.

I remember Holly's mother's makeup table, a Chinese dresser dotted with mascaras and lipsticks that the maid would clean with a thin feather duster, leaving the makeup undisturbed like a crime scene. The Avilars' maid was white and around her the family would chat in Spanish. There were a lot of Japanese brands on that dresser, slimmer, more minimalist than my mother's gaudy, chemical-scented pearlescents. Holly's mother once gave me a lipstick she had tired of and I still have it; a Kanebo, a deep browny orange that looked awful on everyone but her and Holly, but I wore it anyway because it had been on her lips and I thought it might make me beautiful too. My mother was jealous of Maria Avilar, because she looked like she was thirty and because Holly related to her as though she was thirty. I certainly don't recall Holly hating Maria, can't think of anything that would cause Holly to so intimately abuse Maria's fox-fur tool of enhancement. Sitting at the other end of the conference table from Holly, Ivy stares at her lover/business partner incredulously.

"I don't know why I'm even bothering to ask, but why on earth did you do that?"

Holly sighs, a breath rippling through her body like the small wave before the big one that pulls you under. "I wanted to keep my options open."

She wants to shock us. She wants to shock, period, and that's why she persuaded Ivy to give her the startup for this makeup company. Grrrl cosmetics: ugly makeup, pollution-skyline bruise colors to combat all the shimmering pinks on the market. Neither my mother's Florida corals nor her mother's minimalist stains. To Holly's surprise Grrrl caught on and now has its own stand at Sephora. Holly's last stand, where the edgy girls gather. Everyone's edgy in New York, so it's always crowded. I stop by after work from time to time to see them graze. Bruise colors make your eyes sparkle: purple brings out brown eyes, green mascara highlights the flecks in hazel, blue makes blue eyes brighter. Eighty dollars later the Grrrl fans tote their collection of bruises encased in shiny silver, pained and pretty at the same time—and soon to be poor—the model New York City single girl.

"So?" says Ivy.

"I would put it in my ass to practice for anal sex, should I ever choose to have anal sex." Holly was always the most pragmatic wild child.

Maria, who had herself married a Cuban banker, prepped her daughter to settle down with a rich guy. Instead Holly settled down with a rich girl: Ivy, British and well bred, has never shoved anything up her ass, although she does look like a shover, being built like a cement truck. It's charming, the glitter she wears on her face, conjuring that brief window in the seventies when men built like hog carriers could be glam metal stars, standing, balding and beefy, on the bass behind David Bowie. Bowie, in his starburst Ziggy Stardust days, is a framed picture on the wall here, alongside Courtney Love, Robert Smith, Siouxsie Sioux, Dolly Parton, Debbie Harry, and Gwen Stefani. The natural look has no place in the Grrrl universe.

Holly ended up at the same school as Ivy when Holly's father's bank transferred him to the London office. I ended up at the same school on an academic scholarship, which I almost immediately proved myself unworthy of by sequestering myself in the girls' locker room with Holly and Ivy and learning how to both apply eyeliner smokily and graffiti the walls with it.

I was unaware until years later that their parents were really, really getting their full money's worth for the tuition when Holly and Ivy departed for boarding school together and I stayed behind, heartbroken, reading Jackie Collins novels, reading about the lives they were leading: the skiing holidays in Klosters, the riding instructors taking their virginity.

I imagined boarding school as a wonderland, teenage girls looked after but left alone, a perfect point of adolescence, like riding a wave. And also, according to Holly, fingering. Hard as I try not to, her boasting can still turn me crimson. But I never turn as red as Vicki.

Our midwestern coworker, Vicki, the PR girl, is like me a foreigner, but from farther away because Missouri is truthfully far farther from New York than London. She grew up a bank teller's daughter, so of course she was destined to end up subordinate to a banker's daughter. She is, at thirty, the oldest of us. She is also the prettiest, with a wide, flat face with a small nose, a strong jaw balanced by enormous eyes that she exaggerates with sixties' baby-doll makeup, little Twiggy lashes painted on underneath the lash line.

"Okay," I tut, "we get it: You have big eyes."

She bats her false lashes. Why is she wasting them on me?

"When I was a kid, I used to put blusher everywhere. I mean on my cheeks, my nose, my forehead, my chin . . . but I ain't never put it up my ass," says Vicki.

She thinks "ain't never" is charming. It ain't. I cut straight to the chase: "Anal sex, Holly? I thought you were gay."

Holly is always referring to herself as a "crazy dago dyke." This is interesting given that she has slept with at least as many men as she has women. I think she just likes the alliteration.

"I didn't know. I don't know."

Fixing Vicki, Ivy snaps, "Why would you want to blush? Who wants to look like they're blushing?"

"You wouldn't understand," says Holly. "Those of us with no shame gots to paint it in."

They are bickering as usual. It's amazing that they have built this company together. The collection is spread out in front of me, but now all I see is Holly spread-eagled.

"None of these lipsticks went up your ass? Can you vouch, Ivy," says Vicki, "that no lipsticks went up her ass?"

Vicki, reading my mind, is nevertheless asking a dumb question. If she knew Holly and Ivy as I know them, she'd see that they haven't been intimate in months. But if she could see that, she'd probably go right ahead and ask anyway. Vicki is an insensitive shit like that. Insensitive Shit, I think, good name for a lipstick. You put it on and it gives you the courage to break up with him. Holly will probably go for it. She's already green-lighted a nipple rouge called Suck My Left One.

Sex is everything to Holly. She talks about it incessantly. Unsexily. I always feel babyish compared to her. I always did. I wanted men, I even wanted her temporarily, but I didn't want to actually have to do anything. I want to be a high-class prostitute who takes off her clothes, then puts them all back on again and leaves without doing anything. So much of our ad campaign is sex driven. No, not sex driven. Fucking driven. Holly is set. Harder, deeper, nastier. That's the ad campaigns. Those are the names she wants me to come up with. The white face powder called Heroin. Ha ha. The lip gloss with a wand at either end called Double Penetration. I didn't feel too good about that one. It came to me and I said it in a conference and I wish I just could have kept my mouth shut because, of course, she loved it. It became our big push for Christmas—

Christmasy, huh?—and that's when we had our ads banned by *In Style.*

Holly was always like that. Some people are just wired that way. And it always made me feel slightly inadequate. I know she has this soft heart, but she has such an amazing front, it just dazzles you. I mean, Holly wore a black sequined cape to her mother's funeral. Between hymns I couldn't stop thinking, Holly is wearing a cape to her mom's funeral. Why is Holly wearing a cape? We never quite got her back. I still treasure my browny orange Kanebo from Holly's mother. One day I will give it to Holly. I have been too afraid to put it on. It sits on my self-assembled little altar in my bedroom over the fireplace I've never used. I light the candles at night, pray, and put on my Piglet. This is by Hard Candy, a lip stain. I wake up looking like I have been biting my lips. It's a meditation before I tuck away all worldly thoughts and climb into my goosedown bed.

"Put on your Piglet."

I look in the mirror and say it again. "Put on your Piglet." It means something, though I'm not quite sure what. My real lip color is long gone, the way other people no longer know their own hair color. I think it was kind of reddish naturally. So now it's just more red.

When I am in a relationship, I don't wear lipstick at all. I hate the smearing, the retouching, the constant throb of phoniness as you surreptitiously check the damage in your compact between kisses. I wear lots of mascara to compensate, different colors so I don't get bored. When I am about to break up with a guy, he has full warning because I start wearing lipstick again. I wear only matte lipstick in the red and pink color range: a good deep hot pink works well, none of that pale pink glisteny goo that makes me think of porn stars and infected vaginas.

Your lips are supposed to make men think of your vaginal lips, inflamed with desire. But the way women plump their mouths now, it looks like their lips are giving birth. Lipstick doesn't have to make your mouth look bigger. It's all about the color and the shape. A graphic pink can be nice, but a World War II landgirl red is my favorite. I've been planning my pitch for a landgirl range. I hate pitching my ideas to my friends, but I have to. Grrrl cosmetics is, for better or worse, a democracy.

Vicki doesn't get it. "World War Two? That's depressing."

I sigh. "That's when lipstick meant something to women. When it was the one luxury item sent by your sweetheart to uphold your spiritual well-being. There are so many little 'necessities' now. The eyebrow gel, the self-tan. But back then, that red lipstick, the seamed stockings . . ."

"I don't like red," says Vicki. "It's too harsh."

I ignore her. I am so used to ignoring her that I am astounded when she introduces me as her friend rather than as her colleague, although she does that only when she's drunk at one of the parties we throw from time to time. Our parties are the stuff of legend, so say the papers; Vicki gets them to say that. "Dahling," she says on the phone, and I want to scream, "They can't see batted lashes over the phone!" "Dahling," she continues, "I'll see if I can get you in, of course I'd love you to be there, but it will be tough," or "No problemo!" And she winks—they can't see you! "It's done. Ciao!"

Our last theme was "The Devil Inside," everyone with devil horns and neat little pinstripe suits. Holly actually had her pantsuit cut so that part of her ass was showing as her prosthetic forked tail popped out. Of course her suit was so expertly tailored that somehow, somehow it passed for class. Ivy stood to the side, then got drunk and danced and sang way too loud until I took her home. I didn't mind getting out of there: too many starlets and lawyers. Truly the red devil theme was rendered redundant by the crowd.

Vicki is the one who's good with the press and marketing, who can chat up the lawyers and starlets just right. Vicki is the one whose picture made the paper the next day, next to Holly's. "The hot girls behind hot Grrrl," said the caption. Yeah, Vicki is the prettiest, no question. But Holly is the most stunning. Five foot three, with eyes flashing amber against her dark skin, she looks like a convenient serving size of Catherine Zeta-Jones, only covered in tattoos. Not covered: her face, neck, and legs are bare; rather, she is dusted with them. The tattoos fall in the right places like an erotic scent. They settle there at the base of her spine, on her shoulders, on her pubic bone.

Holly and Vicki make a cute couple in the photo.

Ivy and I were out of the party and so we were out of the photo. I minded, just a little bit. I had spent a long time on my spangly red corset and on getting my hair the right shade of wash-in wash-out red. It didn't really wash out and I was left with cotton-candy-pink clumps for a month. It looked nice with my red mouth.

"It's so hard," went on Vicki, "a red mouth."

"Not if you know how to do it properly," I tut.

"I meant . . ."

"I know what you meant."

For the record, here's how to do it properly: To start, pick the right shade. Blue-reds make your teeth look whiter, but they also make your skin paler. Browny brick-reds flatter olive and black skin, but bear in mind that the darker your lipstick, the more sparingly you should apply it. My favorites: Earnest by Delux, Cranberry Lemonade by Fresh, Black Honey by Clinique, Cherries in the Snow by Revlon, and, of course, Grrrl's own Literary Lolita. Absolutely avoid lip liner—it never fails to bleed until you're left with a circle and no lipstick. So just use lipstick, but not with a lip brush and certainly, most certainly, not from a tube. You dab it onto your finger, then dab it onto your mouth, blot twice, and do it again. Then you use the lip brush just to get the corners, to get the Cupid's bow exactly right.

When you wear red lipstick, especially red lipstick that's taken ten minutes to apply, you don't want to kiss lest you rub it off. I swear to God, I think I sabotage my relationships because I miss the red mouth so much. Without it, I feel like I am losing me. There are those kiss-proof lipsticks, but they make your mouth feel so dry that you wouldn't want to kiss. They feather around the middle and bleed in the corners. That's what they look like: dried blood. In my goth phase I would have loved those, but they weren't on the market then and I haven't listened to the Cure since I was fifteen.

Ah, Robert Smith, with his black mascara and squiggly red slash. How I loved him. I shake myself from my reverie and resolve to screw the Grrrl democracy and come back to the landgirl line with Holly in private.

Vicki is stretching to stay awake, still flicking through *Allure*. " 'A war rages,' " she reads aloud. " 'Does black mascara make your eyes look smaller or bigger?' "

"Oh," I say with a sigh, "*that* war."

Sometimes I long to be back in college, trapped in an unwinnable discussion about Sartre. I used to lie awake at night and cry because I didn't write "The Raven" by Edgar Allan Poe. Now I catch myself holding back tears because I didn't think of Piglet by Hard Candy. Of course I know the answer, so I raise my hand.

"Here's the deal: With a light touch it makes them bigger, but you can do only one layer. Green and blue are excellent, aubergine too. Avoid brown, a mistake I made for years, which

3 1833 04804 9792

rather than making them look natural, brings out all the red in the whites of your eyes."

"I thought brown mascara was our big push for fall," says Ivy. It's true, I couldn't understand why we were bothering with a brown mascara, but I was thrilled with the name I came up with: Sexy Rabbi. Ivy rolls the tube back and forth in front of her. "Where does that leave us?"

"With a bunch of piggy-eyed followers." Holly snorts.

Holly can be callous about our devoted customers. She thinks they're all crazy to use our jaundicing products. She uses only Nars herself. I excuse myself to go to the bathroom although I don't need to go. I just need to stand in front of the mirror and be alone with my makeup for a few minutes. I reach into my hand-me-down black Gucci bag with its bamboo handle (Holly left it on my doorstep with a note that said "Its life with me is done. Have it if you want.") and pull out my little cotton case, full to bulging with lipsticks way past their sell-by date. You would think that, working with my oldest friends at a cosmetics company, I could apply my lipstick in front of them. But it's like spending the summer at a nudist colony. It makes you long for modesty.

My face is blank and here it comes. The rush of painting it all on. It feels like masturbation. I don't want it to end. Do I think I'm beautiful? No. Do I enjoy my face? Yes. It's the right one for me. It works, like a healthy body. It soothes me when I'm upset. I see my father in my features and I feel better.

Mouth perfect, I blot with tissue paper and drop it into the toilet bowl, watching it float on its back in the water. I leave them everywhere, my lipstick blottings: in my notebooks, on Post-its, all over my receipts. Grrrl makes real blotting papers, but I myself don't use them. They are too much like organized fun.

I walk back into the conference room and Holly is asking:

"What's all this kohl in the drugstores at the moment? Styli Styl. The ones with the flat angled tips? They're so cheap, but, damn, they do a good job. Do you think we could launch a more expensive one that works less well?"

"Favored tool of the ancient Egyptians," says Ivy.

"A return to old-fashioned values." I nod.

"There was a time," adds Ivy, "when women died from wearing makeup. Elizabeth the first got poisoned by her lead-based whitening powder. It ate away at her skin."

"Her makeup ate her face?" I gasp. "That's one of the most romantic things I've ever heard!"

Ivy is very well read. As a teenager she dropped William Blake like the rest of us dropped Ecstasy. Now her facts come bubbling up and Holly looks at them as if they were farts, embarassing to her. She turns her head or walks out of the room to get some fresh air, away from Ivy's knowledge. It is something I love about Ivy. It is something that makes me question how Holly and I can be such good friends. It is something that makes me wonder how Ivy can still be with her.

Vicki sides with Holly, nose wrinkled in the air as though she also smells the fart, as though we are uncouth, not them. I can see that though Vicki is straight as a die—she had a parade of winsome one-night stands; she even does Internet dating, proudly, proudly showing us her listing on Friendster, her holographic friends, her holographic love with graphic designers—she is competitive with Ivy for Holly's affection. But Holly is Queen Bitch, and that's all that matters to her.

None of us really adheres to the Grrrl ethos. We tell our followers to look scuzzy, but we aren't going there. We want to look pretty. We want to be fuckable. We want to get work and be loved. Ivy's glitter, nothing else on, the purple discolorations real; Vicki's Edie Sedgwick look, disaster socialite girl from farm girl; my mouth, everything else smoothing the way for that; and Holly's immaculate makeup, flawless skin, glossy mouth, wide eyes.

"Anything else on the Grrrl agenda? Anything real?" says Ivy.

"Can I raise an issue?" Vicki answers, and she ever so cutely raises her hand. "It's about Sadie's lipstick blottings all over the place. I find them very distracting."

They are *not* everywhere. Yes, they float in the office toilet bowl like love poems thrown from a bridge to the river. If the markings are not perfect, I crumple them up. When they are perfect bows, I let them float. It seems a good omen somehow.

"You find my lipstick blottings distracting?" I look at the hot-pink chairs, the nuclear skyline painted on the wall, the Clash blasting from the surround-sound stereo Ivy blew part of her last trust-fund installment on.

"This is a makeup company," says Holly, jumping to my defense because Vicki will never stop being the new kid. Even though I have been with the company mere months . . .

Holly gathers her notebook and pulls her stiletto-booted feet off the table. The boots go all the way up her legs, stopping at her thighs, just beneath her hot pants. They are ridiculous. A fisherman/hooker. She makes them look great.

"Oh, yeah," she says as she pulls her hair into a clip, "Isaac called."

The hairs on the back of my neck stand up.

"You gonna call him back?" she asks casually.

"Fuck, no!"

But the truth is, I don't know.

"Yes, you are."

I point at the fruit I bought for breakfast. "It depends. Is this a mango or a papaya?"

Holly rolls her eyes. Marine Escort, a Fresh eye powder now

discontinued, flutters from her lashes to her cheekbones. "You eat it all the time. How can you not know the name of your favorite fruit?"

"That isn't good, is it?"

Isaac Isaac Isaac. The man with the biblical name who gave me the twenty-first-century computer on which I cannot write.

2   BORN TO RUN (WATERPROOF)

ISAAC AND I MET in the parking lot at a Springsteen show. I couldn't find my car or my purpose and had intended to ask Springsteen to help me, at least with the latter, but I was seated so far away from the stage, I could barely see the Boss over the Earth's curve. Isaac, being who he is, had the best seat in the house.

"Have you ever been to Elaine's?" asked Isaac, from the backseat of a shared limo into Manhattan, my ears still ringing from Springsteen's third encore. I couldn't remember where I'd left my car and Isaac persuaded me to leave it there and go with him. "Oh, you must have dinner at Elaine's. I'll take you."

What I should have said then, what I realize now, is: If I had wanted to go to Elaine's, I would have already gone. There were any number of middle-aged suitors who would have taken me.

When I met him, I was still working reception at the Crunch gym on Lafayette. Men there tried to pick me up because I was so unworked out, so disinterested in triceps, biceps,

and quads, my soft arms writing down credit-card numbers
and handing out locker keys with a barely disguised sneer. Seeing me amid all those aspiring hard-body actresses was, I guess,
like going to Sweden and seeing an ugly person. Their interest
was captured. But I rarely returned it.

I got off work early the night of the concert and changed
clothes in the ladies' room before making the slog to the stadium. No one would come with me. No one my age gets Bruce
Springsteen. I tried to get my dad to fly over, and he thought
about it—he researched all kinds of Internet deals—but in the
end he was too busy. I bought him a Springsteen key ring from
the souvenir stand and planned to e-mail him a full report as
soon as I got home, but then Isaac got in the way.

Why Isaac? Perhaps the idea of meeting your lover at a
Springsteen concert was simply too intoxicating for me to pass
up. What a story to tell your grandkids. Except Isaac told me
he didn't want children. And though I never said it out loud, I
knew we weren't in love. And that we had no future together.
How could I be so sure? His stomach slapping against me
when we did it. Let's get this straight. It wasn't the weight. It
was the noise. He never fucking shut up, not even in the sack.

Springsteen looks like he only works out onstage, which is
the ideal. When straight men primp, I feel so embarrassed for
them, I lose my erection immediately. Isaac worked out with a
personal trainer twice a week, but he never lost his tummy.
Sweaty against me when we, ugh, made love. Cringe. Really,
really cringe, like origami folded up into a million corners.
C'mon: younger girl, older man. Successful writer shagging a
girl who yearns to be a writer. I could see how it looked, and
how it looked was the truth. There wasn't a whole lot of depth.
I never met his friends. He never met mine. But the other
truth was, I found being with a great writer exciting.

I'd read his column almost every week before I met him. In

the gym, between credit cards and scowls. He's a hell of a writer. I'd look at his unimpressive white dick and think, "Hey, this is a genius penis." And me to him? Well, he was bathing in the blood of a young virgin. No, that makes the relationship sound dramatic, which it really wasn't. He was bathing in the saliva of a young virgin.

I thought about breaking up with him a number of times. But before I did, I had a secret wish that gnawed at me each week. I wanted to be in his writing. To influence it somehow. Just a name check like in a rap song. Big up to Brooklyn! One love to Biggie Smalls! But in Isaac's language, so that one of his sentences began: "In the words of an up-and-coming young writer, Sadie Steinberg . . ." or "To borrow a phrase from my friend Sadie Steinberg . . ." I knew I was being crazy, but there you go, that was my dream.

When he called Al Gore a douche bag live on air, I thought, Well, is there a message in that? By saying "Al Gore is a douche bag," does he actually mean "Sadie Steinberg, you are the smartest"? I didn't love him, but I wanted him to love me. It's hard to find too many secret love signals in an editorial on Iraq, although I tried. I also didn't like sharing attention, not ever, not with children, not with other women, and especially not with the world. It was easier when I was with an actor or a comedian, someone flip, as it didn't matter, their silly world of velvet ropes and borrowed suits. But Isaac's world did matter: the real world, adult as could be, other adults looking to him for guidance, reading his writing for signs. I felt competitive with the world. The worse the state of the world came to, the more dazzling Isaac's columns became, the less time he had for me, the more makeup I wore. The day war broke out I went to my bathroom and put on everything—primer, foundation, blush, brow gel, eyeliner, mascara, gloss—before I called him.

"I'm busy. I'm on deadline."

"I bought a new lipstick."

"Uh . . ." He hung up, the typewriter in the background an affectation I found affecting.

My dad wanted me to be a writer. His mom said he had to be an accountant and, being from a generation of assimilated Jews grateful to be accepted and taught never to rock the boat, that's what he became. She and my grandfather died of cancer and a heart attack, respectively, a few months apart the year my father turned twenty-four. And he was stuck. So he wanted me to be a writer, to be as far from his constricted office life as possible. I wrote great stories when I was a kid, really advanced. And then I just stopped.

I told Isaac all the ideas I had for my novel, or a short-story collection, or a biography of Rasputin, or, somedays, a biography of John Travolta. "It's going to be this and this and this," I said excitedly, literally shaking with anticipation at the blockbuster I was going to write. He'd kiss me and say, "That's a sensational idea! Do you want me to hook you up with my literary agent?" "Uh, well, I haven't written any of it down quite yet," I'd say, trying to distract him by placing myself on his lap. "So do it," he'd say, hugging me close, "and we'll send it over."

Isaac and I did grown-up things together, drank grown-up coffee, had grown-up sex, talked about art and poetry and, of course, politics. He lectured at Ivy League schools. I dropped out of college after two semesters, but I've read two books a week ever since I was five. I waited for him to call and come to see me, but Isaac's a very busy man. He could get away only now and then, and even then it was only for the night and he would catch a 6 A.M. flight back to Washington.

Maybe it was that, like my father, Isaac's a Springsteen fan, for I see Springsteen as a lesson in how to be a good person. You swap your supermodel starter marriage for a Jersey girl, you hang out with the same bunch of friends for thirty years, you subvert the mainstream by becoming an icon of Americana while championing the rights of the workingman. The lovemaking technique of a Springsteen fan should mirror Springsteen's career pattern: introspective, then bombastic, then introspective. Springsteen love should be wild and all-consuming, end-of-the-world-is-nigh passion. But that's not what we had. It wasn't bombastic—Isaac saved the bombast for his television interviews—and it was hardly introspective (although he sometimes cried when he saw the American flag). What we had, what he could give me, was well-choreographed cheerleading.

"You can do it, kid!" "You're so smart. You're brilliant. Just write it down and you'll have a hit novel in no time." "How's my little genius?"

Isaac won't smoke pot, but he does take pills. He says he sometimes has to have them to work through the night. When he's been on a binge, he often looks at the American flag framed above his desk and barks, "Born in the USA!," his fist pumped in the air.

"Okay, first of all"—I sigh—"you were born in Belgium." Damn army brat. "Secondly, are you listening to the same Springsteen I'm listening to? He doesn't love the America you love. He hates it. Do you get it?"

"Don't ask me if I get it. I get it just fine. I've been getting it for decades!"

That escalated into the biggest fight we ever had. I wanted to smash that framed American flag over his big fat head. But I didn't. I went to the bathroom and punched the wall instead. Then I sat on the floor and tried to calm down until I could remember all the good things he'd done for me.

I should tell you at this point that Isaac is a Republican. He says he's an independent. But he's a freaking Republican. And he's Jewish. Jewish and black Republicans: What the hell is that about?

Perhaps being with a right-winger was the only way I could rebel. After all, I grew up with parents who said, "Smoke pot at home so we'll know you're safe." My father, the stoned accountant.

Isaac is an avid skier and it was always a bone of contention that I wouldn't go with him. I have maneuvered my life so that I only ever do things I am good at. It is a small life but a pleasing one. I have only three high school certificates—French, Spanish, and Russian—but all are A's. I walked out of every other exam and locked myself in the toilet or hid in the nurse's office, feigning stomach cramps. I am good at feigning stomach cramps. I never thought of excuses as cowardly get-outs, rather as opportunities to utilize my imagination and experiment with words.

"Jews shouldn't ski," I said, "or ride horses. Cossacks ride horses. And skis are basically thin, wooden horses."

"You're weird," he answered, and went upstate for another weekend without me. He'd come back exhilarated and tan.

"You would have loved it!" he said, but I knew that I wouldn't have. It was only when he intimated it might be time for him to move on that I vowed to ski him right off that mountain despite the fact that not only had I never skied before, the last sport I had done was climbing halfway up the ropes in gym class when I was eleven. If I could triumph on the ski slopes, I could triumph over Isaac too. It was time for him to move on and time for me also, but I just kept seeing myself at age eleven inching farther and farther up that rope, willing the kid me on, seeing myself make it to the top. Forgetting that once you get to the top of the rope, you can only hold on for so long before you have to come down again. Once you are naked, there is nothing left to do but put your clothes back on.

So on my twenty-fourth birthday, we made the drive to Vermont. It hadn't snowed that week, and when we arrived at Killington, the run was icy. Still, Isaac wouldn't let me start on the bunny slopes. He insisted that I was better off throwing myself off the deep end. Midway down the mountain, I sank onto the snow and started to cry.

"I hate this. I hate you."

"Stand up," he said, "you can do it."

"Fuck off!" I shouted as a three-year-old on skis whizzed by. "I hate you," I reiterated, and realized for the first time, the sensation draining from my toes, that it was really true. I had no more love. It had gone off, like milk.

"There's no other way to get home," he said, ignoring my revelation, "except to ski to the bottom."

"Shut up," I answered. That's what I used to say when I was a kid to things I didn't like. I'd take three bites of my carrots, then look at them and shout, "Shut up!" When Dad tried to teach me how to ride a bike, I was so frustrated, I knocked the bike over and spat on it, kicking its training wheels and yelling, "Shut up!"

I thought that being a woman meant knowing how to make love and breakfast. But I wasn't a grown-up. I couldn't be with Isaac. How could I? He was twenty years older than me. How could I ever be a grown-up if I stayed with him? I saw that we might have looked like father and daughter. "I have to get out of here."

Standing shakily, I began to inch my way back up the mountain, tiny sideways pigeon steps. I kept at it for twenty minutes, though I was sweating so hard, I could feel it making its way through the supposedly impenetrable Gore-Tex of my ski suit, the sweat as determined as I to go the wrong way. Just then I was distracted by another whizzing three-year-old, this one zipped into an astonishing pink Barbie snowsuit.

"Wow," I said, forgetting my anger and humiliation, "what a beautiful outfit." I whipped my head around to follow the pink blur down the mountain. In my head I heard "Follow the little girl!" as though she were a moving yellow brick road.

I followed her and I was perfect, as good as she, two elegant free spirits, the only people on the mountain. But near the bottom, somehow, the little girl and I became entangled. She was fine, not a scratch on her resilient little limbs. Not me. I didn't want to admit I was hurt. I held it in all the way back to New York, as though it were pee, as though when I finally got to go it would be worth the wait. Most masochistic thing I've ever done. Isaac played Abba all the way home and I really thought I might die. Last thing you want when you have a broken toe is a bunch of bearded Swedes sharing your space.

"See that girl," trilled Isaac, "watch that scene, digging the dancing queen!"

"Enough!" I screamed.

"Of what?" asked Isaac, alarmed.

Of this pain. Of acting tough. Of this relationship. Half a love, twice a month. Of Swedes with beards.

"Enough of what, baby?"

I stayed silent. He turned up the music. Through gritted teeth, I reached into my purse and applied my Cherries in the Snow. Skin had torn off the sole of my foot. I tilted the rearview mirror my way. I could feel blood wetting my sock.

"Hey, I need that mirror to see where we're going."

I glared at him and he let it go.

I didn't say anything until we got into Manhattan, when I asked to be driven to the hospital and, as we pulled up to the ER, told him that I never wanted to see him again.

3   GET OVER IT

HOLLY CAME TO the hospital armed with lipstick. Seeing me between the white hospital sheets with my Cherries in the Snow, she exclaimed, "Oh, thank God! You had some. Though this is not what they meant when they thought up the name."

She was wearing combat fatigues and pink stiletto boots, a yellow T-shirt with Marvin Gaye and Diana Ross on the front. I stared at it, my vision a little fuzzy from the painkillers.

"EBay. One hundred dollars. Stayed up all night for this. Sadie Steinberg, don't even think about stealing it."

Her hair was curled. I suspect, despite the hoarse phone call I'd made to her on the hospital phone, that she had stopped to set it in rollers before she came. Her eyes were kohled to a smoky intensity. Her lips were a high-gloss neutral.

Holly smiled, revealing cute, big, horse teeth, and rummaged in her bag, showcasing a small, high ass.

"Sadie, your skin needs evening out." And she came toward my metal bed with a powder-dipped brush.

"I feel weird lying here while you even me out. You're making me feel like I'm dead."

A handsome young doctor with a yarmulke came to take my blood pressure. Holly, who flirts with anything with a backbone, engaged him in chat, little flecks of glitter dancing off her as she laughed. He blushed and crept away sideways like a cheaply animated cartoon.

Holly is a heartbreaking beauty.

"You need to stop using pencil and start using powder," clucked Holly.

Holly took out a new thin brush and swept my browbone black, being careful not to touch my elevated foot. She looked at the thick white bandaging. "You know, this could be kind of a Comme Des Garcons thing you got here. Very challenging."

Holly knows style like ice cream knows sugar. In the last year alone, she has made thick gray tights look cool, not to mention orange nail polish, large polka dots, and Converse sneakers.

"Man," she added as she worked, "you're going to get at least eight Vicodin out of this."

I looked down at the bloodstained sheet. The hospital would wash it out and another person with a different injury would end up lying here, encased in the ghost of my disastrous love affair. It made me smile. As Holly rouged my cheeks, I must have looked like a corpse, but I felt more alive than I had in forever.

I thought of the mess, the love, the intensity. Me, a real-life Lolita with my own older man wrapped up in knots over me. When I first started seeing Isaac, Holly had found me a pair of rose-tinted heart-shaped Lolita sunglasses at a thrift store and left them on my bed as a joke.

"I needed these years ago!" I'd laughed and put them on. I ended up wearing them during sex, but they kept clunking

Isaac's nose and I took them off. I have no clue where they are now.

"I told him I didn't want him here. I told him I never wanted to see him again."

"Huh. I don't know what took you so long."

I do: a writer! A real writer, putting his writer's mind next to mine. Older, wiser, connected. Always encouraging me. In which case, why had I not written anything during the whole time I'd been with him? Nothing. Nada. Not a jot.

Holly looked at herself in her compact mirror, then snapped it shut like a castanet. She kissed me on the forehead. "Happy birthday, my darling."

I had forgotten. I could feel it on my forehead, her lipstick kiss, the seal of something that had been decided and set in writing, but what?

4 PROZAC SMOOCH

I FIRST CAME TO MANHATTAN from a London suburb that smells funny but contains no funny people. I miss it not a bit. London was a doctor's waiting room for New York, full of old dog-eared copies of the *Tatler*, each of which, in a conundrum worthy of *The X-Files*, you have already read though it is a magazine you make a point of never reading. The only thing I miss about London is my father.

He is so kind, my father. Although he is by birth a Turkish Jew, he's also a Buddhist without knowing it. Separated from him, I have transferred most of my love to Sidney Katz, who is lounging on my sofa and of whom I now demand: "If I'm in love with you, then why aren't you in love with me? I don't believe I could feel the connection this strongly if you weren't feeling anything in return."

Syllogistic logic, it's true, but I am desperate. No response. I try a new tack, lowering my voice to a Marilyn quaver. "Please love me?"

Blank stare. This isn't washing. My volume control slips.

"God, you're so cool. You're so bloody cool, aren't you? You don't need anyone. Well, guess what? You need me! I picked you up off the street and brought you into my home and I never did nothing but treat you right."

I sound like a B-list country singer—ramblin' Sadie Steinberg, the Jewish cowgirl—and still he isn't budging. Humiliation burning in my throat, I return to washing the dishes, scrubbing each plate with a force more appropriate to a criminal removing bloodstains, as opposed to Ding Dong crumbs. I never wash dishes except as a last resort. It's a political belief I hold that women, as an act of protest, should not do housework or cook, except breakfast, at which I excel. Pancakes, French toast, omelets. Problem is, if I cook I have to wash up, so I prefer not to have men stay. The men I date, they tend to have better kitchens than me anyway.

Generally with dirty dishes, I put them in the fridge until they're piled up too high to fit and then I throw some of them away. I have the good grace to be ashamed of tossing out perfectly good plates, so I do it late at night, under cover of darkness and dropping off clothes for the homeless at the same time. This plate tossing—to conjure, falsely, a little Greek merriment—is a monthly ritual that smashes a little piece of my self-respect each time I do it. But I can't stop.

So there I am, washing the dishes, needing Sidney Katz to notice me. The act of scrubbing seems foreign, like trying to make a girl come. How could I possibly know what's too hard or too soft? There's nothing wrong with people who enjoy housework. I just don't feel *that way* about it myself.

I peek down and sideways through the triangle of space between my bosom and my arm. His eyes are boring holes in my back. I drop a fork and spin around to face him, drunken Sue Ellen style. "Fucking hell, I love you!"

He looks at me quizzically.

"Jesus God in heaven, I want to have your babies."

He starts to back away.

"Ten or eleven. Or twelve."

Horror in his eyes.

"I want to have ten or eleven or twelve kittens with you."

Sidney Katz leaps into his carpeted cat tree, the highest shelf, away from me.

"We could give away the ones we didn't want." Have them take dirty plates with them. "Think about it."

His eyebrow whiskers twitch and he appears to be thinking. Dad helped me rescue Sidney the week he spent with me in New York. I see my father in Sidney's face.

"May I eat your paw?"

From over his balcony, he proffers a paw wanly and I put it in my mouth.

"Oh, Sidney Katz, you are too delicious."

INVENTORY: I HAVE A CAT that looks like a cow—big splotches of black on white, big eyes as though he's perpetually about to be slaughtered. I spend sixty dollars a month on cat food, which like all the other nourishment in this apartment comes delivered and paid for by credit card. Sidney is one of many cats I have fostered in my home. I've brought them in from their hiding places beneath parked cars, behind trash cans, inside discarded boxes, and nurtured them back to health before placing them with good homes. But Sidney's the one that stayed. He's the only one I associate with my father.

I have forty-seven bras. My mother bought me the wrong bra size for years. Until I left home I had four-boob syndrome: enormous cleavage under all my T-shirts, bulging, uncomfortable, overflowing, and messy. You know when you see your house is a mess, there's no way you can get your mind clean and focused? For some of us it's our bodies that are the clothes on the floor, the haphazard towels, the dishes in the sink. That explains my bad grades and the way I couldn't look the teacher in the eye. When I left home, I got the right bra, and then I couldn't stop—that's my bra problem, which is my money problem.

I've slept with eight men. I have never had great sex. So what am I doing? I ask myself that question every time, which may be why my sex life is blah. It's hurt. It's been uncomfortable. It's been humiliating. It's been dull. It's been athletic. It's been amusing. But it hasn't been that thing, that life-changing, problem-quashing big event, and I feel like a failed feminist, unable to have orgasms on command as a political statement. I always think: The next one, the next one. I have little food in my cupboard save a half-loaf of white bread and one jar of honey. In the fridge I have a mango—or is it a papaya?—and a bottle of deep red nail polish. I have four undeveloped rolls of film dating back at least two boyfriends. I am far too frightened to get them developed, nor can I throw them away, so they languish on the shelf, in photo-shop purgatory. I have shelves. A few. But not enough to keep the magazines from piling up, the CDs from spilling over, the books from resting on the toilet back.

I have a pretty great apartment. When I first moved here, I lived in a sublet share in Brooklyn and would ride into Manhattan on the subway dreaming of my own place. As much as I wanted to live in the city, the ride over the bridge was worth not living there. I'd lose myself in the graffitied buildings that loom as you enter Manhattan, spacing out in the spray-can swirls and insults, some of them beautiful, some of them reeking of boredom. During my second week someone graffitied the building next to the Jehovah's Witness Clock Tower with the word *Montana* in huge baby-pink letters. "Welcome to

Montana," it says, in the signature style of "Welcome to New York." Weird. But I liked its bubbly letters. They seemed joyful and always left me in a good mood to house hunt. When I found this apartment, I was sure it would be a great place to write.

I should be writing. But for now there are simply too many things in my head: The primary two, besides a mouse in my apartment, are that my British accent is going and so are my breasts. The décolletage and decorous inflection are my trademarks here and I cannot bear to lose them, though I know I will. Cabdrivers keep asking me if I'm Australian. Fucking Australian! A land so rife with killer spiders that I can hardly stand to say its name. But it's true, after five years in New York my accent is no longer British, not quite. I hear myself go *up* at the end of sentences where I used to go down, British shame versus the American need to be liked.

Then the breasts, two round spheres that I have always found every bit as comforting as my lovers do. If I could rest my weary head on them I would. I'm twenty-four; how can they be sagging? You don't see the difference, you swear. Fine. But I can see it. I can feel it. It's not right. When I was seventeen, they buoyed me through life like flotation devices. It isn't fair. Life isn't fair, I know, and there are far greater unfairnesses, it's true, but this is my unfairness. And I have been nurturing it for months like an expensive whiskey.

I told my mum when she called to see if I'd gotten her Christmas card.

"I bet they're fine." She laughed. "If they're like mine, they'll be great for another two decades." They're not like hers.

I told my doctor when she was doing a biannual checkup.

"They're healthy," she snapped.

But who, at twenty-four, would not exchange health for beauty?

The only one who will tell the truth is Holly.

"Look at them, Holly. NO, LOOK AT THEM!"

"Hmmm," she says sagely like a Swiss scientist stroking his beard as he figures out an equation, "we'll get to the bottom of this."

So now we're in her office conference room, where she has not one but two DVD players and one is paused on Angelina Jolie's nude scene in *Gia* (1998) and the other is paused on her nude scene in *Original Sin* (2001), and me, I'm nude from the waist up, standing in between them. Her eyes move from one screen to the other, in the manner of a football fan watching a penalty kick on action replay.

"See!" she shrieks. "They aren't as perky as they were in *Gia*, but what was she, nineteen then? They aren't as high up in *Original Sin*, you can see that. But they're still awesome. Her tummy was bigger in *Gia*, wasn't it? So cute. Now go stand right next to the screen."

She gasps. "See! See. They're *exactly* the same, they've moved exactly the same amount. They have sagged, that's for sure, but no more than Angelina's, and you can't say fairer than that."

And because she has answered my question, because she can answer any question, I ask the first thing that pops into my head. "Should I adopt a Cambodian baby?"

"Should we have Thai for lunch? Yes." She picks up the phone and orders as I hustle back into my clothes.

5   PRETTY ON THE INSIDE

"ISAAC WAS IN an English paper today, the *Telegraph*," says my mum, her voice staccato in place of the stilettos she can no longer fit her chubby feet into. "He attacked Colin Powell again; quite witty, I must say."

"Great."

"I will never understand about you and him."

"Me and Colin Powell or me and Isaac?"

"Now don't joke, because I wouldn't so much as put it past you."

With all the celebs my mum screwed when she was young, you'd think she would be proud of me. But I think somewhere deep down she still sees herself as a groupie and me not as her daughter but as younger competition. This particular cloudless morning, our topic is so banal that it is threatening to become deep.

"I get uncomfortable when I read stories about Jennifer Lopez," says my mother, "because, you know, she's you, with better access."

A pouting French waif of a waitress deposits my mushroom omelet in front of me with that Gallic combination of insouciance and loathing.

"Hello, I want to marry you! Go away! Hello, I love you, goodbye! Hello, Ben Affleck, I want to marry you and make children with you! Oh, go away, I'm bored of you. She's clearly deranged."

Then comes her punch line.

"But at least she sticks with men her own age."

"Yeah, yeah, Mum. Not this again."

"Not this again? We have been having this talk since you were thirteen."

It's true. My romantic choices were preordained by a first-edition copy of Nancy Friday's *My Secret Garden,* which my mother had left lying around. In it, women discuss their sexual fantasies. But it was published in 1973, and though the fantasies were nothing that wouldn't pass muster today, the heroes were horribly out-of-date:

"And then Cat Stevens presses his erect manhood against my thigh."

"Martin Sheen buys me a drink, his hand creeping higher and higher up my skirt."

"Elliott Gould takes me tenderly by the hand and asks, 'Have you met my friend Donald Sutherland?' "

It was an anachronistic book for a thirteen-year-old to read at the end of the twentieth century. The fantasy men had gone on to other drugs, were in and out of sobriety, career collapse and revival, other religions, other worlds. And yet I still have a soft spot for the heartthrobs of yesteryear. My first sexual feelings were about Christopher Lee, who, even when he was young, was still very old. Isaac and I talked about old movies and about Crosby, Stills, and Nash and Kris Kristofferson and I validated him because I didn't make him feel old, or so I thought, but actually I did because he felt nostalgic for them whereas I was just discovering them. He didn't believe me when I swore that you could feel nostalgic for things you'd never experienced in the first place.

The movie star I dated came pretty close to being my perfect man for a while. I'm not going to tell you who he is; suffice it to say that he's the greatest actor of his generation.

"Mum, he's the new Brando."

"*I* did the old Brando. That was a challenge."

I tell her the details of my love life that you're not supposed to tell your mum, not because we're so close but because I don't care what she thinks of me. I really don't give a shit. I told her about the time I tried anal sex.

"Oh, really," she said. "What did you think?" Like it was something that had been recommended by Oprah's Book Club.

I told her about the comedian I was dating, who, whether we met in public or in private, used to greet me by grabbing my ass and murmuring, "Mmm, you're like dessert." At the time I assumed he meant I was a guilty pleasure. I tolerated it although in the back of my mind I was like, Hey, would you squeeze the profiteroles? But now that I think about it, he was saying that a little of me goes a long way and that he felt ashamed and slightly sick after devouring me. These affairs: They never lasted more than a few months.

Then Isaac happened. And for a year I would have dropped anything and everything, wherever, whenever, to be with him. He is a brilliant man.

When I'd tell my dad what crimes Isaac had committed that day, I sounded like I was commenting, blow by blow, on a star wrestler: "Then Isaac came up from behind with a broken dinner engagement!" "Then Isaac, completely without warning, went to visit his brother for five days!" I'd ring Dad, weeping softly from behind the locked bathroom door as Isaac banged on it halfheartedly a few times and then went back to bed. For months my father had been pleading with me.

"Cry over an artist. Cry over a playwright. Please don't cry over a journalist." He was talking about himself, the accountant. My father's self-loathing is beyond measure, and it makes me love him more.

"He's a political writer, Dad."

"He's not a writer. He's a huckster."

My mum, ever the erstwhile groupie, shagged Woody Allen in 1973. As I said, Mum had sex with a lot of famous people. It was in the olden days and I don't think all of them treated her that well: They two-timed her or didn't call her when they should have. That's what my dad is really talking about when a celebrity diatribe spews forth. When Mum fell in love with Dad, she felt compelled to tell him exactly who she'd been with and what they'd done, and really, when he gets cross, he's just being chivalrous. He'll see a celebrity on TV, burst into a rage, and I'll know immediately that the man shagged my mum. It's frightening the people she's slept with:

"Frank Sinatra is crap!"

"Merle Haggard is crap!"

"Robert Evans is crap!"

"Jon Voight is crap on a stick!"

"Maurice Chevalier is crap!" That was the worst. That completely ruined *Gigi* for me. His thanking heaven for little girls and me knowing what my mum had been up to. Mum was very pretty back then. Very Nordic ice queen. I think she was amazed when she fell in love with my father, an accountant and not even a wealthy one, and moved to London to live with him. Now she has this insane love-hate relationship with celebrity because it meant so much to her and yet, in the end, it wasn't there for her and Dad was.

A big part of me wishes she had found a way for me not to

have been born in England. I can't remember ever living there, although my accent, my hang-ups, and all my documents say I did for nineteen years. When I go back, I see endless, gray sky and cringe: It looks like a dumpy drunk girl getting naked at a party.

"I'm going to London!," friends will tell me, as though they are impressing me with something luxurious. They think "I'm going to London!" is like a mink coat draped across a naked body. And then when they return:

"It was very expensive."

"It rained the whole time."

"They talk funny. But not in a cute way."

I was thinking today how Isaac ended in January and wondering if my despair might not have been seasonal rather than romantic. When I met him, I was wearing a spaghetti-strap dress and dainty pink sandals, dressed up for Bruce Springsteen. Toward the end I was wearing long johns under my jeans, a turtleneck, moon boots, and a parka. I thought he had transformed me into a schlump, but maybe I should have just looked out the window. All that seething rage and discomfort was probably just the oppressive heat of my radiator.

6 TRUST FUND

IN THE END, it was a haircut that propelled me back into the world of men. Holly came home from work one day wielding black dye and a big pair of scissors. While Ivy and I were busy laughing at a Creed video, she sat behind me and cut four inches off. Then, while we were mocking Jay-Z, she slid in front of me and snipped quietly until I had thick bangs that stopped just above my eyebrows. Then she dragged me away from a Sting video, absolutely ripe for mockery, bent me back over the sink, and dyed my bleached hair the color of a beetle. After she blew it all straight, Holly filled in my lips with a brick-red lipstick. By now, Ivy had turned off the television and was standing before me, squealing with delight.

"I look like an East Village Bettie Page wannabe," I said. "I know it."

"You don't," answered Ivy, quieter than I had ever heard her before. "You look like a French starlet." Amazingly, she was right.

It was a completely magical haircut that made men stop

dead in the streets, in the supermarket, at the bodega. Men of every color, shape, and income. Some whistled, some shouted obscenities, others handed me their business cards. Some actually had decent, interesting lines.

"Pleiades," said a smooth-talking yogi at the bodega.

"What?"

"The freckles on your arm. They're in the shape of my favorite constellation: Pleiades. The plow."

He was handsome, with close-cropped black hair, dark eyes, dark skin. He was buying soy milk, which I was surprised to see they carried, as I loaded up on Ding Dongs. He had the soft voice of an animal trainer. He had just come from yoga, he told me. "Excuse me. I feel a little blissed out."

I couldn't see his body, as everything he wore was huge, his T-shirt and pants bagging ridiculously. He looked like a child in them and I couldn't gauge his age . . . twenty-eight, twenty-nine? Too young for me. I wavered between the good looks and the soy milk, looking from one to the other and in a snap decided that we could never be. The way soy milk sits on coffee, flaking, no matter how you stir it. The bliss. No. It wouldn't work. He gave me his number, but I never called because if he looked closely enough at me in the first three seconds to see Pleiades the plow, he'd probably end up wanting me to spread my legs while he stared at my vagina. I've had one of those before. Knelt there, peering with such intensity that I never wanted to have sex again. I felt a little wistful as I left the yogi, handsome and blissful, but it was for the best.

"Louise Brooks," gasped a Frenchman in a coffeeshop. He looked like a Frenchman from central casting. As we talked, I imagined a beret hovering above his head like a halo. He wanted to take me to a Louise Brooks festival at the revival cinema. But I knew I would feel stupid, like someone going to an 'NSYNC concert with " 'NSYNC" written on her cheek.

I've never been one to mind when men whistle from time to time. I'm the sort of girl who feels validated when a guy looks down her blouse. Plus, it seemed like a waste not to do anything with the haircut. Given all the attention, I even started to fear the moment when it began to grow out, when the roots kicked in, that we might never be able to get it exactly right again. So I started dating.

There was this amazing restaurant mogul I really liked and he liked me back. Even though he was a millionaire, he always wore jeans and a sweatshirt: On our first official date he had on his University of Syracuse sweatshirt. He was one of those men whose looks were enhanced by having gone gray too early and he looked a little like the young Steve Martin. But instead of him making me laugh, I kept cracking him up. He'd dated a lot of starlets, so every other sentence I said made him gasp with amazement, and he even took out a notebook once or twice to jot down something I'd said.

"I have to remember that," he said, smiling and putting his Montblanc pen back in his pocket.

He told me that he had been compelled, just from seeing the back of my head, to introduce himself to me at Magnolia Bakery. Things had been going really well.

And then one night, as he was leaning in toward me in the darkened VIP room of his latest success story, I whipped out a baby photo of myself and made him look at it. The lights were dim and all around older men had their hands on the thighs of young women—models/actresses, whatever. That title kills me. No boundaries in their job descriptions or in their lives, the girls around me melted onto the men who touched them until the men just wanted to scrape them off. I knew he thought I wasn't a whatever. He thought I was interesting, different.

"No, look again. Aren't I cute?"

He looked at my hair. "You are so cute."

"No," I said, angry, "in the photo."

"Yes, you're cute."

"How cute?"

"Extremely."

In the picture I am two years old and my hair is a wild mess of ringlets. I am wearing a pink-and-white gingham romper and my dad, as always, is nestling me on his chest, my curls against his thick chest hair.

"That's my dad." He was wearing an open-neck shirt.

"I'll call you," said the restaurant mogul as he walked me to my door that night. He didn't try to come in.

He never did call me, and rather than feeling hurt or humiliated, I instead felt strangely compelled to e-mail him photos of me as a baby until he had his assistant call and ask me to stop.

7   BUTTERFIELD 8

NOT LONG INTO the short-hairdo era, Holly and Ivy took me out to dinner and asked me if I wanted to work for them. Coming in such close proximity to my near-death experience, I felt like how Elizabeth Taylor must have when she won the Oscar for *Butterfield 8*. I accepted gratefully, tearfully, and immediately knocked back a couple of glasses of champagne so I could forget to feel undeserving.

I had been informally helping the gals come up with product names for Grrrl ever since they started the company. I thought of it like a game of charades or word association. I always loved party games and this just seemed like an extension of that, but with futuristic lip-plumping technology. "Pink—fuchsia—shocking—sexy—ass-slapping—Ass-Slapping Pink!" Ass-Slapping Pink was an immediate hit. I wondered, when Ivy congratulated me on its success, whether the women wearing it followed the instruction as they wore it. I wondered just how much power a girl who names makeup might be able to wield.

That Friday I went into Grrrl's Fifth Avenue offices and signed a contract, which felt a little strange. Although the lawyer who oversaw it had a gray suit and immobile features, Guns n' Roses was playing in the background and the pen I signed with had purple ink. I was contracted exclusively to Grrrl cosmetics for one year and they would pay me forty thousand dollars plus health benefits. A single girl can live on that in Manhattan as long as she eats only two meals a day. I picked breakfast and lunch. For dinner I'd usually have a bowl of Cheerios.

On my first day of work, I wore a black skirt, black jacket, white blouse, and patent-leather heels. I even walked to the office in Reebok sneakers then changed into the heels, like a real nine-to-fiver. The gals looked at me in disbelief.

"What are you wearing?"

"Office clothes?"

The next day I wore a denim miniskirt, thick turquoise wool tights, and a top I had copied from a Stella McCartney window display. It was just a long-sleeved cotton T-shirt with a lot of colored circles on the front. I sat in my apartment and drew them in pencil with a compass and then colored them in with paint from a hardware store. The gals thought the top was great and immediately set out to rip off two of the paint colors for their new mascara.

I loved my job right away. It felt like life was a constant Rorschach test. Look at this lipstick. What do you see? And what is a Rorschach test, or indeed any quiz with multiple answers, but a chance to talk about yourself? My first week at Grrrl, I named the nail polishes for the spring season: Fragile Ego, Wallflower, Sophisticated Inebriate, and Jailbait. It was the party collection.

Men from the computer software company downstairs were always stopping by to chat with me or Vicki. I was jealous that all the men loved her.

"They do not," demurred Holly. "I don't find her attractive at all. You can't be five foot nothing and built like a child and then go around wearing ballet slippers and barrettes in your hair."

"You can," I sniffed. "Almost every girl in the whole of the East Village wears ballet slippers and barrettes."

"But they have tattoos." Ivy frowned. Her frowns came few and far between and her smiles have carved deep grooves beneath her cheeks. "They have piercings and their thongs peek out over their denim skirts. Vicki has that clear skin and glossy hair. She's always so nicely turned out, like her mother dressed her. I see this invisible stage mother instructing her to do pirouettes in the middle of parties."

"I've never seen her pirouette, but I have seen her do kind of a scissor kick on the sidewalk."

"Yeah. I hate that. I don't want to be mean, but she's thirty years old. She seems real attention-seeking. All I'm saying, since you brought it up, is that any man who is attracted to her would have to be a pervert."

If you think it sounds brutal to describe a thirty-year-old woman as old, you should see the things I read in my mum's diary about the thirteen-year-old Led Zeppelin groupies who laughed at her when she was twenty-four. When she was my age.

8 WALK OF SHAME

WHEN I CAN'T WRITE, I take a lot of baths. Although I have been on a roll at Grrrl—Junkie, Jet Lag, Jaundice for the purple, green, and yellow eye shadow trio; Applebum and Cherry Orchard for the new blushes—I can't write my novel, so I've been taking a lot of baths, two or three a day even when I spend eight hours at the office. I try to think of a different thing to do each time and space them out so that I feel I'm achieving each session. Soap. Exfoliate. Wash hair. Wearing red lipstick the whole time. I have no novel, but Isaac always said I have very soft skin, the softest of any girl he has been with. In the bath I write my novel, in my head. And it leaves as the water drains.

The weather hasn't helped my feelings of gloom. It's snowed a lot in March, which it really, really isn't supposed to do. I keep thinking the snow has ended and then get caught. It starts and stops like the fourth day of your period. We have a full week without snow and then, on Wednesday, there comes this downpour that keeps kids out of school. Going to the Grrrl offices one March day, I'm wearing long white trousers, and by the time I get to work they're gray and soaked through to the tops of my knees. Evidently the same has already happened to Holly and Ivy because when I walk in, they're walking about without their pants, just wearing matching Spiderman tops and knickers. Ivy's are boy-cut and quite modest, but Holly's are a good two sizes too small. I love that she doesn't tug at them, but lets 'em wedge where they want to and forgets about it. She is more comfortable with herself than any of us are.

Their corduroys are hung up over the radiator in our office. Vicki, who is sitting down at her desk, stands up to give me a hug hello, which seems more than a little grating once I realize I will be receiving it every single morning. I see that she too is without her lower garments. I take mine off and place them on the radiator in the conference room. Soon we are an entire workforce of half-dressed women. We look like a performance-art installation.

Laid out on the conference table is an advertising mockup for a line we have coming out of tough-wearing nail polishes that will last through anything. It is of a female foot wearing a stiletto whose heel appears to be a weapon grinding into the bare torso of a man. Just visible through the toe of the pump are glossy black toenails.

Holly had me name the nail polishes after tough bitches: Ivana, Imelda, etc. I wanted to name them for art heroines— Gala, Arbus—and commission a young female artist to paint a series of miniatures using our polishes. Vicki said we should endorse inspirational women: Mia, Winona, Dido. Simpering idiots just like her. I'm surprised she didn't suggest the fucking Olsen twins. And, yes, I know they prefer to be called Mary-Kate and Ashley, but then billionaire blondes tend not to ignite the best in me. Vicki's just a poor blonde and I have a hard time not kicking her up the arse each time she speaks. If Holly wants to build the new marketing campaign on bitchiness instead of sex, why can't she just let us all be bitches in the office? Because we all are under the surface, each after our own agenda. But we have to sit under the sadomasochistic ad campaigns and act like feminism is our raison d'être. Funny kind of feminism. But what do you expect from a company that makes its cash from telling women they should highlight what's wrong with them?

This communality is frustrating. Vicki keeps offering her opinion and we are all supposed to listen. Why? What are her qualifications? She wears lots of makeup. That is good enough for Holly and Ivy. And maybe they're right. They're the millionaires, not me. Born millionaires know how to make millions. It's frustrating. All I know are my father's mess of itemized bills and my mother's same old moans of "Why can't we take a holiday this Easter?" She insists on marking all the Christian dates on the calendar and all the British ones too—every bank holiday; May Day; Saint George's Day. Our holidays—Purim, Hanukkah, and Yom Kippur, yes, even the ones where you're supposed to fast—Dad and I just go get dinner together. Without her. We asked her to come, but she won't.

"Fine," she says, "enjoy yourself." As my mum heads toward sixty, I often get the feeling she still has the voice of her anti-Semitic doctor dad in her head: "My baby girl with a Jew?" I'd judge her harder for it, but, you know, who can truly find peace when they know they've disappointed their daddy? Yet I can't be around that unhappiness. You can't choose your family. Occasionally people get lucky: Dad and I got it right; we are great friends. You know how some girls want to put couples together on the street: "You go with him." "Ech, he's much too straight for you." "She's too tall." I want to put families together too. Send Vicki to live with Mum.

I sit at my desk in my turtleneck and knickers and try to think of a new way to market red lipstick. Vicki reminds me that people should think they have to buy all three, a set that can't be separated. Well, gee, thanks for that, Vicki. But she's right. They are basically all the same color and they each cost eighteen dollars. So I called one Chico, one Harpo, and one Groucho. If you didn't see that the colors were all the same, you'd have to be one of those people who plays along with psychics: "Yes, I *do* know a dark-haired woman who may bear me ill will." In my experience makeup junkies are the exact same people who pay to see psychics.

I feel a pang of guilt when I show the gals my suggestions for the new reds. They think the names are great.

"But then it's easy, isn't it?" says Vicki.

"It isn't easy," I hiss, "it's art." I haven't even worked there three months. Still, I scramble on with my theory: "Cherries in the Snow is Revlon's bestselling lipstick of all time. But it isn't the color that makes it. That's just another shade of red. It's the name. Cherries in the Snow? That's imagery worthy of a real writer. Truman Capote could have written that."

"Chico. Harpo. Groucho," says Vicki, slow and spiteful, "that's Dostoyevsky."

She pronounces it "dos-TOY-yefsky," conjuring a wooden dreidel sold in a children's Judaica store. I hate her, I hate her, I hate her all over her body as if I were in love with her. It's bonkers, this seething; it's childish and useless. She's just a dumb girl, so what's the problem?

As soon as I met Vicki, with her blond halo of curls, I wanted my old hair back. Once the girls colored my hair, I never left the house without putting on red lipstick carved into my unrealistic bow. I lost weight because I didn't want to eat in case I messed up the lipstick. I remember as a kid how much I hated it when my room was touched, like I had lost control over the only thing I had. I feel like my face and what I do to it is all that I have control over.

Ivy turns on Vicki. "You shut up, fatty," she gibes. Ivy calls everyone "fatty." She is trying to reclaim the word *fat* from being an insult to being a compliment.

The row simmers down. Not much of a row, I know, but hey, I'm not in a relationship right now so I take what I can get.

"I need to take a slash," says Holly. She has retained from her time in England only the most vulgar slang. Kitted out, today in earrings that dangle all the way down to her collarbone, she beckons me to the bathroom with her.

"Give it to me," she says, hand outstretched.

"Give you what?"

She rolls her eyes. "Your Cherries."

I fish inside my bag and pull out the tube, which is getting pretty gnarly. She takes it from me, presses me up against the wall, and applies the lipstick to my mouth, not at all the way I do it. Four strokes exactly, half of my top lip, the other half, half of the bottom lip, and the final quarter. I can see, if I ever doubted it, how she is in bed: swift, confident, a little self-satisfied. Then she applies it on herself, the same join-the-dots pattern, but I see it this time in slow motion, gasping as the color appears before me. She never wears lipstick that costs less than twenty dollars. She steps back and studies her work.

"This is just red."

She's asking me a question, but so cheap with language is Holly that she usually expects you to supply the question mark or the exclamation point in a sentence. The answer to her question is "Kind of." Yes, it's red. But that's just part of the story. I look at our mouths floating side by side in the mirror and I see Lauren Bacall in black and white, the deep gray on her elegant mouth somehow, undoubtedly, Cherries. I see a

1950s afternoon tryst, the first woman on the block to get divorced, the first to find herself. I see a girl who really loves a man's body rather than getting through sex with her eyes closed and her hands to herself, a girl who finds her lover's whole body beautiful. I am not that brave girl. Not yet. But each time I apply Cherries in the Snow, I have hope. . . .

"It's a *great* red," I reply. Holly stares at me, at my mouth, but says nothing. I feel like I am waiting for a queen to announce whether I'm getting leniency or the guillotine. Finally she speaks: "I get it."

Relief. Suspicion. "What do you mean?"

She puts her arm around me. We are the same height in the mirror, give or take an inch. She sees this and straightens up, taking the inch. "We need our Cherries in the Snow."

"Really?" She doesn't know what this means to me.

"Look, our company, the ugly, edgy makeup, is cute and all, but we need something that will last, live past us. Honey, I plan to die young. I want to know that there're dream-filled sluts out there using my products long after these skinny bones are gone. . . ."

I never would have described her as skinny. Compact is better. The pun is not intended. Rather destiny has entwined her body type and her career.

"Our company's been going for five years. We've got our core audience, I know, but these girls are going to grow up eventually, find out that, actually, edgy is all very well, but what they really want is to be beautiful. One product, one name. That's what will do it. The product doesn't really matter. But the name . . ."

"That's my job, huh?"

She nods, kisses me on the forehead, and walks out. I look in the mirror. She has a nasty habit of stamping me with her scarlet seal of approval. Great. It will not budge. I brush my bangs over my eyes. But I am too overwhelmed to be pissed at her.

At lunch, Holly goes out and buys some cherries and we place them in the snow on our windowsill, then stand back and watch, as though they are about to do something. They do look wonderful.

"I hope I look like that when I'm stretched out on my white sheets with a man." I sigh.

That's what we're doing when we hear a cough and turn around to see a guy carrying a brown paper bag. It is the handsome yogi I met in the bodega the month before. I recognize him immediately even without the carton of soy milk in his hand. Brown eyes fringed with long lashes, close-cropped black hair, mocha skin. I can't quite place his ethnicity: skin too dark for a European Jew. Sephardic maybe? Like my dad. Away from the harsh bodega lighting, he looks ten times handsomer than I remember him. His body is different. Maybe it was like that before, ripped dancer's abs and other words I remember from my time at the gym but never gave a shit about until they were standing before me, Springsteen-ian with lack of effort.

The cherries glow behind him, a chorus of approval; they lift themselves from the snowy windowsill and dance around his head, forming a heart shape that encircles his close-cropped skull like a halo. A 3-D painting of a saint. Saint cheekbones of the doe eyes. I sigh. There is a gentleness to his features that makes me feel calm.

"Oh, my fucking Christ!" shrieks Holly, breaking my calm, and leaps into his arms, wrapping her naked legs around him and causing the cherry heart formation to crash to the floor. Ivy stares from Holly to him, her ears visibly pricking up. And out. She looks like Spock.

"What's up, my favorite dyke?" He has a soft voice, like an

animal trainer's. Or from the way Holly clings to him, pretzel-style, a lesbian trainer's. Holly unravels herself and he places her neatly back on the same ground above which I feel myself hover. "This, girls, is my old friend Steven Marley."

"Oh, wow," says Ivy. "Hi, I've heard so much about you. I can't believe it's you." What looks like it might be a blush of jealousy on her cheeks subtly morphs into a blush of confusion. My objectifying turns a shade of intrigue. Who the hell is Steven Marley?

"Your work," adds Ivy, "is amazing."

"Thank you," he answers. "You must be Ivy. I've heard so much about you. You're the better half." With a single sentence he soothes the inflammation eating at Ivy's soul, and she smiles shyly as she shakes his hand. She seems small next to him, an accidental and additional kindness on his part. For all her ballyhooing about reclaiming the word *fat*, I see how much she enjoys the tininess of her hand in his.

Having delighted Holly and Ivy, he turns his attention to Vicki. What, am I invisible? Am I cute only by the light of the bodega? I wait for the bowling ball of charm to knock out Vicki and she's waiting too, her mouth twisted into a truly terrifying grin, gummy and wet.

"Hi." He nods briefly, giving her just enough time to say "Hi, I'm Vi—" and then he turns straight to me.

"Hey." Vicki blinks, fluttering her lashes. But he doesn't stop looking at me. He stares so hard I start to wonder if I too have dancing fruit behind my head. He has the same confused look that Sidney Katz gets when I have to blow-dry him after his biannual bath.

"We've met before, no? In the deli? I was on my way from yoga. You said you'd call and you never did."

You say deli, I say bodega. Oh, it would never work out between us.

"You didn't call him?" says Vicki out loud, then realizes she said it out loud and skulks to her desk in shame. We have covered a spectrum of reds—exuberance, jealousy, shame—and this guy has been in the office only three minutes. Except he isn't really a guy. He is, quite indisputably, a man.

Each muscle on his stomach waits for a response. I feel so bad for not calling that instead I say, "I have stretch marks. Look." I point like a museum guide. "Look here. And here. And also here."

"Oh," says Marley, placing his bag on the floor, "is that a good thing?"

"In certain cultures." Holly laughs.

"I have trousers," I add quickly.

The whole office loves it when I slip into a Britishism and they always repeat it back at me in an accent somewhere between Helena Bonham Carter and Dick Van Dyke in *Mary Poppins:* "I have TROW-sers! I have TROW-sers!" they shriek. Marley looks befuddled.

Then I go to get the trousers. I come back with them on, half-dry, still gray-streaked. Holly, Ivy, and Vicki are back at their desks and Marley is still standing in the middle of the office. As I walk back toward the girls, he calls after me.

"I like them."

"What?" I ask, too embarrassed to turn around and face him.

"Your stretch marks. Graphically appealing. They're cool. They're pretty gorgeous actually."

I go back to my desk, blushing. I take a test sample of red lipstick, scratch out "Harpo," and write "Humiliation."

Vicki is peering over my shoulder. Her round face looms over me. "Why would anyone want to buy something called that?"

"They wouldn't," I snap, and toss it in the garbage can.

"Hey, those cost money!" barks Holly. So I retrieve it, put it back on my desk, but cover it with a tissue so I won't have to look at it.

"I'm double-parked. I'll be back, babe," says Marley, and walks out, the yoga classes rippling through him and toward me like a special effect. I am disappointed he has used a word as generic as *babe,* but maybe saying it to a lesbian negates that. I look out the window and down to the street, where a 1970s Springsteen muscle car is parked in the slush. I know it's his before he climbs in.

"What is he doing here?" I ask.

"What he is doing," says Holly, mimicking me, her vowels flat, her ass squashy against my desk, "is a mural. Remember like in high school, the mural in the hallway?"

"We all went to school in England," interjects Ivy. "There were no murals, remember?"

"Well, in New York public schools. Which means state school in England," explains Holly.

"I get it. I've been here five years, not five minutes."

"Coulda fooled me." She smirks.

"Oh, anyway, can you tell us why he's here?" Ivy is gobbling her words as she does her daily pizza slice, impatient as Holly offers up the facts in a thin person's morsels.

"Well," says Holly, "we're gonna have Marley do a mural in our conference room. He's the best. The best graffiti artist out there. Although he isn't out there no more. That kid makes millions."

"Is he some kind of design adviser?" asks Ivy.

"Right, design advisory tomfoolery. But he's coming out of retirement to punk up the conference room. I bumped into him at a party last week. Haven't seen him in a hellava long time."

"What party?" says Ivy. The air is thick with what is quickly becoming obvious tension.

Holly ignores her. "And he says he's been itching to go back to a full-scale mural. So I said, Hey . . . have free rein."

"I think it's a great idea," says Vicki.

"Thanks for telling me," Ivy says huffily.

"Ah, you'll love it."

"Maybe I will, but you should have told me."

"I think it's a great idea," says Vicki again, like she's practicing different intonations.

"I think it's gre—" I put my hand over Vicki's mouth.

I think up a lot of my best names in that conference room with its empty walls, dead air, lack of sapphic lust, and Vicki's babble. I hope his free rein is not going to interfere with my free thought. But mainly I am pissed at him for being cute and more so at the gals for contaminating my space with cute. I turned him down once already and he comes back and I feel all gooey like I'm in love. I don't need that at work. I don't need that, full stop. Or, as you Yanks say, "period." Either way, this can only be disruptive. I am trying to think of the name that will be our Cherries in the Snow. That's what I have to concentrate on. Not his eyelashes. Ugh. This goo, it feels like the way I felt over Ryan O'Neal posters when I was thirteen. But this man's real, three-dimensional; I could do something with him. I feel like he likes me back and we could get married and have ten thousand babies and see . . .

"So?" says Holly, watching me watch him out the window. "He's cute, right?"

"I dunno, probably. I was looking at his car. Cool car."

"He's a cool guy."

"He's a boy."

"He's twenty-eight!"

"Right, so like I said, he's a boy. I really only go for older men; come on, you know that. A walker and I'm in."

"But he's sooo dreamy," says Holly, swooning. "Those glasses, with that body! So Clark Kent."

"I thought you were supposed to be gay."

"Dude, I could drink pussy from pint glasses, but, oh my God, that man is hot like crack cocaine!"

I sink into my chair, defeated.

"He's hot."

"See!" screams Holly, leaping from foot to foot as though they are hooves and she is a mythical fawn-girl troublemaker. "I knew you'd like him!"

"I didn't say that."

"You said it!"

"Anyway," I say nonchalantly, "it would never work. I saw him buying soy milk at the bodega."

"So?"

"I love coffee."

"And?"

"You know how soy milk sits on the surface of your coffee no matter how much you stir it?"

She stares at me.

"He's twenty-eight!" I squeal.

"You're twenty-four!"

"Girls mature faster than boys."

"Yeah. You're really mature."

"Can you shut up now, please? He's going to be back in a minute."

But when he returns to the office, sequestering himself in a corner with Holly, try as I might, I can't help sneaking looks at him. I feel dirty, like a man trying to take a surreptitious peek down a girl's blouse. I notice he is wearing a little blue wooden bracelet with interlocked red hearts, a kiddie thing you buy in toy stores at the counter as you pay for your real purchases. Vicki notices too.

"Ooh!" she gasps, skipping over, "I want that!" And she grabs for it, but he moves his wrist away. He does not like her and makes it quite obvious. Brownie points for the twenty-eight-year-old.

After twenty minutes or so, he leaves and, I swear, as soon as he does, the room has less oxygen.

"He's gay, right? Tell me he's gay."

"He's gay," Holly says as she shakes her head.

"How do you know him?"

"We go way back. Hung out back in the day."

"Back in which day? What are you talking about? Have you slept with him? How could you keep him a secret?"

"He's pretty secretive. And no, amazingly enough, I haven't slept with him. I tried it on, big time. But strange little boy is into monogamy."

"Did you see that little heart bracelet he had on? What was that about?"

"Oh, that's Montana's."

I deflate.

"So he's taken?"

"In a sense."

"What in a sense?"

"Ask him yourself. He'll be back in a minute."

"I will."

Marley comes back up the stairs with a shiny red apple in his mouth. He looks like a male model being spit-roasted.

"What's up with your dinky heart bracelet?" I ask before he's even halfway toward me. Holly, Ivy, and Vicki scatter like pins in a game of nihilist bowling.

"That's my daughter's bracelet."

"Oh. You're married?"

"No. Separated. We were never married actually."

"Does she live with you, your kid?"

"If she did, I wouldn't walk around with my circulation being cut off."

"Doesn't she want it back?"

"She gets to wear it when I get to see her."

"When's that?"

"Once or twice a month, unfortunately. She's in California. Work has me here for now."

"Holly says you're a graffiti artist."

"Sort of. I used to be. Sold out long ago. Now I advise ad agencies and graphic design companies. I only do pieces very occasionally for special friends. Like Holly."

"How do you get inspired to write your graffiti?"

"Nowadays, supporting my eight-year-old daughter in the manner to which she has become accustomed. Is this an interview?"

"Sort of. I write too."

"You do graffiti?"

"No. I'm a novelist."

"Wow." He doesn't doubt me. More brownie points for the twenty-eight-year-old. Twenty-eight, close to Isaac's age, half my father's age. If I could turn him into numbers and math and science, maybe I won't be so attracted to him. The un-science of lust. But I want to talk to him too. Talk at him.

"Yeah. And all novelists have to have other jobs. It was either this or academia."

"I didn't go to college."

"Neither did I. I dropped out."

"I couldn't afford it. Now I can afford it and I have such an inclination to learn. But I have a baby."

"Oh, so you didn't want her."

He raises his eyebrows. "You're very forward."

"It's just that you're so young."

"That's why you're forward?"

"No, I'm always that way."

"Oh. I thought I was special." He feigns feeling wounded and then I see he's not faking it, it's real.

9   JUNKIE

"DID YOU NAME THIS?" asks Marley, picking up a blue-and-green-swirl eye pencil called Junkie.

"Yes," I say proudly.

"Have you ever known a real junkie?"

"I'm not sure. Why?"

"I was one. Funny to see that experience diluted to eye pencil. I'm not criticizing you."

He writes on the wall with it.

"Hey, that's a sample. . . . That's our wall. . . ."

"Sorry." He is baffled. Of course, a twenty-two-dollar eyeliner does not make sense to a man who buys soy milk.

"You disapprove of me."

He doesn't answer. "It's the drugs that gave me the courage to climb as high as I did. Got off them when I met the mother of my child, and I never really did anything that good again."

"Hey, it looks like your life turned out all right."

"Yeah. It did."

Marley keeps coming and going that day, up and down the stairs, carrying bags of spray cans, thin as fat joints, thick as beer cans.

He is there for three days. Doing his thing. The muscles in his upper arms flex beneath his T-shirt like lovers under a duvet. On the second day I peer at him through the window of the closed door. His back is to me and his ass crack is showing.

"Oh. Hi," he says warily, when I pass him in the hallway, as though I have caught him trespassing. We are not allowed to look at the mural until it is finished.

"That's just his old graffiti mindset," says Holly. "You know, he went to jail a bunch of times."

I go back to my desk, cross out "Chico," and fill in the label: "Crush." I go to the bathroom and put it on, smiling at myself in the mirror. It suits me, a true brick red. I am starting to feel like my old self again. He doesn't look like an artist. He looks like a carpenter or a plumber, or a 1970s car mechanic, sliding out from under a Chevy on a hot July morning to say hi. I feel ridiculous for having a crush on a guy painting our walls. It feels so porny: "I've come to fix things around here."

"Oh, thank goodness. Things around here really need to be fixed. Oh, by the way, my friend just came over to use my shower."

"He's such an amazing writer. That's what they call graffiti artists," Holly says, and I think of my laptop at home, not switched on except to e-mail my dad. My head is full of stories, but every time I look at the blank white page offered, like a sacrificial virgin, by Microsoft Word, I have to turn it off again.

On the third day, I get braver. I go over to where Marley is working and look through the door's window until he comes out. I kind of stand over him in my short skirt and generally lean on things. I do a backward handstand against one of the walls, hoisting myself up against it. I try to act really casual, like I too am just doing my thing. Ivy sees me and is shocked. She says I should wear a T-shirt that says "I'm really good at sex. I'm very bendy." I explain that I was just trying to communicate yoga style. My knickers flashed; it seems like something Holly would do. Except she would have no knickers on. Mine are white and large. I chose carefully that morning. All has been meticulously planned. It always worked on boys in the playground. But Marley isn't a boy, he is a man, and when I come down out of the backward handstand, I don't quite know what to say. I stretch my arms above my head, waiting for something brilliant to come to me, but it doesn't, so I race out of the room.

I sit at my desk for the rest of the day, my back aching from the floor show. Holly persuades me that I can't go home with a backache and no date. She keeps egging me on, so at 4 o'clock I go back to the toxic-smelling room and ask him, "Would you like coffee? Or a Coke?"

"I have a Thermos," he says gravely, as though he's saying "I have a plan."

"Did someone make you the Thermos? Someone pack it for you this morning?"

"I did."

I am doing little circles on the floor with my toe, waiting for him to ask me out, when he adds, "I had a dream I was going to fill the Thermos before I woke up. Then I got up and did it. Sometimes I dream I'm going to make toast, and then I get up and make toast. Don't you resent banal dreams?"

I don't have a comeback, so I ask him out. Although he has already asked me out and I never called him. But somehow that has been forgotten. "You wanna go to a movie?"

"That would be fantastic. I don't drink Coke or coffee. And neither should you. It's green tea. Detoxifying. You want some?"

"You know how many toxins are in your paint fumes?"

"Three hundred, the prime one being arsenic."

THE NEXT NIGHT we go to a movie he picks. Before he arrives, I drink a lot of coffee and Coke—a "Fuck you" and a fight to keep my mind focused on my lipstick project. It backfires. I am shaking when he arrives. I fall into his arms and let him hold me. I rest there for a while. He does little chakra points on my back and I calm down.

"Hey. That's amazing."

"Just Eastern good sense."

I tell him I'm trying to think of the name of the lipstick that will change our company.

"Wow, big task."

"You're making fun of me."

"No, I'm not. You wield great power. You could make a real mark with this."

A real mark with lipstick that lasts two hours if you're lucky.

"This is interesting."

"So you and Holly, did you ever . . ."

"No. Not my type."

"Ivy will be relieved."

"And you?"

"Holly needs to have a spiritual crisis."

"So what did you talk about? Why were you friends? I knew her mother."

"You *knew* her mother?"

"Yes. She was a beautiful woman. All my lovers have been older. A lot older."

All. Holly's mother. Wow.

"Does Holly know?"

"Of course."

Of course she wouldn't be bothered. Of course it wouldn't affect her trying to seduce him.

"It didn't last very long. Months, I think. But it ended with dignity. Like her. She was a beautiful woman. Holly, I have less in common with. But she's a good girl somewhere in there. I think."

"All my lovers have been older too."

"How old are you?"

"Twenty-four."

"Wow. I mean I knew, but younger than me? That's a first."

"How old are you again?"

"Twenty-eight."

We drink in silence.

"When was Holly's mother?"

"After my split with Jolene."

"Jolene, like Dolly Parton?"

"Don't talk Dolly to me, I'm from the South."

"You are? You don't look like . . ."

"I'm from everywhere."

I like to know people's ethnicity. Not knowing my friend's ethnic background is like when you call people on their cell phones and have no idea where they are when they answer. It makes me feel unanchored. Mariah Carey, what are you? Rosario Dawson, what are you? I am a Sephardic Swede, now your turn.

You don't have to name every color. If he's from everywhere and I can never name the color, well, then, he's the exception in my life. He buys me a strange guarana drink and tells me his friends call him Marley. Everywhere in the East Village kids high-five him, skateboarders wheel up to pay their respects. He seems embarrassed, but the blush barely tinges his dark skin.

We sit in the darkness watching a documentary about homeless people who have built communities under the subway. He puts his hand in mine. Afterward we go to a late-night Polish café, where I order the raspberry cheese blintzes with a chocolate cupcake on the side. As is my wont, I take five bites of my blintzes and wish I had ordered something else. The café's lighting is making me nervous. I'm sure my blue mascara (which I wish I had not named Mars Attacks!) is coming off as tacky instead of eye-opening.

"I don't want this. Do you want it?" I push the plate toward him.

"What am I, a vacuum cleaner?"

"Nah, sorry. That's just what I do with my father."

"No thank you. I don't eat sugar."

"You don't?"

"Or dairy."

"You're lying!" I hear myself screech.

"That would be a dull lie."

"You're right. My God, when did this happen?" I sound like I'm asking him when he had a vasectomy or when he lost a limb.

"Oh, about a year ago."

"No sugar in a year?"

"No dairy in five. Jolene was . . . is a health freak. Is a health freak. She exists without me."

"I know that feeling. How do they continue without you?"

"It's a funny one, huh?"

We go back to my apartment. Sidney Katz eyes him with ill-concealed distaste. Marley sits on the edge of my bed because there is nowhere else to sit. I am overcome with nerves and rack my brain for something clever to say. Instead I say: "Don't you think it's weird that in 'Do They Know It's Christmas' by

Band Aid, Sting sings the word *sting*: 'The only water flowing is the bitter sting of tears.' That haunted me as a child."

"Not the starving Ethiopians?"

"I was distracted by Sting singing *sting*. And why was the American version called 'We Are the World'? Such jingoism!"

"I never thought of that. You're right."

I look at the green electronic clock. "Two A.M. I'm pretty much always right."

"Good to know."

He leans over and kisses me. I look up at the ceiling as his lips press against mine. And then nothing happens. He sleeps next to me and doesn't touch me. No, he does touch me: He holds my hand and we fall asleep for a few hours. At seven I creep out of bed, but he pops awake like a trick can of peanuts. Boo! No time to brush my teeth or put on clear mascara. Clear mascara, an eyelash curler, and an eyelash separator, the mandated tools of the morning liar.

"Listen, I have to write. I like to do an hour every morning before work."

"Why do I find that so sexy?" he asks, wrapping his arms around me.

"I have no idea."

He kisses me on the cheek, which after being kissed on the mouth is like being downgraded at the airport, gathers his coat and scarf, and leaves. I sulk for fifteen minutes. Then the doorbell rings. "Special delivery." It is Marley, carrying a croissant and cup.

"Oh, great, coffee."

"Uh, no, it's green tea."

"Oh, great." Yuck. "Thank you."

"The computer is off," he says, peering past my shoulder to the desk.

"I write longhand first. After I've written it in my head. You know, meditated on it."

His bright eyes brighten. Such dark eyes so bright. I resolve to ask him to spray-paint my computer. Stain of Isaac away, cleared away by Marley.

"By the way, the mural is done. Just thought I'd tell you."

I CAN BARELY MAKE IT through the bus ride, waiting to breathe in the three hundred toxins' worth of toxicity he has painted onto the office wall. I imagine they depict me and him sitting in the dark of the movie theater, the cherry heart behind his head blocking the view of the people behind us.

As soon as I get to work, I head straight to the conference room to look at Marley's mural. The girls are already there, standing in awkward silence, Holly's arm uncharacteristically around Ivy's shoulders. The room smells so strongly of paint that I have to squeeze my eyes shut and it takes me a few blinks to get them open again. The mural intermingles each of the Grrrl workforce, Holly, Ivy, Vicki, and me, with the celebrities from our wall of fame. I would say we're chatting, but we appear to be either boring or molesting the celebs, among them David Bowie, Courtney Love, Robert Smith, and Siouxsie Sioux, all beautifully and lovingly depicted. Holly is tuning Courtney Love's guitar. Vicki is holding Courtney's naked breasts in her hands. Ivy is giving Robert Smith a piggyback ride. I appear to be leering down Debbie Harry's cleavage. David Bowie has a book in his hand—on closer inspection it's a Yiddish to English dictionary—and looks like he would rather be elsewhere. Vicki runs, crying, out of the room.

"Hey, what's the big deal?" I ask her.

"He made me look like a . . ."

"Like a what?" snaps Holly.

"Like a lesbian!"

"The problem being . . . ?" says Holly coolly.

"I'm not one!"

"Not that there's anything wrong with that," I add jokingly.

"There *is* something wrong with it. In Missouri."

"Does it look like you're still in Missouri?" asks Ivy, standing closer to the mural, right up close, as though it will all come into focus and make sense.

Holly claps her hands and says, "Okay, everybody"—there's just us three in the room now—"back to work."

"Well," says Ivy, "I think it's fucking awesome."

"Well, I don't." Vicki sniffs from the door, a tissue stuffed in her nose.

"That's because you want everything to be pretty and nice." I sniff back.

"I want it to be the truth."

"You work at a makeup company!" Holly laughs. "You think we deal in truth? What the hell do you think you're selling?"

"What's wrong with pretty and nice?" Vicki simpers.

"Honey, you may be working at the wrong company. In case you haven't noticed." Holly points up at the ad campaigns on the wall, the gap-toothed girl in black lipstick.

"This is *exactly* how I see Grrrl," says Holly. "This is exactly how we should be represented. We're all freaks. Our audience is freaks. That's a good thing. And we should be so lucky that Marley, who could have charged fifty thousand dollars for this mural, has done it for free."

"I agree with Holly," I say.

"I don't," whines Vicki. "We don't even look pretty."

"What's pretty?" Ivy sighs. "Who gives a fuck about pretty?"

"I do," says Vicki, bawling. "The consumer does."

"The consumer knows shit," I say. "Every time the British government holds an opinion poll on whether or not to bring back hanging, the people vote overwhelmingly yes. And are ignored. Because a government's job is to be more civilized than its people."

"Okay, history girl," spits Vicki.

"I had a crush on my history teacher," I say.

"Who didn't?" Holly sighs.

"You didn't know him. You were gone by then."

"No, but all history teachers are hot. Like all bass players are hot."

"And the best track on any album is always number seven."

"Let's just get back to work, okay? The truth is, we need a crossover commercial hit. We're running on borrowed fashion spreads. The mags love us. The models love us. Drew Barrymore loves us. But the people in Ohio . . . they got no love for us. The big boys in Paris will put up with that for so long. They may put up with it forever. But the fact remains . . ."

"We need our Cherries in the Snow," I say.

"Exactly."

"Cheerios in the Snow."

"Good start."

I SIT IN the conference room with the paint fumes.

Poison Apple lipstick?

Braceface lip gloss?

"What about a line of slut makeup called One Night Stand?" I call down the hallway. "A bronzer called Dishonest? A miniature package of mascara remover called Walk of Shame?"

"Done," Holly calls back. "Done and done."

And though I'm glad she likes them, none of those names are "it." None of them are "the one." I eat a lot of cheese that night before I go to bed. Brie, Camembert, and Stilton. I'm hoping to have some funky dreams and that the name will come to me in a vision.

10 FLOOR SHOW

IN THE MORNING I am woken by the phone. I am furious because I'm halfway through a dream. Elizabeth Taylor is writing with lipstick on a dressing-room mirror, just like she does in *Butterfield 8* before she storms out in her negligee and fur coat. But it's not Liz in the negligee and copious eyeliner: It's me, me in a big black wig. I crane to see what I'm scribbling. And then the phone rings.

Fuckety-fuck fuck fuck!

I assume it's my dad, who usually calls at 8 A.M., just as he is taking lunch in London. "Papa?" I say crossly, stepping into my bunny slippers. My once-white pajamas had gone pink in the last laundry. No answer.

"Dad?" I ask again, digging in my nose for bogies with my index finger.

"Uh, no."

On the other end of the line is my enigmatic crush.

"But I'm very flattered to be confused with the man you love the most."

I giggle stupidly, hoping the blush of sleep will pass my stupid off as sexy.

"Would you like to have dinner with me tonight?" Marley sounds scared.

I usually play a game, fake flicking through a calendar, asking if I could get back to them, leaving them hanging until five. But I couldn't. Not with him: "That would be lovely."

Tea with scones and clotted cream would be lovely. Meeting Dame Judi Dench would be lovely. Having dinner with Marley would, I sense, be something else. Something familiar and other at the same time, like his complexion, which I spent the other night biting my tongue not to ask about. God, let my first question this evening not be "What *are* you?" Me, the Swedish Turk, interested enough in someone to be impressed by their ethnicity.

I THINK ABOUT IT all day at work. Holly refuses to tell me. She is amused, which suits her about as well as green eye shadow suits me. Not at all.

"Try a taste test," she teases.

"Disgusting girl."

I swivel my back to her, reach into the bottom drawer of my desk, and look at my lipsticks, then riffle through the box of samples until I find the brown spectrum, which I wipe one by one on my lips and turn to her for approval.

"Puerto Rican?"

She shrugs.

"Cuban?"

"Nuh-uh."

"Dominican?"

"Pffft."

"Sephardic Jew?"

She rolls her eyes.

"Indian?"

"Maybe."

"Feather or dot?"

"I'm not even dignifying that, Sadie."

Holly leans over my shoulder. "Oh, you two together are going to be great."

She selects a mochaccino from the bottom and hands it to me. I put it on carefully and blot.

"It's not fair! It's not fair!"

"You sound like a teenager." She shudders. "God, you were a miserable teenager."

"I was not! I was cheerful. That's why you liked me."

"That is not why I liked you."

"Why *were* we friends?"

"Too young to know better. Please let this be an end to you and older men."

GETTING READY FOR MY DATE. I apply individual false eyelashes to the very outer edge of each eye, thinking, as the glue dries, that I wasn't so sad back then when I was a teenager, not desperate, but I could feel the sadness beginning to creep in and that my depression was really the equivalent of women getting face-lifts before they need them. I decide my fear of turning twenty-five is preemptive, like women who get Botox before they get wrinkles. I'd like to think I've dealt with everything early so that my happiness won't start to sag too badly for a very long time.

I had spent my teenage years up until the present day worrying about my malaise. I don't imagine a teenager has time to feel malaise when he's had a baby. Maybe that is why Marley seems so solid.

We were going to the sandwich bar near my office, but then I ask if he feels like going to Balthazar and he makes it happen, which seems to be the way things go with Marley. He's like Santa with a paint smell. The restaurant is hopping. A very pretty black hostess with no bra and a gray tank top greets us, flashing perfect white teeth at my date. I held a pencil under my breasts this morning before leaving for work, seeking to further chart their decline. It wouldn't stay, dropping to the floor with a clang. I imagined my breasts following it. The hostess jiggles unconscionably as she leads us to our table. She tucks me into my seat and I feel like I am being put in a high chair by a beautiful nanny my papa is secretly fucking. I know for a fact that my dad never cheated on my mum. I'm not so sure about her. There was a time Engelbert Humperdinck came through town and she got very cagey. I was only five, but I remember it well. She wouldn't tell me a bedtime story any night that week.

Marley is wearing a black wool turtleneck and brown corduroy pants, and is sporting stubble. He looks great, and all of New York's beautiful women are gathered in this restaurant. Two Italians weaving past us to the restrooms honk their way through a conversation. They have short skirts and long glossy black hair; you could see the future in that shine, that shampoo scent could turn any man into a pervert, squeezing closer for a smell. I'm so jealous of those women. I have hair envy, table envy, food envy.

I hate feeling like I'm on a date. Correction. Like "we" are on a date, since he has to be there too. It took a long time for the music teacher at junior school to explain the word *duet*. I could not understand it. I tried and tried, but each time I glared at the other girl as her voice joined mine, even when we were onstage at the Christmas pageant. "The world does not revolve around you," people say. I look at them politely, like they are slightly mad, and I don't want to antagonize them. Jesus, the videotape my dad took of that Christmas-pageant duet debacle is not fun to watch.

"Do you videotape Montana?" It sounds creepy.

"I draw her." That sounds creepier. "I wanted to be an artist. A real artist." He is embarrassed. "I got sidetracked. So I like to draw her. She draws me too. She draws on me. I save a little from each trip." He bends his ear and shows me pink marks.

"But I do have photos somewhere." He fiddles in his wallet. I notice green and then hate myself for noticing it.

Both of the pictures are old baby shots. In the first, she has wisps of blond hair that someone has coaxed into a bow. She's wearing her long white christening gown, disappearing into its folds, her hands curled into tiny fists like she's going to deck the photographer. In the second, she is toddling toward the photographer, reaching out a chubby arm to touch him. The blond hair has grown into a thick hairdo, bangs starting at the crown of her head and stopping above her eyes, which are the pale blue of killer jellyfish. She's wearing a sailor suit.

"Now, is she really a sailor," I ask as I sip my lemonade, "or is that just a costume?"

He pauses for a minute, squinting a little. I flutter my semi-false eyelashes and he laughs.

"Ah, no, that's a costume for her second birthday," he says. "I should have a more up-to-date photo in here. I'll get one, I'll get one soon."

I dig into the bread and butter.

"When Jolene got pregnant," says Marley as he places the photos daintily back in his leather wallet, "I worried at first that I would feel I'd lost a part of me. But within forty-five minutes of Montana's being born, God, I loved her so much. I just wanted to squeeze her and hold her, and there's only so much you can squeeze a baby. I remember how much I wanted her to be able to understand words. It used to drive me crazy that she couldn't."

"I can imagine," I say, although I can't.

"Oh, but she learned so fast, it was as if she could see me suffering."

I try to imagine Marley suffering. I see his brow furrowing, deep lines rippling on his forehead, his tears running from his brown eyes, spilling onto his daughter and making her grow. I close my eyes and imagine myself growing, bigger and bigger like a beanstalk, breaking through the roof of the restaurant.

My mother always used to tell me I was "compact" and that I packed a lot into a little space "like Linda Ronstadt," she said, showing me an album from 1979. Linda looked gorgeous in cut-off jeans and a tank top. I discovered the rest of her albums one day when I was at Virgin. I wondered if my mum had stopped buying her records because she thought her music was getting worse or because she thought Linda was getting fat.

"So you're an only child I'm guessing," says Marley, interrupting my resentment nostalgia.

"Correct."

"I'm one of six."

"Wow."

"You can't imagine what it's like to fight for your mother's attention."

"Is Montana going to be an only child?"

"I'm not planning to have another kid. I love this one so much, it already squeezes the rest of my life out."

"Did you take that love for your little girl and use it to leave Jolene?"

"I used my own will to leave Jolene. It took a lot. She raised me. I was with her from the age of eighteen. She could have gone to jail for me in certain states."

"But she didn't."

"Not for that. She did go to jail though. She was cuffed for protesting the closure of a local abortion clinic. Montana was in her stomach. I've never been more hysterical in my life."

"So Montana was born a little criminal."

"You could say that."

"Good. Then I will."

Now it's in my head: the little criminal. I envisage her slipping out of her sailor outfit and into a little artful dodger getup, flat cap and ripped blazer with secret pockets to hide stolen wallets.

The menu is presented to us. I like a restaurant where they hand you the menu instead of flinging it. I had always wanted Isaac to bring me here and now I'm glad he didn't. I want to lose my restaurant-date virginity with Marley. I'm nervous. I need to calm down. I immediately scan to desserts.

"Ooh, I know what I want for pudding."

"What do you want for your main course?"

I look halfheartedly at the entrées.

"Frisée aux lardons." I'm not sure what it is but it sounds lazy, like someone with bed head in front of a TV.

"Salad with bacon and eggs. That's not enough. You need something else. Some more protein. They have really good mussels here, apparently." A dreamy look comes over his face and he murmurs, "I love mussels. I love to look at them."

"Why?" I ask curiously.

He looks like a little boy as he says with glee, "Because they look like cunts!"

The word he says, which I cannot bring myself to repeat, snaps like a castanet, a mussel in a shell. Then he sighs and mimes opening up a shell and peering at it sideways. I turn to see if our fellow diners are looking. They don't seem to have noticed anything, engrossed in being blown-out and European. I think about it again. The "c" word. There had been no violence to it. The pronounciation was a caress.

It is an extraordinary thing to say on a second date, before you've even slept with the person. It's gross. It's very, very odd. It is, most would agree, social suicide. It makes me love him immediately.

"Excuse me."

I go down to the ladies' room and hang out there. There are breath mints, hairspray. The lady is a Chechen. I know because I ask her, stalling for time so I won't have to go back upstairs, to my romantic doom. What a job, hanging out in the restroom all night, a secret underworld cavern. There's a seat with a mirror, so I sit down.

"I think I just fell in love."

"Congratulations," she says, accent as thick as my mother's.

"I don't know."

I look at myself in the mirror. "Fucker! Absolute fucker!"

She turns her head and I see the crucifix hanging around her neck.

"Excuse me."

"What made you fall in love?"

"Something he said. Something sweet he said. Oh, boy. I'm gone. He has a daughter too."

"How old?"

"Eight."

"Lovely age. Is she nice?"

"I don't know. I don't see why she wouldn't be. How do I look?"

The low-cut polka-dot dress was a big mistake, too much

tits rising and falling with every word I utter, like backseat
drivers, bores at a cocktail party constantly interrupting. I look
at them. "Get away from me!"

She tilts her eyebrows.

"This is too much, no?" I ask.

"No. I don't think so."

"Oy yoy yoy, I think so. Do you have a safety pin?"

She does.

"Better," she says.

"Can I stay down here with you?"

I didn't want to be in love, especially not with a young man,
a complicated young man with a young daughter, a man who
said the "c" word on a second date. The father, not the daughter, although it seemed likely that she was also a foulmouthed
outcast. That's why she had to wear a sailor outfit in photos.
The image of his ostracized eight-year-old, unable to make
friends because of her odd manners, made me feel so bad for
him that I went back up to the table as fast as I could.

"Are you okay?"

"Yep."

"You weren't having problems?"

"Not toilet problems."

This had to be the most vulgar dinner ever to occur in the
hallowed halls of Balthazar.

"What happened to your voluminous bosom?"

"It was distracting me."

"Me too. You look nice."

"I am nice."

I was so grateful when my frisée aux lardons came that I ate
it way too fast. I would have looked a damn sight more elegant
if I had snorted it.

"Whoa there; you've got quite an appetite."

"Thank you." I blush.

"Not quite crimson." He touches my cheek with his dark hand. I take it in mine and look at it.

"Not quite mocha. So what are you?"

"What am I?"

I open my bag and tip out the lipsticks, roll them toward him across the table. He looks at them one by one, at the labels I have stuck on them: "Puerto Rican," "Sephardic," "Native American." "This is what you're calling them?"

"No, no. I was just . . . thinking."

He opens one and twirls it up and down. Then he replaces the lid. "All of the above."

"Really?"

"You nailed it. You know me so well."

"So your family . . ."

"Montana is my family. That's it."

"That's enough, huh?"

"Feels that way."

"Wait a minute. Did you do the Welcome to Montana sign at the end of the Brooklyn Bridge?"

"Yes, I did! The day she was born."

"I used to look at that when I was riding the subway. I'm so jealous. Imagine being appreciated by the city like that."

"Well, I know it's not a trust fund for college, but it was the best I could do. I was only twenty."

"How did you make it all work?"

"I had to. That's the truest answer I can give."

"Are you anti-abortion?"

"I'm pro going with the flow."

"That's a pretty heavy flow you went with there."

"You're not wrong."

I am awash with childishness. Well, if he has enough, why is he taking me out to dinner?

"You're beautiful."

"So I'm told."

I am being a brat. He laughs.

The mussels come and I try to pretend he hasn't said what he's said as I watch him eat—not watching but looking up sideways.

"You did that when we kissed. You didn't look at me."

"I couldn't. Jesus, I'm fucking freezing."

He smiles. "I love it when someone says *Jesus* and *fuck* in the same sentence. My Catholic-school upbringing."

I put on my jacket. "Catholic. Ewww. My mum's Catholic."

"My mom was Catholic, but she's dead."

"My dad's Jewish and he's awesome," I say.

"Just goes to show. So you want dessert?"

I really, really do, but we are running late for the movie and I feel gypped, always do, the way other women do when they shave their legs and don't have sex. I put on a pretty dress for this? There is nothing more gorgeous than a girl in a dress eating dessert. Holly told me that. She says it makes her want to come.

"Let's get it to go," he says. He insists on paying. I see he has paint on his wrist. He guides me out with his hand on my hip. It feels sharp; all of me feels sharp in his hand. Senses attuned. Everything is noisier, colder than when I walked in. The hostess smiles broadly at me as we walk out, and for some reason I believe she is happy for us and I forgive her her beauty.

We walk over to the Angelika theater, me in my fancy dinner outfit carrying the carton of profiteroles. My black polka-dot dress with the sky-high red heels that are so comfortable they are the official choice of every transsexual I have ever met, made slightly less chic by the nude fishnets that cause me to slip perilously as we try to make it to the movie. My white fake-fur coat sits boxy on top of the skirt, which billows up around it, and I have double reason to wish I was for once wearing tights instead of stockings. Tights and leggings and snow boots and a windbreaker.

"Last time you were dressed down." He sounds disappointed.

"This is my superhero outfit."

He holds my hand.

"Motherfuck I'm cold."

"Creative. Why so freezing?"

You have made me cold with your warmth.

"I'm wearing stockings."

I say it so resentfully, with the wrong voice completely. It sucks all of the sexiness out of it, so planned. The look was a great idea: black arches, red lipstick. I had thought, as I applied it, that it was '50s pinup, but now I see that my outfit has veered too close to Mexican gang girl. I've read they wear all that aging makeup because they're statistically unlikely to reach middle age. That's how I feel about romance, I who have played Lolita so long. That's what I want my memoir to be called: *I Who Have Played Lolita So Long.*

We sit near the front. I get very upset by the film, in which a beautiful actress is made to look ugly. It seems somehow a terrible symbol for Grrrl, for what we are selling and what those poor little girls are buying in their quest to differentiate themselves from the crowd. At the end of the movie the actress is murdered. Of course she has to die. How else is she going to get cred? For a terrible moment I imagine it being the next stage in Holly's marketing strategy. "You wear the bruise collection. And then someone hits you on the head with a hammer. And when they print the crime-scene photo in the paper I want to make sure Grrrl gets a prominent credit."

I cry and cry. Afterward I run to the restroom. The red of my nose and eyes looks terrible with the red lipstick. I am a mess.

"Let's clean you up, Sadie Steinberg."

"That's a pretty name," says a woman behind me.

I wash my face with the bottle sample I save for just such an occasion from my soon-to-be-released Walk of Shame collection.

Then we hop a cab to my place.

TINGLE

I LOOK OUT THE WINDOW and he comes up behind me and starts to kiss my neck. I go to the bed and take off my dress. I don't think he is admiring my red-and-white polka-dot underwear properly, so I stop him and arch my back, turn around so that he can see the little gap at the back, the stockings ruined, ripped off as soon as we got back as if shaking an Etch A Sketch clean. I hate being half dressed. I just want to be undressed completely so that we can screw and get it over with and I can put my clothes back on.

I am about to unhook my bra when he says, "Let's sleep."

"Really?"

"Really."

It is the best sleep I've had in a long time. I try to wake up all pretty, but when I open my eyes Marley is leaning over me, cooing, "Mmm, you have dragon's breath." "I'll brush my teeth," I snap. "No, no, leave it. I like it. It's real." I'm hungry, but Marley is rubbing his hands all over me in a manner far more exploratory than the night before. He nuzzles my neck and scoops his hand between my legs, running his thumb over my polka dots. I lean into his ear as if I am about to talk dirty and whisper, "Feed me."

I am thinking a slap-up breakfast—bacon, eggs, home fries, and coffee—but Marley drags me by the hand to the local health-food store, where he orders berry smoothies. With soy. As we wait for the blender to empty its purple contents, he bites his nails. "Hey." I slap them away and start kissing him. Once we start to kiss, neither of us can stop. After a full minute we are woken from our reverie by the angry voice of a middle-aged woman.

"There is a time and a place and this is not the time or the place." She has long gray dreadlocks and a Malcolm X T-shirt.

"There's food here," she adds, which seems odd. I think of her long dreadlocks grazing the salad bar.

"I'm sorry," I say, but as soon as we are outside, smoothies in hand, I hiss, "What a cow."

"No," Marley says sadly, "she was right. It was very rude."

The smoothie is too cold against my teeth. "Jesus, we were just kissing."

"No. I was doing more."

He resumes biting his fingernails, a most unbecoming trait for a man, so girly and neurotic.

"Why are you doing that?"

"Because I want to put my fingers in your cunt. And I don't want to hurt you."

Two grand mission statements. My cunt, as it has now been named, begins to blush. I hold myself against him, the heat radiating. Please take me home please take me home. I don't say it out loud.

"Okay."

I have said it out loud.

I down the smoothie and my tummy is instantly full, but I still feel light. Hand in bitten hand, we pass Saint Luke's, the redbrick wall along its gates tagged with ugly blue graffiti.

Marley is outraged. "That's just wrong. God, I'm glad I sold out and stopped."

I squeeze his hand and he kisses the top of my head.

"You should stand up taller, Sadie. There's at least two inches I could get out of you."

"What are you talking about?"

"You have a beautiful body and lousy posture. You're not engaging your powerhouse. Basic Pilates. Very easy to incorporate into everyday life."

"You're into that?"

"Oh, yeah, I've been practicing Pilates since I was seventeen."

"Which is a whole what, eleven years?"

"Don't you think about getting older?"

"No." I have been wearing a bra to bed every night since I was fourteen so my breasts won't sag.

"Montana does it too; so does my ex. We still do it together."

"You do it together?"

"You know . . . We're close."

"So what happened?"

"Um, she was older than me. She was my Pilates teacher."

"Ohhh."

"What does that mean?"

"Well, of course, a boy . . . a man like you, had to have been taught by an older woman."

"I like to think I'm self-taught. That's what I like to think."

I turn to him and press him against the graffitied wall of the church. "I like you very much for someone who does yoga and Pilates and uses the word *cunt* so often."

He laughs. "What do you call it?"

"Hoo hoo. My hoo hoo."

"My daughter calls it her noo noo. That's funny. I can't bring myself to call it your hoo hoo."

"So just don't call it at all."

"All right."

"We'll leave my vagina out of this."

"Okay, we'll have a relationship and we'll just leave your vagina out completely."

"Good."

Then we go home and have sex and it changes everything. My vagina is very, very involved. I hate it when men go down on me, drippy and gooey and it's always all about them. But his tongue is soft and almost dry, like a cat's tongue. I am ugly and naked immediately and he makes me come so fast I forget to arch my back and twist and turn, all those things to signify I am enjoying it. Instead I just come. Muscles grab and grab at him, insane crazy woman, "Don't go don't leave me!" hysterical and sobbing, all those things we can't say out loud. My vagina is going to give me away. I feel a little shellshocked. He is the first man who has ever made me come. All those older men and then this little pisher. He holds me close, his arm around my waist. My belly used to be flat. Now it is round, all these little changes every day.

After we make love, he curls up beside me and I look, really look, at his cock. Not the flash of my father's penis, an accidental sighting, a penis swinging inside a loose dressing gown, whereas Marley's is for fucking and is thus a cock. I look at the color and the shape, trying to figure out the workings of the man I love.

"Can I touch there?"

"Yep."

"It doesn't hurt?"

"Nope."

"Which part is most sensitive?"

"Here."

It is a living, breathing *Cosmo* how-to article come to life. After I am finished investigating his penis, he makes me toast and tea. Then he hops back in bed, where I am arranged on the sheets thinking of the cherries in the snow, glad I have my red-and-white polka-dot knickers, which are back in place.

"What was that about last night, all the Bettie Page stuff?" he asks, snuggling next to me.

"What do you mean?"

"All those poses you were doing."

My heart contracts like the evil twin of my orgasm. There is a release, but it is bile in my throat. I try not to cry.

"Hey, hey. I'm sorry. I thought, This girl is either very experienced or very naive."

I try to hold it together. "Somewhere in between."

"It's no big deal. This morning was just so great, when you stopped acting."

"I acted for a long time," I cry, and tell him about Isaac, about the others. My clothes are everywhere, like voyeurs, bums, drunks crashing a party. Dresses have thrown up socks. I hate my apartment. I hate it.

He moves his hands across my de-braed breasts.

"I used to draw tits like that when I was a kid."

"You say *tits* and *cunt* and *cock*."

"It is what it is."

"You don't think it sounds ugly?"

"I was raised with ugliness. That's not it."

"Would you want Montana to say those things? Or hear those things?"

"I just want her to be a good person. To be kind and generous. That's good enough."

"And to not eat sugar."

"And to not eat sugar." He kisses me.

When he finally leaves, I whisper, "Can I come to your place next time?"

He strokes my hair. "Maybe."

"Mrs. Maybe and her amazing baby," I mock, which my mother used to say to me. She'd also say "Oh, I was so proud I was crying like a turtle" and "Oh, that man is such a pompadom."

AT WORK THE NEXT DAY I tell the girls how amazing he was. Vicki is a little churlish, which I can't understand. I sit looking at my lipsticks and I just see the color of his cock. "You should do kind of a pinky-red with purple undertones," I suggest.

"Are you thinking about his cock?" snaps Holly.

"Nooo! God, you're disgusting."

"I know you are, but what am I?"

I spit back as instinctively as I had when we were nine. "I know you are, but what am I?"

"Infinity."

Vicki looks up from her work. "What are you people, children?"

Vicki has her cat pom-pom socks on. I burst out laughing. I try to stop, but I can't, and then Holly does too, and I remember trying not to laugh in assembly and seeing the gym teacher's ugly feet squeezed into stilettos. Vicki storms to the bathroom. Ivy goes to comfort her. Holly, composing herself, looks at me.

"Oh, I don't give a shit."

12   TANTRUM

MY COMEUPPANCE is that as I do my work I start to feel ill. I have had, throughout my life, frequent bouts of cystitis. In England it's called cystitis, which sounds like the name of the girl who got kicked out of Destiny's Child. In America it's called a urinary tract infection, or UTI, which, like so many American things, sounds like you are being watched via covert homeland security cameras. The long and short of it is, when I get an attack I feel like I have to pee all the time and then nothing comes out and then when it finally does come, a torturous dribble, it hurts like hell. I get cystitis if I have sex, if I think about having sex, if I wear noncotton underwear, if I wear tights instead of stockings (accidental sexiness from something supremely unsexy). Because I have to go to the bathroom every few minutes, people who don't know me think I'm a cokehead.

Nausea spreads through my body like a Mexican wave. Cystitis. Big time. I go home at lunchtime. I still can't get used to Holly being my boss.

"Uh, I don't feel so good."

"So go home."

I don't have to pretend or sniffle like I did at my last job.

Marley has called and I call him back and tell him I'm not feeling too good and he offers to come over. He arrives wearing a raincoat and wet hair.

"I feel really sick. I have a tummyache from hell," I tell Marley. I do not want to tell him my problem on a second date, which technically we still are on. He has made me come and now he has made me sore and both are rather intimate. I am glad I am with a father.

"Owwww!" I lie on the floor and cry. I do not want to have to tell him this so soon, that I can't do sex right, that I am not built for it. I want to be a sex goddess. I am a sex nymph. Ina of the slim ankles was my favorite goddess when we studied classics at school. I don't know what she did besides have slim ankles. That was good enough for Zeus. I could be her cousin, Sadie who reads *US Weekly*. Godly powers for unheroic acts.

As he makes me drink water and chamomile tea, Marley puts *Finding Nemo* in the DVD. All the water is making my cystitis feel diluted. I am feeling a little better. But then the sad story kicks in: You give a fish Albert Brooks's voice and I'm screwed. I miss my dad so bad that even though he's not a fish and I don't have a deformed fin and in further news I'm not a fish, I get upset and it all starts to hurt again.

"Montana was bored by this," says Marley as he brings me my tea. "She's not really used to watching TV, so a screen just confuses her. She always thinks she wants to watch a video and then she lasts about twenty minutes before she's bored."

I think about his parenting skills compared to my father's. I imagine them being the same age (my father was only a few years older when he had me), talking at the playground as we play, me and Montana in the sandbox, everyone admiring the two handsome fathers. Then Jude Law comes up and everyone is a handsome young father together.

"Mnnppp, mmmm, uh-huh-uh." I stifle sobs.

"I want to help you. I can't help you because I can't understand you. If you tell me what's wrong, I'll help."

I let my reaction sobs, which are like reaction shots, subside. "My wees hurt and I want to talk to my dad and my land line's been cut off and I don't have long distance on my cell."

"Your wees hurt?"

"I have cystitis. You have given me cystitis."

"I have given you what?"

"A urinary tract infection. From fucking."

"Oh, no. Oh, don't say that."

"It's true. It hurts."

"Oh, my God. I feel horrible."

"You don't need to," I scream from the floor as I clutch my stomach.

"Okay, here's the phone. Maybe after that we should take you to the doctor." He passes it to me. I feel a little baffled and dial the number somewhat testily.

"Papa?" As soon as I hear his voice I want to go back to baby tears, but Marley is standing over my shoulder. "My wees hurt."

"Well, what do you want me to do about it?"

"Feel sorry for me."

"I feel very sorry for you."

"But it hurts."

"I'm sure that it does."

"I think I have an infection. What shall I do?"

"Go to the doctor. I have to get back to work."

Handing back the phone, I repeat my father's instruction. "He says go to the doctor."

"I already said that." Marley shrugs, stroking my stomach.

"I wanted to hear my papa say it."

"I'm somebody's papa." He kisses my stomach as I groan. "Do you have insurance?" he asks.

"I forgot to pay the bill. It hasn't kicked in from work yet."

"We'll figure it out." He zips up his raincoat: punctuation at the end of his promise.

IN THE WAITING ROOM he holds his credit card between his fingers and keeps flipping it over and over like a gangster flipping a coin in a film noir. With his other hand he holds my fingers. Of course the second we walk into the waiting room I start to feel a bit better. I look at a magazine as the minutes tick by. I see that Minnie Driver is a proponent of a new kind of yoga.

"Some spastic invented Cool Yoga. You do it in freezing temperatures. How retarded is that?"

"That was Montana's mother," says Marley softly.

"What?"

"Montana's mother, Jolene, is the one who created Cool Yoga. I'd like to take some of the credit, but she was already plotting it before she even met me."

"Is she rich?"

"Extremely. You haven't seen her exercise videos?"

"Noooo."

I try to change the subject. He tries harder.

"She's also experimenting with a line of bath products. Bubble baths and soaps that feel icy against your body."

"Nice." I start flicking through the magazine even harder, as though it is a workout. I'm going to pitch the foot-in-mouth workout. I find it sheds pounds quickly. You get too embarrassed to eat. We sit in silence for some time, he stroking my stomach now.

"*Spastic* is not a nice word. I'm sorry."

"It isn't a nice word. But no worries."

I slow my flicking down and actually begin to look at the photos. "Ooh, cute." I can't help myself, wowed by the power of Scarlett Johansson attending a premiere in a yellow Christian Dior dress.

"You think so?"

"You don't think so?"

"I don't know."

"Is she cute?" He shrugs his shoulders. I flick the page and point at Demi Moore. "You like older women. Is she cute?"

"Too much makeup. Too skinny."

Then he stops me before I can turn the next page. "Jennifer Connelly has beautiful eyes."

"She does not." I scowl. "She's got dead eyes. And I hate her nose. She has a pig's nose. Brunettes are supposed to be warm, not cold. They just found someone to fill the intelligence gap."

I start to panic. "You love her. You want to marry her. You were thinking about Jennifer Connelly in bed." I tug at my curls. "She has *straight* hair." I sob. The sick patients turn to stare at me. I hope none of them is about to hear that she is dying or pregnant or I will color her good/bad news forever. One lady pats her pregnant stomach anxiously.

"All I said was she has pretty eyes."

"Beautiful, you said beautiful." Like a prosecutor. I stand up and pace around his chair, clutching my abdomen in agony.

"Do you want me to go away?"

"NO! Don't leave me!"

The doctor sees me, prescribes an over-the-counter medication, which Marley immediately collects, and then we go home and he tucks me into bed. My eyes are puffy.

"I don't know what that was about, that was really, really

weird, freak-out, bad behavior," I say as I knock back my medicine. Then, most unlike me, "Sorry."

"That's okay. Look. It's nerve-racking being in love."

"Who's in love?"

"You're in love with me."

I gasp.

"And," he adds in the clear voice of Sidney Poitier accepting an award, "I'm in love with you."

I am flabbergasted.

"So we're equal."

"We're equal?" I don't know what to say, so I roll over and put my head away from him on the pillow.

He strokes my ear. "Sleep awhile. I'll leave you my phone in case you need it."

When he creeps out, I call my dad.

"I did something bad."

"Uh-oh."

"Well, let me just preface this by saying that Jennifer Connelly has a nose like a pig."

"Now, Sadie, you say that a lot about actresses, but let's try to think what a pig actually looks like. It sort of has a wide round nose that appears flat from the front but from the sides sticks out and up. So that isn't really accurate. Jennifer Connelly has a nose more like Pinocchio, wouldn't you say?"

"Yes."

"Don't you think this is a bit silly? Marley sounds like a nice guy."

"He does?"

"He waited for you at the doctor's after you threw a fit? Sounds like a keeper to me."

"Thanks, Papa."

I fall asleep.

. . .

SIDNEY KATZ PAWS ME AWAKE. When I pad into the living room, I find my medicine has been laid out for me, with a pile of magazines next to it. Flicking through them, I see that, before leaving, Marley defaced every single photo of Jennifer Connelly with a beard or a mustache. It is such an oddly tender gesture that it makes my knees wobble. Love love love. He comes back in the evening.

"Now, let's get some soup on," he says, moving toward my gas stove.

"No!" I leap up like a teenage boy about to have his drawer full of porn discovered. "It's never been switched on."

"How long have you lived here?"

"Four years."

"And you never turned it on?"

"I just told you that."

"And I didn't quite believe it. Ah, well, let's turn it on."

"No!"

"No?"

"I'm superstitious. Maybe something will *happen* if you turn it on."

"Yeah, something will happen. You'll get hot soup."

He turns it on as I put my fingers in my ears. The smell of chicken soup seeps into the living room like a hit single.

"Eat this."

"I don't want to."

"Eat it."

"Mmmm, yummy." It is really good.

"Like I'd give you something yucky."

"You wouldn't?"

"No."

And then, having seen me at my worst and having offered defaced photos of an Oscar-winning actress, we are together. We lie on the daybed, arms and legs entwined.

"How's your hoo hoo?"

"Pretty perky, actually."

He pats it through my dressing gown.

"So this love thing you mentioned . . ."

"Yeah. It's not very convenient. I have a child."

"I am a child."

"You are. Great. What am I thinking?"

"I don't know."

"Me either. Oh, well."

13 MYSTIC JUKEBOX

PICKING ME UP FROM WORK, Marley hails a cab to go to his place, and as soon as we get in I memorize the number of the cabdriver just in case he kills us. It's not because he's Arab that I think he might have something sinister in mind; it's because he's listening to Billy Joel. I really don't want to die, but if I do die, I want someone to get in trouble. Not vengeful, vigilante trouble, more the kind of trouble that stops banks from giving you a mortgage.

"M987," I say to myself as I snuggle up beside Marley. I touch his hand, then his thigh, then I nuzzle his neck, then I tilt my head up to kiss him.

"No," he says softly, in the kind of voice you use to say "yes."

"What?"

"I can't do that. Making out in cabs. I feel like it's disrespect-ful to the driver."

"Oh. I'm sorry." There're times I can't help but feel he's reprimanding me. That's what you get for dating a dad.

I look up at the license and see that M987 is actually Osama

Mohammed. He hung his taxi license upside down, poor bastard.

"It's okay," Marley says, and gives my thigh a little squeeze. I squish myself away from him and lean my head against the window. I watch the Lower East Side speed by, a blur of bodegas and graffiti, the scent of Chinese cabbage accompanying it like a soundtrack. Osama is going too fast, but I'm enjoying it. At least someone in the taxi isn't hung up on taking his time. Is that fair? Yes, Marley's gotta take his time: He has a kid, he has a complicated romantic history, and the last big impulsive thing he did made him a junkie. And yet I can't help thinking . . . love *is* the drug. It is addiction, it is irrational, it is madness, the best kind of destruction, a kind of self-destruction that, after it implodes, reforms itself as something better. At least that's the way it always seemed from listening to Bruce Springsteen. I sigh. And instantly, in one of those magical moments when you get to be DJ and listener at the same time, Billy Joel fades out and "Born to Run" comes on the radio.

"Hey!" I turn back to Marley in shock, but he merely looks at me because he doesn't realize that I just played mystic jukebox.

I know this song by heart, like a poem. Because, in fact, I once learned it by heart for a school poetry recital. Dad helped me break it down into chunks. He wrote it down on little flashcards for me and had me say it back to him. He waited out in the school auditorium to watch me triumph, which I surely would have done if I had not been disqualified for choosing a song instead of a poem. Dad took it well. We spoke-sang it together in the car on the way home. Now I sit in a yellow taxi on another continent from my papa, with a young man who looks like he might be related to him. And

I say: " 'In the day we sweat it out in the streets of a runaway American dream.' "

And I am actually in America. And I am actually with someone I could run away with. And, actually, at the speed upside-down Osama is going, we kind of are runaways.

" 'At night we ride through mansions of glory and suicide machines!' " I sing, in a voice so soft that, to my surprise, I am in tune. Marley leans his forehead against his window and starts to sing too.

He steals a glance at me, then leans in and whispers, "Your breasts are bouncing." I can't think of an answer, so I keep singing and soon enough Marley is kissing my neck. As we pull onto the Brooklyn Bridge, he cups my face in his hands and starts to kiss me, hard and loose like a kissing version of Bruce racing up and down the ramp at Wembley stadium with a guitar on his back so the whole audience, even those in the cheapest of cheap seats, can see him. I glance up at Osama, who looks stonily ahead.

"Marley, you are a man of principle."

I'm thinking of Bruce on an eight-track and my father at the wheel when I say it. But once it's been said, I'm thinking of Marley too. Although, to the best of my knowledge, he has met neither my dad nor Bruce Springsteen, by the time we pass the Welcome to Montana sign and drift over the Brooklyn Bridge in dream time, they're all drinkin' it up together backstage at the Stone Pony.

Upside-down Osama is driving a cab in America as it ought to be. It has been a good ride. I am surprised to note when I see him in the rearview mirror that Osama looks cross.

When we get out, I make a point of tipping him five dollars on a fifteen-dollar fare, to compensate for the horrors he has seen. The UTI has gone. I left it somewhere in Chinatown, among the red cabbages. Before Marley so much as undoes the first button on his jeans, he makes me promise that I am completely healed, and I do such a good job of convincing him that I am, it isn't until we're making love that I realize it's the truth.

14   LADIES MERELY GLOW

I GO TO THE BATHROOM to touch up my makeup, my crotch already tingling with the first fizz of the relapsed urinary tract infection. Although I can see the next five days of cranberry juice, live yogurt, and milk baths panning out before me like the regimen of a health spa for whores, I still feel happy.

I check in the mirror and see mascara running down my face. Ugh. To be so intimate with someone and not know your cheeks are inked with black. He knows what your insides feel like, but you don't know how your own face looks. But that's the risk of sweaty sex. You don't get to look pretty. This is Holly's dream ad campaign right here, looking back at me in the mirror. I wipe the mascara off as best I can. I can't imagine how many times I have had uninhibited sex to make a man like me, probably no more than I made myself try to get a man to like me. And I look so ugly either way, face all twisted and red. How do people with mirrors on their ceilings ever reach orgasm?

I splash my face with water and then, turning my back to

the mirror, lean against the sink to try to catch my breath. I realize I have been sitting there, breathy and blank-brained, for a while, and suddenly I feel too embarrassed to return to the bedroom. Those fifteen minutes seem like a two-week period of noncommunication and I can't work up the courage to pick up the phone. It is doubly neurotic since I know Marley is passed out cold. Realizing that I have some leeway, but still afraid to return to the bed, I scoop myself up off the sink and go to look at Marley's house. We did it in the kitchen, which is surprisingly roomy and well stocked for a bachelor boy. The living room is large and ill lit, hung with eerie, childish artwork that looks like the prison work of a serial killer, that naif stuff Marilyn Manson sells to Johnny Depp. But on closer inspection each is signed Montana. Of course. The prepubescent white elephant in the room, framed neatly and hung lovingly. The centerpiece is a coffee table/Scrabble board Marley told me he had made himself on his last birthday.

I know, of course, the bedroom, clean and light like a room at a B and B, two dogeared *New Yorker*s on the bedside table contributing to the illusion that this is a weekend getaway. And, truth to tell, it feels like a weekend getaway and that's what's making me nervous. I want to meet the kid. I don't want to be the weekend getaway. As much as I dreamed of finding someone to be a Springsteen-ian runaway with, I don't want to be a getaway at all. I want to be home. I want to be the place he's thinking of if he ever has to click his heels together three times and say "There's no place like home."

And I figure the only way to be that is to meet his daughter. The only way to be his true love is to befriend the one woman he will always love more than me, and always should love more than me, no matter what.

Montana's name is written on her door in the same bubble script as on the billboard. She is only eight years old, but already she has her own logo. I touch my hand to it and whisper, "Please like me. Please please like me. I like your daddy so much." I kiss my fingers and place them on her doorknob like it's a mezuzah and I'm just about to turn it and take a peek when I think: She should be the one to show me her room, when she feels like showing it to me. I remember how crazy it used to make me when my mum would take harmless flicks through my harmless little diary. Even the most loved and pampered eight-year-old feels like she has nothing that is truly hers, and I remember feeling that my mother being in my room without me was a huge transgression. I edge away from the door before I can change my mind and wander back up the hall to Marley's room. The door is closed and for a moment, moving my fingers to the knob, my hand looks tiny in front of me, the knob way too high to reach without standing on tip-toes. I stretch up, clad in a winceyette bunny-print nightie, and when I get to the other side, it has transformed back into a big girl's black lace underwear.

As I climb into bed, Marley pulls me on top of him.

"I saw your daughter's room."

He kisses me and says, "Don't look so frightened. She isn't here."

I climb off him and back between the sheets. "That's why I'm here, huh?"

He nods breezily, but I feel like I am about to be sacrificed.

"Yes," he says, "that's why you're here. She gets here tomorrow since you mention it."

"How long will she be here?"

"Well, I've been meaning to talk to you. A while. Back and forth. I'll be looking after her a couple of nights a week."

"How come?"

"Because I'm her father. And because her mother is launching her line of Cool Yoga bath products here. She's going to be working overtime. So I won't get to see you quite the way we have been. I'm excited to have her with me, but I feel bad about this, like I'm betraying her or being a shitty dad: I really feel pissed that I can't spend all my time with you. It's been so delicious."

"Why can't you do both?"

"What do you mean?"

"Why can't I be here when she's here?"

"It's pretty early on to meet her, don't you think?"

"No, I don't! You've already told me that you love me."

"And as soon as I told you that I loved you every fiber of my being screamed no no no! Retreat! Retreat!"

"What am I, Iraq?"

"I'm sorry, but it's the truth: I got that sick feeling I think I last had when I ate steak after being vegetarian for ten years."

"What am I, meat?"

He sighs. "I think what I'm trying to say is coming out wrong."

"I think so, maybe. You wanna try again?"

I feel bad 'cuz I sound a little harsh. Then I see in a flash that besides all his other talents, Marley has the coveted gift of being able to make you feel bad for telling him when he makes you feel bad. That's a real girl skill, that one. Vicki works on it nonstop. But her face isn't half as sweet as Marley's, the daddy with the baby face.

"Oh, man. Look." He shrugs, his cheeks flushing pink. "I never date girls your age because they always, without fail, cheated on me. I was so good to them and I was always left with egg on my face."

"I'm sorry." At the same time I feel a terrible urge to punch those girls from the past, I know, in my future, that there is no telling I won't do the same thing they did. Marley, his eyes glassy, is still leafing through their datebook, opening the car door to find them with another guy, sitting behind his gal as she's necking with another guy in the movie theater.

"They weren't even being malicious. Not at all. Girls in their early twenties are just finding themselves. Older women know their sexuality, they're done with experimenting."

I've done enough experimenting to last me a lifetime, but I don't tell him that. Besides, I'm not going to interrupt him. He's on a roll now.

"I want to find a woman who won't walk out, because she'd be walking out on me *and* Montana. I want to find someone I can grow old with, be sick with. I can't imagine anything more romantic than cleaning shit off your dying lover's ass." The shine comes back to his brown eyes. "It would be like making love."

"Gross!" I holler, unable to contain myself.

"I have a baby. I know fluids can be beautiful. I made a chart for Montana's poos and wees. That's how you know everything's functioning right. Her poos were an occasion for celebration. 'Gold!' I'd call them. 'We have gold!' "

"Gross."

"You've said that twice now."

"I know, and I usually say it only once or twice a year."

He seems really offended by this.

"Don't you get it? It's beautiful."

"I'm trying to get it. It's just that I'm twenty-four. And I don't have a child. I'm trying to get it. I just think if you'd let me meet your kid, it would be easier for me to understand. Don't you think?"

He ignores me. "It's okay, Sadie. It's hard to get. But I suppose I thought you, with all your mess and cat hair, would get it."

"I don't have cat hair. My cat looks after it for me."

I look down at my T-shirt. It is coated. Every time I pet Sidney Katz he sheds an entire sweater. "Okay, so I'm covered in cat hair and my apartment's a pigsty. But I love the mess. It helps me feel free." Bullshit. Bullshit. Bullshit that I want to get on my hands and knees and shovel up and burrow under the earth.

"Jolene loves cleaning up. Loves it. Neat freak. She spent two thousand dollars on a vacuum cleaner."

That he is comparing us already . . . Is that good or bad?

"That sucks."

"No, it's wonderful. I can't tell you how great it is to be around."

I look over at my pile of clothes in the corner, which have somehow crept into a new corner, now at two bases. I'm cornered. I am about to give up, leave, when he kisses me. Just leans forward at the end of his sentence and plants one on my mouth for no reason.

Goddammit. Why has no one kissed me like this before? Twenty-four years old and everyone has been joking with me all these years? What a ripoff. I want my money back. I want to go to each of their houses and stand outside until they give me my kisses back. I'll melt them down, sanitize them, and regenerate them in the shape of this: the real thing.

And yet . . . and yet . . . the real thing can't be really real until I meet Montana. And he doesn't want me to. Which means he doesn't mean it when he says he loves me. Okay, slow down, Sadie, take a breath, not a hop, skip, and jump. Don't put two and two together and get insecurity.

I search for my next sentence out the window. The sky is slushy gray like the bathtub ring from dyed blond hair. I am so glad I'm not a blonde anymore. That ring used to drive me crazy. The blond was never neat enough and never slutty enough. I was neither Grace Kelly nor Debbie Harry. I was just a mess. He has great hair, Marley, thick, dark, wavy. Movie-star hair.

I look back at him; his face has clouded over. "What are you thinking, Marley?"

"I was just thinking about making love to you. And you coming. And me coming. I just think what we have is so exceptional. I would be so devastated if . . ." He can't finish the sentence, so I finish it for him.

"If I thought it was rubbish?"

He nods sadly and I see that he has taken his own hop, skip, and jump, resulting in a cavalcade of suspicion beneath those lashes and under that heart. I take his hand, which, cut, chewed-nailed, and paint-stained, hides nothing.

"Marley, I really do want to meet Montana. And I want to meet her not as her father's girlfriend but as her father's friend. I should be genderless."

He holds my hand tight and laughs. "With that rack? Good luck!"

"And we can't show affection in front of her, none, not even holding hands."

He turns serious. "I don't know if I can cope with not touching you."

"Well, you're going to have to. We have to think long-term."

Immediately I regret saying it. *Long* and *term*. Conjures up images of Margaret Thatcher clinging to power until her approval rating went so low that even her own party couldn't stop the freefall. I imagine myself in a two-piece suit, one of her frilly affronts to femininity around my neck, orange bouffant of hair, soupy glances from Ronald Reagan.

Marley changes the subject. "Don't you have to write? I thought it was so gorgeous the way you got rid of me that first morning so you could work on your novel."

"You did?"

"Oh, my God, I went home and jerked off."

"Disgusting."

"Don't worry. I don't do it anymore. I can't do it without you."

I mime blushing behind an eighteenth-century fan.

"You're too kind." I stay behind my imaginary fan an extra beat and try to figure it out. "Wait, so is that a yes? Am I meeting the little darling? Do I get to shake hands with my jury, my archnemesis, my celestial soul mate, my future?"

I look out from my fake fan to check that I didn't say any of that out loud. From the way Marley is dreamily masturbating, I take it that's a no. Breath of relief. My indoor voice has started to kick in. First sign of the apocalypse. Perhaps I'm growing up.

15 THE HAVE-LOTS

GORKY'S, open from 6 A.M. to midnight, is the best café in the Village to write in. Sometimes I have a bash at my novel; more often I bang out names for Grrrl. At the front left window table is the seat where I came up with "The Have-Lots." It was, in a single morning, the cosmetics equivalent of the five-year period when Prince released *Lovesexy, Purple Rain,* and *Sign o' the Times.* The music at Gorky's is great and played at precisely the right volume: nostalgia rock—you know it so well you can hear it without listening and it doesn't distract from your own words. Often *The White Album.* Sometimes Donovan's greatest hits (and they are great); occasionally Sheryl Crow. The amazing thing about the Beatles is that they always sound of the times. That's how you know they're the most important band in the history of rock.

There are a couple of group tables and several coveted desks in the recessed dark corners and by the full-length front-facing windows. At night the clientele seems to be teachers marking homework, during the day aspiring screenwriters gossiping about who got their short into Sundance between slurps of coffee. The waitresses call out exotic names—"Paloma," "Tatiana"—as they bring unexotic food to the inspirees.

Today I sit across from an actor memorizing lines for an audition. "But don't come back," he hisses between sips of tomato soup, and "Oh, you want a cigarette?" He makes little Al Pacino tics. His lines in the script are circled. I see him staring into the air and psyching himself up. He is not going to get the part. He sings along to Donovan.

At the table across the way there is a twentysomething guy I think I recognize from a UPN sitcom I once saw, and he's staring at pretty girls, of whom there are a number. One says, "How you doing?"

"Pretty good. Doin' some work." He looks away. I know they have never had more than a conversation and they don't even know each other's name, but he is acting like he didn't call her after sex. I am so happy to be in a relationship. He should be so lucky. The politics of coffeeshop chat screw with my concentration and I close my laptop without writing a line.

That night, when he is peeing into my toilet, I knock on the door and ask Marley, "Am I your girlfriend?"

He stops peeing, kicks the door ajar, kisses me, and answers, "You're my special friend." He sees my face fall and adds, "My very special friend."

Hmm. I climb back into bed and start reading *The National Enquirer.*

"I wish you wouldn't read that shit."

"That's what you wish? That you waste your wishes on?"

He grabs it out of my hand and kisses me and Jake Gyllenhaal and Kirsten Dunst's grainy kiss shot has nothing on us. I am trapped in the inky embrace of a tabloid, out-of-focus kiss. But his daughter doesn't know I exist and I feel like a mistress. Most women spend the courtship waiting to hear "I love you."

I got that out of the way so fast that I'm now waiting to hear it from his daughter. If I ever meet her. Which he hasn't decided about yet.

The next morning I intend to go back to Gorky's on my way to work, determined to sketch my heroine, a civil war (still not sure which) mistress of a missing soldier. You have to get there early because tables go fast and then they're occupied for hours and hours. There's one in the corner and two by the window, and these are the optimum work spots. Depends on the time of day too. The sun gets in your eyes in the left-hand corner if you're facing the wrong way. You could wear sunglasses, but a person writing a novel with sunglasses on is just offensive. The other patrons don't know I'm writing a masterwork that's going to be remembered alongside *Anna Karenina* and *The Brothers Karamazov*. Or, at least, that I plan to. Only problem is, I don't remember *Anna Karenina* or *The Brothers Karamazov*. One has a woman and one has some brothers.

Reading those books in sunglasses may be a greater punishable offense but only just. I want to go up to the other laptop tappers one by one and slam the monitor down on their fingers. Crap crap crap. You'll never publish. You'll never finish. You're playing Tetris. Your sweater is ugly. I am the only real writer here.

What does a real writer look like? I would like to say plainer than me, but I think I'm not quite beautiful enough. I've noticed from all the magazines I have to read each month to see where Grrrl has been featured that real writers nowadays have to be slim enough to model clothes. *Harper's Bazaar, Vogue, Elle,* the *New York Times Fashion Supplement:* Here they are, like goons. I tear them out and keep them in a box under my bed. Thomas Beller in a sweater by DKNY. Lucinda Rosenfeld in Armani. Jhumpa Lahiri in Michael Kors. Flicking through *Elle,* I once found Candace Bushnell in Dolce & Gabbana. I ripped it out. Her teeth were exceptionally white and she looked like she hadn't eaten in several weeks. I put it in my cookie jar with my Kit Kats and Newman-O's to punish her.

Sitting, thighs squished wide on my narrow toilet last night, I flicked through *Vogue* and found an excerpt from a Plum Sykes novel accompanied by photos of the author in Alexander McQueen. I wiped, flushed, washed my hands, all the while keeping one eye on paper Plum in case she should try something, like stepping on Sidney Katz's tail with a stiletto heel. Then I scooped her up, ripped her out, and dropped her in the cookie jar with Candace Bushnell. This weekend I will bury it with cake under the earth in Washington Square Park, coconut and chocolate fudge with pink sprinkles.

That night I dream of Plum and Candace bursting from birthday cakes, but their glam frocks are covered in earth and mold and their skin is green and peeling. I shake myself awake, determined to get up and write. My dad sent me a Hello Kitty alarm clock that meows instead of beeps. Novelty alarm clocks aren't so amusing at 7:00 A.M., and I smack it off with a viciousness I seem to harness only in the space between asleep and awake. Sidney Katz has already woken me up at 5:00 A.M. with kitten paw service. This is when a cat puts his paws on you and flexes his claws in and out, kneading away as though you are raw dough in the shape of his mother. I was a little freaked the first time he did it, pressing at my bosom, maternal loss seeping out of his paws and into my chest. When I got him, he was a street kitten whose mother, a delicate pastel-wash tortoiseshell, had been instantly adopted. "You want me to be your mother?" I asked incredulously. No one had ever wanted me to be his mother before. It had never crossed my mind. I got used to it pretty quickly. Now I hold his face in my hands as he kneads me and coo, "Who's my little baby?"

Even though it's raining, I finally drag myself out of bed and over to Gorky's at eight because it is either that or stare at the ceiling. I also fear I might be close to developing bedsores, so slothful have I been this weekend. I step into my thermal leggings, which make me feel like I am wearing a diaper, and pull on my gigantic black fur snow boots, which make me feel like I am wearing the results of a bear hunt, slap on some *Dynasty*-red lipstick, and head into the snowstorm: Joan Collins bear hunting in a diaper. It isn't the look I was going for and I hope it won't affect my writing.

Outside the café I see a beagle puppy tied to the railing and immediately inside I spot Philip Seymour Hoffman. Both look rumpled and needy, only Philip Seymour Hoffman is dry. Remembering that beagles are the breed most commonly used in lab experiments, I keep turning to check on the puppy through the window as I wait in line to order. The puppy is killing me, gazing balefully straight at me, which I know sounds a lot like the time I went to see Bruce play at Wembley and he looked me right in the eyes. Every time someone pushes back from his or her bagel debris and rewinds his or her scarf, I keep hoping it is the owner, but it isn't, and I am left with the same dumb half smile you have when you're waiting for your blind date to walk in.

The three diners with whom Philip is eating focus intently on him. As he eats lustily, they barely graze, so fascinated are they by his every word.

"The thing about having a baby girl," he says, dirty blond hair collecting at his shoulders like unpaid bills, "is that the first year is just pure unrequited love."

His companions hold their forks in front of their mouths, unable to manage a bite until he finishes his thought. One girl at his table keeps looking around, deliberately catching people's eyes as though to say, "Don't look at him! It's so rude! Why will no one let Philip Seymour Hoffman dine in peace?," when everyone is actually looking around for the waitress to bring them their French toast. I was going to have a pain au chocolat, but when I get to the counter I decide I should try to eat healthy, so I order lemon butter crepes and coffee.

I hover near two potential leavers so they'll leave more quickly and I can plug in to the outlet by their table. As I mentioned previously, a window table is a find at Gorky's, so before they even have their jackets zipped I plug in and put my computer on the table. If anyone else did that it would be extremely impolite, but I figure the cultural importance of my novel excuses bad manners, now and for the rest of my life. Unfortunately, I find myself a little blocked. Leaning back in my chair, I let my fingers hover over the keyboard, moving but not ever touching the keys, as though I were a psychic healer. When the waitress brings my breakfast it turns out the crepes are in fact a crepe and I inhale it in four bites. Thankfully, at Gorky's they let you stick around long after you've finished your meal. Just in case, I move my fork in figure eights through the sugar remnants on my plate, hoping to stave off hoverers and look so deep in thought that I might hopefully find myself lost in thought. It doesn't work. My mind soon wanders to Marley.

I sneeze and a woman across from me says, "Bless you." I love it when people say "Bless you." I feel special. It is very easy to hurt my feelings and very easy to make me feel good about myself. When someone says "Bless you," the room becomes bathed in holy light and it makes me believe in God. It's like when you get a wrong number but the person at the other end is nice about it. It's so discombobulating when you dial a wrong number and the person at the other end says "No! Who? What?" and there's a TV turned up way too loud and the people in the background are speaking a language you've never heard before. You feel so alone in the world.

"I love how they put the little fake stripes in the fake bacon," says Philip Seymour Hoffman, poking cheerily at his vegetarian breakfast.

When he leaves, the people at his table talk about what a nice man he is. "Can you believe what a nice man he is?," as if anyone expected him to be a raging asshole. One of his companions, now bereft at his departure, picks up *The New York Times* and begins reading in silence. Turning to the theater pages, he suddenly calls out, "Hey! She's my friend too!" I wonder who his friend in the photo is. Someone else with three names. Sarah Michelle Gellar. Or Lee Harvey Oswald.

To my immense displeasure, two guys with computers plunk themselves down opposite me at my table. Both have white laptops, and against my orange iBook it looks like our computers are having a threesome, with mine in the center, and I feel uncomfortable and pack up. Another day with no writing done.

On the way out I pet the shivering puppy for a while, looking from the dog to the remaining diners until, finally, a preppie girl in a polo shirt and Ugg boots comes out and smiles at me nervously. "Is this your dog?" I ask, and through pearlescent pink lipstick she utters a defensive "Yes." "Did you know that beagles are the dog most commonly used in lab tests?" She looks at me, frightened, and says, "Please take your hands off my dog." She starts to untie him quick. I turn to leave, but as I zip my jacket something makes me look back down at the dog and say, "I love you." It is said with the oddest, most sincere and aching intonation. The girl hurries off in the other direction, the dog turning his head to face me as though he wants desperately to reply but is afraid of inflaming his owner.

When I get to work, I'm ready for Holly to bitch me out for being late. It's 10:00 A.M. and she and Vicki are out at breakfast together. Ivy seems a little put out and not very inclined to chat. The products are on my desk and they transform before my eyes to shivering puppies tied up and left outside cafés. We have never tested on animals; that is my favorite thing about Grrrl. Not my favorite thing even, but something that helps me sleep at night.

"We don't test on you," I tell the lipstick beagles on my desk. They don't care. "Why did you leave us so long?"

"What do you mean?"

"Why will you not give us names?"

"I've been so busy with Marley and then I thought I had inspiration for my novel, but I didn't. . . ."

"What is a puppy if it doesn't have a name?"

They transform back into lipsticks and I scribble down "Sick Puppy." That'll cut it as a maroony eye shadow, but not as a lipstick. I snap my fingers. "C'mon, c'mon." I write that down as well: "C'mon, C'mon." Good name for a mod lipstick, pale white-pink. It's good. We can use it. But it's not *the* name. Ah, fuck it. It's not going to happen today.

I call Dad and tell him about the puppy at Gorky's and about Philip and he says, "Have you ever seen a film that didn't have Philip Seymour Hoffman in it?" I think hard, but I can't remember one.

Dad is in too much of a rush to talk for long because it's tax time, he says, which is weird because it's usually when he needs to do a lot of work that he's on the phone to me the longest.

"Sadie-Pops?" He'll elongate my name into this nickname and I know he's sitting with his legs stretched out in front of him and his back off the chair, testing to see how far he can go without falling off. He loves to do that. How many glasses he can balance on top of one another without them crashing. How many bags of salt and vinegar crisps he can eat without feeling sick. How many kisses he can give me before I squeal "Gerroff!"

Today Dad and I don't talk very long, and though I understand, I can't help but feel sad. I wish we could share an office, like Carole King and Neil Sedaka, and he could do his tax returns across the desk from me as I come up with names.

As I am trying to wish the ache away, my phone rings.

"So," says Marley, "baby girl, you want to meet the other baby girl?"

"What?" I squeal. "When?!" Ivy's interest is piqued and she sidles over and stares at me, her cow eyes rimmed red from crying.

"Tonight. Come to my house at seven."

I mean to sit Ivy down and find out what's going on, why she's been crying, but once I hang up I am in such a tizzy that I never get around to it.

16 RAZZLE-DAZZLE

HOLLY, NOT AWARE that I got in late, lets me out of work early so I can go home and pick out what to wear. She understands—of course she understands—that this is of the utmost importance.

I consider going very adult, very kindergarten teacher, in a sweater, khakis, and pearls, but then I opt to go the other way. I lay out jeans, Converse high-tops, a pale blue T-shirt with pink polka dots, and, the final touch, little flannel duck hair clips.

I run a bath, my heart beating into my throat. I turn up David Bowie very loud, then louder and louder, trying to drown out my heartbeat, until I realize that music made on coke probably isn't the best way to slow your heart rate and change it to Joni Mitchell. I bathe, I shave, and then I do a strange thing: I shave off my pubic hair. I start out trimming things, neatening them up around the top, and then I just keep going. I want to be like Montana. It's better if she doesn't know

I'm an adult. Not that I'm planning to show her what I've done. It just gives me some weird feeling of equality.

I take a cab across the bridge because I am too nervous to remember how to ride the subway. I won't be able to work my MetroCard and I'll accidentally take the train to Queens. We pass the Welcome to Montana sign and I hold my breath. The cabdriver is, of course, fuming with anger about having to go to Brooklyn, especially as I tricked him by getting into his car, closing the door, and asking to go to the Lower East Side before sneakily changing my mind. His silent anger fans my nerves until they are tickling at my ears, tangling up with the pigtails I put my hair in.

I stand on the doorstep for some time, raising my finger to the buzzer and then putting it back in my pocket. I do this several times and then finally I sit down on the stoop and call Holly. "I can't do it."

Apprised of the situation, she threatens that if I do not immediately hang up and ring the bell, she will call Marley at home and tell him I am sitting on his doorstep like a spastic. I ring the bell and close my eyes. It seems like I am there forever.

"Hello?"

There is a mouse scurrying around the dishes of my subconscious.

"Hello?" the mouse squeaks again. I open my eyes and I am blinded by blond.

"Montana?"

She has Marley's face and it makes me want to faint, seeing this face I have sat on . . . on a little girl. Marley in photo negative: she is pale, blue-eyed, with long flaxen hair cut with stylish and very adult jaw-length bangs. I tug gingerly at my duck clips. She's awfully tall for her age.

"Are you Sadie?"

"That's me."

"Are you my papa's friend?"

"I am your papa's friend."

"Please come in."

I see Marley hovering behind her, grinning broadly. I want to kiss him, hug him, lick him. "Hello," I say soberly, and reach out to shake his hand just as he reaches out to guyishly slap me on the back. Montana goes in and out of the kitchen bringing dishes of hors d'oeuvres.

"Thank you, Montana," I say as I dip a carrot in some hummus, "how lovely." She sits down beside me and peers at me real close as I try not to choke on the carrot.

"You like it?"

"Yes, thank you." I swallow and turn my eyes to Marley for help.

"Montana picked it out herself," he says.

Big whoop. The kid picked out hummus. Get the medal ready.

"How clever of you. I love hummus." I sound altogether too excited about hummus and I sense that she has already labeled me dull. She goes over and sits in Marley's lap and I am about to drag her off him by the hair when I remember that he is her father. He tickles her and she laughs and laughs, much too loud, and I think, Hmm, that girl's gonna fake orgasms, but I feel very very jealous, so I try to join in the tickle fight. I have blocked out much of the rest.

My defense, later that night when Montana is in bed, is that I was nervous and I wasn't sure if I was supposed to treat her like an adult or act like a child. Play by play: I wrestled her to the floor and she stuck her finger up my nose. We lay on the floor and giggled and I patted myself on the back for bonding so fast. Then, during dinner, veggie burgers with tahini, I saw her picking her nose, digging away. I remembered my dad saying "You can pick your friends, you can pick your nose, you can pick your friend's nose." Kids love my dad. I went over to her and stuck my finger up the other nostril, grabbed a bogie, and popped it in my mouth. I wanted to seem affectionate and close to her, and you can't get much closer than inside someone's nose.

She went bright red, her finger frozen in her nostril. Marley stopped breathing.

She looked absolutely stunned. "Did you put my booger in your mouth?"

"Yep," I said cheerfully. She didn't cry. She didn't move.

I opened my mouth and revealed the little green slime on my tongue. "Do you want it back?"

"Yes."

I carefully picked it off and handed it back. She hid it from me in her tightly clasped hand as though it were jewelry, all her worldly goods. Then she went into the bathroom and closed the door.

Lying in bed with Marley that night postlovemaking, as far away as he can be and still be on the same mattress, he says, "Bad move, Sadie. Bad move."

"What?" My face crumples.

He is really angry, shaking his head. "You do not invade a child's space like that, take from her without asking. We're adults."

I want to say "Well, how would I know that, I don't have a kid." But instead I just turn away from him and cry. I want to take my orgasm back. All of them. How could he let me do that and then say that, holding it in him as he made me let it all out? Criticism should never come within the vicinity of lovemaking.

"We are supposed to set boundaries for her, she's a kid."

"I'm a kid too."

"A kid? That's some real Michael Jackson defense right there."

I am devastated. I seriously think about jumping out the window. I see myself falling. I am naked. I don't want to jump out of a window naked. I don't mind people seeing me splat, but I don't want them to see that I already have stubble where I have shaved off all my pubic hair. "I'm going home," I huff. And I do. And he lets me.

I AM ENTIRELY CONVINCED the next day at work that it is over. Holly and Ivy comfort me and even Vicki is nice as she can be.

"It's weird to wear that little kid's bracelet," Vicki snipes, bedecked in pom-poms.

"It's the damn duck hair clips. They started it. If I hadn't worn them, I might have felt like a grown-up and acted like one too."

"Sorry," Vicki says, and goes back to her desk, where she makes calls for the rest of the morning.

We have an afternoon conference with a potential Milan buyer. I can see that he likes me, but all I can do is stare at Marley's mural, feeling it closing in, closing in, the water rising up around my heart. I drop a cookie in my coffee and my heart copies it, submerging completely so that I can't breathe. I fish desperately for the cookie and pull it out in lumps, coffee spilling all over the table, all over Vicki's faux white wedding dress.

"Hey!" she yelps.

"Sorry," I say halfheartedly.

"Say it like you mean it," says Holly, who loaned her the dress, which was loaned to her by Alexander McQueen.

"Shove it up your arse," says Ivy to Holly, and we all look at her, stunned, including the buyer.

"Excuse me," Ivy says, and leaves the room.

17   BUTTER ROSE

WHEN I GET HOME, I climb into the bath and stay there for hours, refilling the hot water every time it gets tepid. Sidney Katz sits next to me on the toilet and comforts me with his round green eyes, his white fur ruffling with the breeze from the bathroom window. I hold my breath and duck under the water. I must have been in there a good one and a half minutes when the buzzer drags me to the surface. Wrapping myself in a towel, I hit talk on the speakerphone, but I can't hear who needs me. Assuming it is Holly, I put on my father's kimono and unlock my bolt.

It is Marley at the door and he has Montana with him, her skin absolutely white, with pink dots on her cheeks. She is wearing a velvet Princess Coat and white tights with Mary Janes. She has exactly the look Vicki is going for. Vicki would have demanded to know where she'd gotten her coat.

I ask them in for a cup of tea as though they are a pair of visiting vicars. He says yes and that Montana would like to use my bathroom. Montana doesn't say anything. She has a cupcake in her hand. It is vanilla with pink frosting. It has to be from the vegan bakery on Sixth Avenue. I know the sugar is made with fruit juice. I can't help naming it in my head: Butter Rose.

Marley leads Montana to the bathroom, and when they come back, she is still holding the untouched cupcake in her hand.

"Are you going to eat that?" I ask pleasantly.

"In the fullness of time," she answers. That freaks me out so much, I have to go and hide in the kitchen, pretending to make tea. Montana sits delicately on my sofa, eyes glued to the television. She has the remote in her little white hand and is watching *The Powerpuff Girls,* which I had been half-eyeing from the bathtub.

"I like Bubbles the best," I say brightly, poking my head around the door.

She doesn't answer. She breathes quietly and calmly, as though she were conserving energy. Her long hair is backlit by the blue of the television.

"Is there anything I can get you?"

She doesn't turn around as she declares, "I would like a plum."

I scramble back toward the kitchen to see if I might have a plum when I know full well that I do not.

"Wait," she says, lifting her index finger, still facing the television. "I would like it sliced." Although Marley insists that I really needn't, I pull on my jeans and sweater and dash to the bodega to find her a plum even though it is winter and they are out of season. When I come back, they are cuddling on the sofa, laughing together. I go to the kitchen and wash the fruit, which is something I never bother to do for myself, then I dry it and start slicing. In my anxiety to get the plum sliced and in front of her, I cut my thumb. I cut it pretty deep. I scream and

Marley rushes in to see what is going on, with Montana trailing behind him. She sees the blood and starts crying, and Marley picks her up and hugs her and shushes her as I stand there, blood dripping down my wrist.

I am in the bathroom, trying to clean myself up, Montana still weeping in the next room, when I hear Marley yell, "I'm going to take Montana home. I'll call you later."

Marley comes back that evening after he has dropped Montana at her mother's hotel. He apologizes for rushing out. "Montana is very sensitive," he says. "She frightens quite easily."

So do I, I think. I sit quietly on the sofa where she had been. Finally I ask, "Why is it okay to name children after some American states but not others? Why Montana and not Missouri? Why can you name a child Atlanta but not Ohio?"

"Atlanta is a city."

I eye him closer. "Why did you name your daughter after a state renowned for housing militiamen and right-to-lifers?" I am challenging him and I don't know why.

He leaves sadly and I cry myself to sleep. He calls me every day that week, but I don't call him back. I can barely work. I have the makeup-naming skills of Vicki.

"Pink." I jot it down miserably on a tube of cream blusher. By the end of the day I have managed to come up with Bright Pink. I go home and flick through vintage *Vogues*, looking for the color, for the name, the color and the name. I know that if I can find it then I can find myself. I fall asleep propped up on my bed, my notepad in my hand. I wake to hear Sidney Katz chewing on it.

Finally I ring Marley on Saturday and Montana answers the phone.

"Hi, Montana. Can I speak to your dad?"

"To Steven?"

"Are you allowed to call him by his name? Aren't you supposed to call him Daddy?"

"No," she says softly. "I'll pass your message along."

"Thank you."

"Wait."

"Yes?"

"I have to get a pencil. And some paper."

"Can't you just remember the message? 'Sadie called.' That's it. It's pretty easy."

"I'm writing it down. 'Sadie called.' " She spells it out: "S-a-d-i-e c-a-l-l-e-d."

By ten P.M. he hasn't called me back, so I storm out of my pajamas, pull on a T-shirt, jeans, and a silk scarf, and go over to ring his doorbell.

"You can't just go around ringing people's doorbells, you know, unannounced," he says, laughing, as I stand there like a caroler.

He kisses me in the doorway and we fall into his bed. I say "fall," but I suppose, in fact, we inch our way under the covers, as though wriggling on our arses down a steep hill, since Montana is asleep in the next room. Once we are in bed and he is in me, it is delicious, really delicious, like a hot fudge sundae when the fudge is actually hot. It is the kind of sex that allows you to leave yourself, zone out as you do over the perfect sundae, a ripe nectarine, the definitive tuna melt. I have noticed that the people who lose themselves in food—gulping, chomping, chewing ecstatically—are also able to lose themselves in sex, or rather are only able to lose themselves in these two acts. They make their grim way around art galleries, sullen and unimpressed as children. They storm out early from operas. They are unable to commit to much of anything that lasts longer than an MTV clip. But eating and sex are for them—for us—transcendent states of sublime concentration.

When I come out of the trance, refreshed but a little sore, the name for the new blusher seems quite clear. Postcoital Pink, I say in my head.

"I'm so sorry about earlier, Marley. I just freaked out."

"You know it's okay. I do understand. It's a big package I come with."

In my head I snicker, Hee hee, "big package." But I don't say it out loud and I wonder again if this might be maturity. What I do say is "Marley, is it okay for me to be here?"

"Probably not. Not really. But I want you to be. I need you to be. Please stay forever."

"For*ever* ever?"

I WAKE UP in the middle of the night, needing to pee. I have fallen asleep naked and, dazed, I try to retrieve the clothes that have been peeled and tossed aside like the prickly skin of a sweet fruit. As I grope around in the dark, all I can find is my scarf, but I put it on anyway. When I go downstairs, I notice a piece of paper and a box of Crayolas by the phone. I wrap the scarf more snugly around my neck and go to read the message Montana had taken. I want to see if she has spelled my name right. She hasn't. It says, in scrawly crayon: "Pig buTT caLLed."

18 MAXED OUT

DO I HAVE A BUTT LIKE A PIG? Or is it just a random play-ground insult, rude word du jour? Montana has tapped into my worst fear. I clutch the message in my hand as I sit on the toilet, but now I can't pee. My pig butt squashes damningly against the cold seat. I turn on all the taps, like I did when I was a little girl, but I am too crushed to squeeze anything out. I sit there, think-ing, the taps running. "I am so likable." I inflate my likability, as my bladder strains, casting myself as a cross between a *Sesame Street* host and the baron-shagging nun from *The Sound of Music,* visions whirring in my mind of me leading Austrian schoolchildren in a round of "My Favorite Things." I am on the mountaintop in a dirndl, and all twelve von Trapp children have Montana's face. I can't remember the words so I make them up:

> *When your cooch hurts*
> *From too much sex*
> *When you're feeling fat*
> *I simply remember my favorite things . . .*

I catch my reflection in the mirror, singing, naked, with a scarf around my neck. I fear Montana can see the specifics: not just that I am a lady who spends time with Marley, her father, but that I am a lady who hugs and kisses him, who has sex with him, lots of different kinds of sex. I imagine her keeping a tally of the times he has gone down on me, the times we have done it doggie style, the times I was on top. I sit there and think and think and I must be there for some time because suddenly the door creaks open.

Montana. In a pale pink nightgown. Clutching a Barbie. Pointing the Barbie at me as she demands, "What are you doing?"

I crush the message tighter in my hand. The pee comes flooding out. Montana stands and watches. I don't know whether to wipe or not. Just get up and run. I am frozen there.

"I'm peeing."

"The faucets have been running forever and then you started singing. It woke me up."

"Oh, I'm so sorry."

She doesn't move. Marley and I had decided that I would leave early that morning, before she could see me, that we would work my presence in with great sensitivity. But she catches me, her blond hair shining in the dark like a flashlight.

"I was talking to your daddy last night, and we talked for so long and I got so tired, I couldn't even make it home. I had to sleep on the sofa."

My nipples have grown stiff by the drafty window.

"I see."

"Would you like some breakfast? Some toast? A plum?"

"It's the middle of the night still."

"Of course it is. Silly old me."

She stares at me, a human lie detector dressed in a pink

nightgown. I shift on the seat, which I am starting to fear I might never leave, and say timidly, "I'm going to get up now."

Montana turns on her heel and walks back upstairs. I raise myself very slowly as though I am under arrest. "Thank you," I say to her departing shadow, then I creep back into bed with Marley and stare in horror at the ceiling. I feel, not for the first time in my life, like a doormat. Every time I close my eyes I see the glow of her golden hair.

How could Montana be the child of Marley? The mother. God, the mother must be Claudia Schiffer. The abs-of-steel yogi. The businesswoman beauty. A tear slides down my face and settles in the dip of my collarbone. Marley turns over and puts his arm around my waist, his head on my chest.

"I love you, baby," he murmurs. I don't know if he's thinking about me or Montana. Me. Me. It has to be me. Montana, I assure myself, is no baby. It's hard to believe she ever was. I picture her, wrapped in a blanket and cradled in Marley's arms, saying, "I would like a plum. I would like it sliced."

I lie awake the rest of the night and creep out at seven as we had planned. I hail a cab back to my place and crawl into bed. I wake up at three in the afternoon, confused and heavy-headed. That night I go out dancing with Vicki. We planned it a week ago and I can't get out of it. When I see how she is dressed, I wish I had tried harder. She is wearing ballet slippers, a tutu, and a white mohair sweater, her hair filled with tiny barrettes from the drugstore. She hops and skips past the velvet rope, and then she hops and skips on the dance floor, then some fool hoists her up and she hops and skips on the podium.

Montana would eat her for breakfast, I think darkly. I have on red lipstick even though I'm not single. In the bathroom, under the evil fluorescent light, it really does look like blood, dry and morbid. Vicki is peering delightedly at herself in the mirror, putting on more sparkles, rearranging her barrettes. I ask if I can borrow her pearly pink lip gloss and she shrieks, "Of course!," shoving it in my face as though it were a bottle of smelling salts with which she hopes to revive me from a fainting fit. I edge away from her and wipe off my lipstick. I have to go through a fat wad of tissue to get it to come off. Eventually my lips are bare and I pat them with the cotton-candy gloss. I open my eyes as wide as I can, mimicking the expression that greets me across the desk when I arrive at work each morning. And Vicki has never seen a Shirley Temple movie. Extraordinary.

"Wow!" says Vicki. "You look great! You should always wear your makeup like that!" That "always" carries with it so much office gossip and resentment that I wipe the gloss right off and reapply my Cherries. It feels like I am applying a life force. I breathe a sigh of relief.

The whole time I'm out with Vicki I'm thinking, This is time I could be spending with Marley. We wouldn't even have to be doing anything. I'd just rather be lying stock-still watching him breathe in his sleep than in a club full of people I don't know doing dances I can't remember. I get home at 1:00 A.M. but wait up until 2:00 so I can call my dad in England. He is brushing his teeth. I hear him spit and rinse. I hear Mum snoring in the background.

"I am in love, Papa."

"I have been in love with you since 1978."

"From the very second I was born?"

"It's the truth. I lost my parents so young. When I had you, I had a blood relative forever and ever."

Cradling the phone between my ear and my neck, I wipe my makeup away with a cotton ball. "Did you and Mummy want another child?"

Dad closes the bathroom door. "I did. She didn't."

"She didn't? Was it because of me?"

"She didn't want to lose her figure," he whispers.

"She lost it anyway."

"Don't tell her that."

"She deserves to have lost it."

"Be kind."

"Dad, I know, but it's hard. It's really bloody hard sometimes."

19 BLEACH-BLOND JEW

SOMETIMES WHEN I am trying to think of names it helps to go shopping and look at my makeup out in the world. Every single time I walk through the door of Sephora I get scared that the Grrrl counter will be gone. Then when I see it's still there I get scared to see that it exists—living and breathing like a monster come to life. Ah ha, inspiration already: a range of makeup stitched together with nuts and bolts sticking out of the packaging. I'll call the line It Lives! Holly should go for that, even though there aren't any sexual undertones. Oh, wait, all the cleavage in vampire films, the penetration of the teeth puncturing the neck. There *are* undertones. Somehow we could make the lipstick design incorporate cleavage. Although that would make it look even more like a penis. All the better for Holly to brag about.

I have my suspicions about Holly's famed sex life. The give-away is that she finds novelty sex toys amusing. You know: cakes in the shape of an ejaculating erection, gummy boob candy, flavored condoms. Strippers—she thinks strippers are hilarious and will hire them at the drop of a hat. She sent a "cop" to the office for Vicki's birthday not long after I started working at Grrrl. He tried to grind in my lap. I gave him such a fierce look that he backed off. I felt guilty—he was obviously just an un-employed dancer, probably gay too—but I couldn't help it. I found it so depressing, so unfunny and unfun. I guess Ivy wasn't exactly down with it either. She hid in the bathroom.

I decide to make this a quick trip to Sephora so that I can get back to the office and pitch It Lives! I'm supposed to start getting bonuses soon, for coming up with ideas for new prod-ucts, on top of the names. I need those bonuses. Even though I have a real job now, I find myself more broke than I've been in a long time. Unfortunately, I have something in common with Vicki: We are the only two of the Grrrl group who can't call home and ask for a loan. I don't know that I could ever do that anyway. My relationship with Dad is too precious to put him under that kind of pressure.

The girls (and gays) shopping in Sephora seem to be neatly divided into those whose bank is being broken by their purchases and those for whom it is a drop in the ocean. A lemongrass-scented drop in a skin-softening ocean. So what's new on the shelves?

I get pissy at all the new lines that hit the shelves week after week. They pop up like fungi. Something called Pop. One called Pout. Pixi. All such cutesy, cutesy names, all anti-Grrrl ethos. Does that makes us special or does it just mean we're out of step? They're pretty and glossy, glittery, glam. Little girls gather around to coo. We've got to get a preteen line on the streets pronto.

Around the corner from Pop, Pixi, and Pout are Nars and Vincent Longo. Here the *Vogue* girls graze, reading the labels on the backs of the products as though checking the calorie counts. At Shiseido the packaging is sleek and so are the customers, dressed in black pants and crisp white button-downs. At Fresh, naturally slim girls who don't cover their freckles with foundation try fig perfume on the insides of their wrists. I round the corner to our counter, my stomach in knots in case it isn't there anymore. As I do so, I hear braying laughter.

"Oh, my God, that's too much!"

The Grrrl stand is still there, and picking up and reading the names of the products is a short man, perfectly muscled, with dyed blond hair. He has a face that is one chromosome from handsome but another from simian, like Ben Stiller's. He is a small, blond, braying, gay-ing Ben Stiller. He turns to me.

"Have you seen this?"

"What?"

"The name of this face powder is Heroin. And see this lipstick? It's called Ass-Slappin' Pink." He cannot contain his mirth and hands the lipstick to me so that I can share in the jollity.

"Actually, I wrote it."

"What do you mean, you wrote it?" He puts one tiny hand on a tinier hip. In the other he carries a Magnolia Bakery box. "I don't understand."

"I work at Grrrl. Our office is around the corner. I'm the woman whose job it is to come up with all the names for the makeup."

"Shut up!" He shoves me in the collarbone. "You are a genius!" People turn to look. I do a small wave. "A genius!" he continues. "I'm such a huge fan! I stop by here every week to see what new names you've come up with. Here, take my card."

I look at it: David Consuela Cohen.

"Awesome. Well, I'd better get back to work," I say graciously.

"But I want to take you to dinner." He whines the offer as though he's asking to be allowed one more hour of TV.

"Today?"

"Not now, silly billy. Sometime soon. I'm only in town for the week. I live in Los Angeles."

He pronounces "Los Angeles" with a Spanish accent that comes out of nowhere.

"What do you think I do for a living? Go on, guess. No, I want you to guess!" He moves one hand up and down his tight green T-shirt, at the breast of which I notice the Vivienne Westwood insignia. His jeans have at least sixteen pockets.

A clown? A go-go dancer? An extra from Deee-Lite's "Groove Is in the Heart" video?

"I don't know."

"I'm a fashion publicist, silly! I represent Petro Zillia, Imitation of Christ, and Miss Sixty. Among others. Do you need representation?"

"Oh, no, it's okay, we do it all in-house. Vicki Arden."

"Ugh. That stunted little bitch. Excuse me."

"You're excused."

"What I mean is, do *you* need representation?"

"Me. What for?"

"I could get you a spread in *Interview. Paper*'s 'Fifty Most Beautiful.' You're a cutie!"

"Thank you."

"You'd look great in Petro Zillia."

I have no idea what this looks like. "Thank you?"

"Listen. I want to get back to the showroom and send you some stuff. To keep. For free."

"Okay. Thanks." I hand him my card.

"What size are you?"

"A six or an eight."

"Oh. We generally only carry a four. But I'll see what I can do. Shoe size?"

"Eight."

"That I can do. Ooh! The woman who makes up the names for Grrrl. What a thrill!"

"Bye." I back out of the store slowly, facing him, as you're supposed to when being menaced by a shark. He turns away from me and goes back to picking up the makeup and screeching with laughter.

When I get back to the office, Vicki and Ivy are at the conference table eating pizza. After all this time it still smells vaguely of paint. I don't know how anyone can eat in there. Vicki has taken two slices of pepperoni and added a raspberry licorice to make a happy face on the pie. Ivy is mopping the pizza grease up with a napkin before she eats her slice.

"What are you doing?" I ask incredulously. "Are you . . . are you dieting?"

"No!" she says defensively.

"Okay." I throw my hands up. "Where's Holly? I have a great idea. No. Wait. I just had another. I have two great ideas."

"No clue. She was supposed to be back here at one-thirty. We have a conference call to Paris at two o'clock."

Speak of the devil, Holly swans through the doors as though entering a saloon. Although there's just one door, she pushes it as though it's divided into two. She's wearing a sheer white blouse beneath which her lacy cream bra is clearly visible. She has on gold vertiginously high heels with a diamond ankle bracelet. Uncharacteristically, her linen skirt is wrinkled.

"You're late," says Ivy.

"Only fifteen minutes," says Vicki.

"We have a conference call at two."

"Well, is it two yet?"

"No."

"Then calm the fuck down."

"Okay, okay, guys, listen. I have two ideas."

Holly turns her attention slowly from Ivy to me. "Shoot."

"It Lives!: makeup bolted together like Frankenstein's monster."

Holly looks at her nails and says, "That could fly for Halloween."

"And lipsticks named after people who should have gotten married. Or stayed married. Or come from different generations but should be together. Angelina Brando. Madonna Bowie. Elizabeth Clift. Courtney Stipe. And I think the whole line should be called Ava Sinatra. It's really beautiful, don't you think?"

"That's kind of gay," says Holly.

Ivy raises her eyebrows but says nothing. So I do.

"That's kind of a casual slur."

"What? I can say it. I am one. I'm a dago dyke."

"Yeah, right," says Ivy under her breath.

"See, now there's something!" says Holly. "What about a line of Lenny Bruce lipsticks, the words you're not supposed to say: dago, kike, wop, nigger . . ."

"Stop!" I yell.

"This is my company, don't tell me to stop!"

"Actually, this is *my* company," hisses Ivy. Holly shuts the fuck up.

20 PANIC ATTACK

I STOP BY MARLEY'S HOUSE, wearing a pair of fancy Marc Jacobs shoes that have inexplicably been sent to me at the office. Ivy says it is explicable, that through my meager gift for naming makeup I am becoming something of a minor downtown celebrity. An hour later David Consuela Cohen calls.

"Did you get the shoes? Aren't they rocking? Do they fit?"

"They're from you?"

"Do you know anyone else who represents Marc Jacobs? I hope not."

"Thank you so much."

"I told you I would hook you up!"

The shoes are summer-grass-green suede with a round toe and high heels. I notice the card in the box saying that Marc loves my work. "What work?" says Vicki nastily, and I can't really fault her. Jesus, anyone can become a minor celebrity in New York. You can be a celebrity juicer, like the guy at the health-food store who has lines down the block for his echinacea, kale, and ginger smoothies. You can become a celebrity graffiti artist, like Marley. And I guess, much as it strains the imagination, one can become a celebrity lipstick namer. My ego buoyed, I slip on the shoes and am instantly able to name the red lip palette trio Ivy has laid before me: Marx, Lenin, Stalin.

"A lipstick called Stalin?" asks Vicki. "Don't you think that's a little much?"

"Lady!" says Holly. "This is New York! And this is fashion. Nothing's too much."

When I get to Marley's house he and Montana have just finished doing a yoga session together. She can't stop looking at my shoes and I can't blame her. With Marley in the kitchen making us some dinner, I ask, "Do you want to try on my shoes, Montana?"

"Why would I want to try on your shoes?" She stares at me.

"They're pretty?"

She flicks a lick of blond from her rosebud lips.

"They're okay."

"Go on, try them."

She gingerly places one small white foot and then another in the green high heels. She walks around the living room in circles, click-clacking, clawing her toes tight to keep the shoes on, smiling broadly to herself. Then she comes out of her reverie. She ever so gently takes the shoes off and then ever so violently kicks them into the bathroom.

"Whoa, those are suede!"

Marley comes back in. "What's going on?"

I opt not to tattle, but she tells him herself, almost boastfully. Yes, a boast.

"Now, Montana," says Marley, "you're behaving badly. I'm going to leave you in the bathroom with the shoes to think about what you've done. We don't condone violence, not even to inanimate objects. You know the rule. You can take it out on Daddy, but that's it."

He shepherds her into the bathroom and shuts the door. Immediately she wails and wails. After five minutes she's still wailing and I'm starting to get a little nervous. "That's kind of harsh, Marley. They're just shoes."

"Look through the keyhole."

I look through the keyhole. Montana is crying and wearing the shoes at the same time, walking around the room in circles, admiring herself in the mirror. Marley grabs the shoes back, and I beg off early. It only seems fair.

AT WORK THE NEXT MORNING we go through the papers and magazines for the latest Grrrl mentions. This is technically Vicki's job, but we all enjoy it and so sit in the conference room, cross-legged on the floor, under Marley's mural. Ivy leans back against the wall and I notice for the first time what a long, swanlike neck her round head rests on. Holly is chewing blue bubblegum, which nicely suits her dark skin. Holly even makes colored bubblegum look elegant. Vicki is prancing about, getting excited about her birthday party. The others are going straight from work to help her set up. I think of ways to get out of it. I forgot to feed Sidney Katz, I say. Then, reading Page Six so as not to have to listen to Vicki prattle, I see that Isaac has just been on a panel at the Four Seasons as part of the *New Yorker* literary festival. My face turns red. I throw the paper at Holly.

"Motherfucker! He's in town and he didn't tell me."

"Why would he tell you? You don't care. You don't care about him, you broke up with him, remember?" says Holly insistently.

But I do care. Just seeing Isaac's name brings up all sorts of strange feelings in me. Bad feelings. "Listen, I don't see why I should be tied up. Marley has this other woman. The ultimate other woman."

This is bullshit. I haven't looked at another man since Marley. Who am I kidding?

"That's not fair," says Ivy. "He's a good man. You treat that boy right, you hear me?"

With perfect timing, Marley calls and asks what I'm up to tonight. Montana has gone back to L.A. with her mother. And immediately I segue from seething and jealous to calm and excited.

"Do you want to come to a party with me? It's Vicki's birthday."

"Hmmm," ponders Marley, "our debut as a couple."

"Yeah. I guess."

"Okay."

"Okay." It's true. Our debut. I hadn't thought of that. All our schemes and dreams have been of us alone in a room.

ON OUR WAY TO VICKI'S for our coming-out, I stop to pick up some flowers at the florist across the street.

"Give me ten minutes," says the fat florist, "and I shall create a bouquet for you such as Gianni Versace might have made for a favorite niece!"

I go to the bodega to buy water and when I come back he has made something purple.

"How nice!" says Vicki when I give her the flowers. She puts them immediately to one side, which annoys me although it's exactly what I'd have done too. Vicki has on pink pajamas with bunny rabbits on them, a shorty with frills at the thigh. She is getting very thin, her round pumpkin head becoming angular. She has those big eyes and artfully applied mascaraed long lashes. She looks like Mia Farrow crossed with something Mia Farrow would want to adopt.

"Whoopeee!" she says, and "Yaaay!"

" 'It's my party and I'll cry if I want to,' " she sings, and I wait for her to burst into tears. Her birthday cake has the Wild Thornberrys on it, there is a Powerpuff Girls piñata, and then she puts on a fucking Wiggles CD. The Wiggles are *not okay*; they're from some nonspecific country and they frighten me.

She bashes away at the piñata.

"Oh, poopie!" she says as the thing bursts. She is worse than ever, using her birthday as a free pass to exercise her psychosis. *The Fox and the Hound* is playing on a screen. None of the other guests seem to notice how weird it all is. They think it's hipster cool instead of hipster demented.

I look through Vicki's bathroom cabinet, as I always do at a new home. Everything is in miniature. The trial sizes you buy at drugstores: little shampoo, little conditioner, little toothpaste.

"That's rude," says Marley, "don't do that."

But I can't stop looking, transfixed by a miniature deodorant. Marley closes the bathroom door.

"Look at the Hello Kitty toilet cover. I couldn't pee into that. It's like peeing into a cat."

"That's disgusting."

"That's disgusting." I nod at the Barbie toothbrush.

"Remind me what the point of this girl is?"

"You know, I never stopped to think about it. Perhaps she's good at her job?"

But I really am not sure. "I used to be blond, you know. I mean, I am a blonde."

"You don't seem like a blonde. You seem like a spiritual brunette."

"What do you like?"

"I don't care. I don't understand men who have types. It's creepy. I like women."

"Your baby is blond."

"And, God, I wish she weren't."

"Really?"

"Really. The racist in me. Or the egoist. I want her to look like me."

"She does."

"No, she doesn't."

He kisses me.

Suddenly I hear: "Sadie and Marley sitting in a tree, k-i-s-s-i-n-g!"

"Oh, hi!" says Vicki, popping her head in. "There you are! We're about to play pass the parcel."

"This is weird," Marley whispers in my ear, and it makes me tingle, but Marley could read his tax return in my ear and it would make me tingle.

We pass. "Oh, lush!" says Vicki. "This cake is a spiritual experience!" That's when I know I have to go.

WE SPEND A WEEK TOGETHER. We see a bunch of movies and he holds my hand through all of them. He readjusts the hold but never lets go. He has one hand on me while he cooks for me. He gives me a key. I go to work, feed Sidney Katz, play with him, and then head back to Marley's each night. Sometimes he has flowers for me. Other times he is waiting naked at the door, lips puckered. I kiss him happily, but he says, "Not enough. More."

Sometimes we kiss for hours and other times I am barely in the door before he's inside me.

"I'm good in bed, aren't I?" I ask.

"You're amazing."

"But I don't think I was before. So am I good because of me or because of you?"

"Because of you! If you slept with other people now, you'd know that for sure."

"But I don't want to. Do you want me to?" I am so confused.

"Maybe you should."

I am stung. He sees it and pulls my face close to his.

"No, don't sleep with anyone else." His eyes are on fire. "Don't sleep with anyone else ever again."

He is breathing heavily. "Oh, God, I'm sorry. I try not to get jealous. But sometimes just thinking of you out in the world each day, riding the subway with men looking at you, it makes me want to—"

"Hey, it's okay. It's okay not to be chill all the time, Marley."

"Where I come from . . . chill, even too chill, is preferable."

"There has to be a middle ground."

"Yes. Yes."

"Where is your family?"

"The only family I have is Montana and Jolene. The rest could fade into the earth for all I care. The rest don't matter at all. Please don't ask me again."

"Okay. Okay."

He takes a deep breath. "Kiss me."

I kiss him because I love him and lust him and best of all it seems like I am being asked to help, and, even better, that my help hits the spot. He goes into his office to work for a few hours and closes the door. I sit on the other side of it, pressing my cheek against the wood, and I can smell him through it.

THE FOLLOWING MONDAY Montana returns.

All evening Marley can barely contain himself, he is so excited about Montana's arrival. "My baby is coming! I'm going to see my baby!"

"That kid misses a lot of school lately. You see her all the time."

"I do lately, don't I? How wonderful!" He whistles himself a happy tune. I think it's "Bela Lugosi Is Dead" by Bauhaus, rendered in the style of a barbershop quartet.

"What are you whistling?"

"The Wiggles."

"Ow," I say, "you're hurting my ears."

"Sorry"—he hugs me—"I'm just so happy. It's been too long."

"It's been a week!"

"Come on, everyone, it's wiggle time!" He sighs. "Montana used to love them. Now she likes the White Stripes."

"That's kind of weird."

"Well, she heard the mix tape you made me and that was her favorite song. So we bought all their albums and now she draws pictures of them. Look."

He pulls me over to the fridge where new pride of place is a scrawling that does look a bit like Jack White. And she has rendered Meg unlovable. I know then that I have only yet seen the tip of her competitive iceberg.

"Actually, a friend of mine is interested in publishing them. Children's renderings of their favorite rock stars. My friend's little girl is always drawing pictures of Rod Stewart."

"And someone's really going to publish them?"

"Yep."

I want to contribute so badly. I go into her art room while he's showering, and I start to draw the Beatles. Seems an easy place to start.

"Hey, look what I did."

"The Beatles."

"It's good, right?"

"Yeah. Is it for me?"

"It's for the book."

"It's a children's book. The cutoff age is eight. Montana just made it."

"Yeah, but they wouldn't know. I'll just write Sadie Steinberg, age six, and send it in."

"Uh, I don't think so."

"I want to be published. I want to be published so badly." My voice is tiny.

"You will be." Marley wants to do some yoga for half an hour, and he knows I won't join in, so he comes up with a way to entertain me.

"Go finish your novel. Go now. You're wide awake. Here's a pen and paper."

"But I use a laptop."

"You can make do. Go on."

I sit in the office and stare like I always do. Think of my dad but my fingers won't move. After a while, Marley peeks his head around the door.

"Did you write?"

"Yes. I wrote this whole thing about this girl who disguises herself as a boy so she can fight in the Civil War . . ."

"Which civil war?"

"Oh, I don't want to talk about it. I'll just show you the book when it's done."

"Awesome! I'm proud of you. It can be hard to focus."

"Oh yeah, I'm past all that. I don't find it hard."

"Well, I'm gonna go to the airport now, pick up my baby. Can you do me a favor and do the dishes for me?"

"Okay, sure, I'll do them."

Ugh. Code orange. I look at them. They aren't even piled up like mine. There are four of them and a pan and a spatula and a bowl. I look at them. I read a magazine. I watch TV. I eat an apple. Finally I run a little water over them and put them on the dish rack to dry. Marley and Montana walk through the door holding hands. He kisses me and peers into the sink.

"You did a crappy job of doing the dishes, mate."

I hate being reprimanded in front of Montana.

"Jolene's fine with you staying the night."

"She is?"

"She's a wonderful woman. A very unusual woman."

So I stay, and in the morning Montana creeps into the room. I pretend to be asleep. "Do you love me?" she asks Marley.

"Yes, I love my baby."

"Then why aren't you with your baby? Come sleep with your baby."

She climbs into bed. I pull the sheets around me. She crawls over my head.

"I made this for you"—she has two drawings in her hand—"one for you and one for Mommy. This is Mommy. See?"

"Thank you. That's lovely."

She stares at me.

"Should I move?" I ask.

"If you would be so kind," says Montana.

"I'll go get breakfast, I guess."

"How sweet," says Marley. "Montana, isn't that so sweet of Sadie?"

She declines to answer.

I trudge down to the kitchen and make toast and tea, steeping the bags just right and watching the bread so it doesn't burn. In a cupboard below the sink I find a tray and carry it up to the happy couple. They are snuggled up together, reading the papers, he the arts section, she the comics. Neither looks up.

"I made toast and tea."

Still studying the comics, Montana says evenly, "I am intolerable of wheat. And I don't drink tea."

"You don't?"

"I am a *little girl,*" she hisses, flicking her neck up to face me, her eyes burning into mine.

"Montana!" snaps Marley. "Sadie has made you breakfast and you have not said thank you and you are being ungrateful. This is not the Montana I know and this is not the Montana I love."

Good for you, Marley. Finally! I feel a twinge of joy. Until she bursts into tears. Crying and crying. And crying.

"My papa yelled at me. My papa doesn't love me no more."

"Doesn't love me *anymore,*" I correct her.

"Sadie!" he snaps at me, and though I try valiantly to hold it in, I start to cry too. Montana sobs louder. Not to be outdone, I take little gulps of air, letting him know that, unlike his daughter, I am at least trying to pull myself together. She sees what I'm doing and it enrages her. She flips flat on her stomach and starts kicking her legs up and down on the bed. Her feet, pointed like a ballerina's, beat the duvet one after another with a satisfying *whump!* She has excellent technique. I'm too old to do the kicking-your-legs-up-and-down thing—in public at least—so I try the twenty-four-year-old's version (I think it might be something I once saw Sue Ellen do on *Dallas*): Leaning against the wall, I slide my back slowly down the plaster until I am crumpled on the floor with my head in my hands.

"No!" barks Marley. "This is not okay! None of this is okay!" He jumps out of bed and storms out of the room, closing the door behind him. The slam of the door gives us both a fright. We look up at each other and stop crying immediately without any in-between stage. Tears frozen midstream on her cheeks, Montana looks at me and slowly whispers, "I hate you, fuckhead."

I am too shocked to reply, so I pretend I haven't heard her. When, after retreating to the bathroom to cool off, Marley gingerly reopens the door, he finds us side by side in bed reading the paper. I have persuaded Montana to take a sip of tea and she, without proclaiming it acceptable, has downed the whole cup. A few drops of rain begin to plop from the sky.

"Plop," I say.

"Plop!" repeats Montana delightedly. "Plop! Plop!"

Running with the moment, I add, "Doody."

"Doody." She giggles, then, "Poo. Ploppy poo poo!" she screams.

We look at Marley to see if he has anything to contribute to the conversation.

"Huh," he says warily, "it's raining. I guess I'll go to the video store and get something for us to watch, hey?"

"If you want," says Montana, and, going back to her comics, flicks a derisive wrist at him.

"So you'll be okay. Together. You guys?"

"Daddy! Have you no eyes to see? I am *trying* to read."

"I have eyes. I have eyes . . . ," he answers sincerely, as if he were defending himself against a legal accusation. "I know you're reading, but what would you like me to get?"

"Nothing cartoony," she answers, "something with real little boys and girls, please."

"Okay," he says, "I'll see what I can do. Love you."

He looks over at me while Montana focuses on her paper, so I'll know I'm included too. I smile and make a tiny soundless kiss at him so Montana doesn't notice. He smiles back. After I hear the front door close, I risk interrupting Montana's concentration and say, "I love being indoors when it's raining."

"Me too," she answers, putting her comics aside. "It never rains in California."

"Then you should spend more time here."

"I'd like to."

"You would? Your dad would love that too." I add, "Fuckhead."

She smiles.

LATER THAT AFTERNOON the three of us go grocery shopping. They take me to the local health-food store. To me, health-food stores smell the same as vintage stores—like death, not vitality and life. Like dead people's clothes. Turns out the creators of the foods might do well naming makeup with me. Instead of animal crackers they have Snackimals and glutiNOs. I would not want to eat a cookie that sounded like it was reprimanding me. There is a range of desserts called Go Ahead! To me these scream Go Ahead! Try crack! Go Ahead! Try a threeway, *not* Go Ahead! Eat a fat-free fudge cake.

Marley buys almond rice bread so we won't have to tolerate wheat. He is very particular about his food, a pushy side that is entirely absent in his personality. They say that artists get their darkness out in their art so they can be happy in life. I think Marley gets his assholeness out by controlling his food, so he can be easygoing in life.

Tofutti Cuties are thrown in the basket. Faux ice cream sandwiches—they aren't that cute. Wheatgrass. "Have a shot."

Montana does hers. Marley does his. Why do I feel like I'm succumbing to peer pressure?

I down it in one gulp, thinking of the first time I swallowed come, how I eventually grew not to like that taste but to manage it.

That night in bed I ask, "We're in a serious relationship, right?"

"Well, you've met my baby."

"She's a little girl."

"My little girl." He sighs. "I'm only twenty-eight, but I have to be older, I have to think seriously when I meet someone because I have another life, her life. Does that scare you?"

It does. It terrifies me. He's someone's daddy and he'll never act like mine.

"No."

I decide to sleep in my own bed that night. After we make love and Marley has fallen asleep, I creep down the stairs and catch a cab back to my apartment. I have a bath, lie on my bed to dry off, watch TV, listen to music and dance, play with my cat. And then I turn on my computer. My nails please me as they hover over the keyboard. They make a good sound on the keys as I clack away. I begin to write. I write all night. Sidney Katz purrs at my feet, then climbs up and sits next to me. I have been neglecting him, his big cow eyes say.

"I'm so sorry, baby boy." I scratch behind his ears. "I still love you the most," I whisper, "I love you the most."

Outside the window trannies scream a screaming fight. I look out the window for a while, clicking my knuckles, which are starting to hurt. Then I put on my headphones and keep writing. I fall asleep like that. When I wake up, I look at the screen and there are pages and pages of words. Then I look at the clock. Time for work.

22 LOVE DON'T LIVE HERE ANYMORE

WHEN MARLEY CONFIDES THAT Montana has been asking about my job often, I offer to bring her to visit the office. Although the gals make a big fuss over her frilly pink dress, I can see that Montana feels out of place. She glances nervously at Ivy's denim halter top and says in a small voice, "You look just like Britney Spears, but fatter."

Ivy, whose skills with children are unparalleled, says, "Oh, my God, thank you so much," and smothers Montana with kisses. Montana recoils, falling, involuntarily, into my lap. She sits there, and I look over her shoulder to try to figure out why she is still sitting on me. She cocks her head and sighs. "I'm tired."

"Well," coos Ivy, "then you just sit there and I'll paint your nails." She picks up Montana's small, limp fingers. "You'd look great with fire-engine red." Montana stares at Ivy's hand. I can see that she is still young enough to suspect that fat might be contagious. She snatches her hand away and tucks it into her pocket.

"No thank you," she says, then adds, "thank you so much," like a hotel manager trying to shoo away an undesirable guest without causing a scene.

"Well, maybe," says Holly, whose skills with children are not as finely tuned as Ivy's, "you'd prefer to play with our latest eye shadows. You can do it yourself."

Angel Hair and Baby's Breath, the names we stole directly from the Nirvana song.

I see when Holly says the word *play* the way Montana bristles, and I remember feeling the same exact thing when I was her age. "She's not going to 'play' with the makeup," I step in, "she may want to sample it for us, try it out and let us know what colors work the best."

Again she cocks her head to face me. She glares, trying to determine whether or not I am taking the piss. She raises herself up off my lap, goes over to the makeup mirror, and begins to help herself to all the samples. She doesn't play, not like a child, not like a teenager. She meticulously replaces the cap on the tube of blush she tries, closes the lid on the tray of lip glosses, cleans the goop from around the mascara wand. She takes the white face powder that I am embarrassed to have named Heroin and dusts herself with it. She is so neat, so prissy, that when she turns around to face us, I fully expect her to be done up as expertly and tastefully as Diane Sawyer. In fact, she has smeared blue cobalt across her lids, splashed two balls of pink so high on her cheeks that they sit beneath her eyes, and encircled her mouth with red liner until it resembles a dead body that has been chalk-marked by a really drunk detective. She looks like a kid. It is the most I have ever liked her.

"Wow!" says Holly.

"That's some job!" stammers Ivy.

"No, it's not," Montana replies. "My hands are too little. I couldn't make the brush go how I meant it to go. I wanted the line around my lips to be perfect, but I got it wrong, so I just decided to make it worse."

My God! She could have been talking about my life!

"It didn't turn out how I meant it at all," Montana says, and starts to cry.

"Hey," I tell her, pulling her close to me, "nothing ever does."

Ivy takes a wad of cotton and starts to swab her clean.

"See," I say, "it only takes a few strokes to get the slate clean again."

She looks at her bare face in the mirror.

"Wanna have another go?" asks Holly.

"No," she answers softly, then turns to face me, "you do it. I was trying to copy yours."

I am so flattered, I can feel my heart turning into the shape you draw on a page.

She sits still as a stone while I paint, to scale, my face on hers, and when I am done, she pulls herself inches from the mirror and stares intently. I have done a great job.

Montana turns to look at me, the humiliation of tears ancient history. "Yes," she sniffs, "that will do."

"Thanks, Montana."

"When I am a large lady, I will wear makeup every day to my job as a ballet dancer."

"You'll wear a lot of makeup."

"Yes," she agrees, then turns to Holly. "You'll need to make me a makeup that doesn't fade no matter how many pirouettes I do."

We look at her.

"*Pirouettes,*" she adds, "is French for *twirling.*"

I don't like the way she said "large lady" and study her face. It is all aglow in the shadow of shadow, too excited to be malicious. But seeing her little face light up as she dips in and out of our products has given us all an idea. Only Holly has the balls to say it.

"You know this preteen thing?" she says. I grimace because I know what's coming next. "Well, how 'pre' do you think we can push it?"

"Oh, come on, Holly. Makeup for eight-year-olds? That's fucked up."

Montana turns on me. "You said 'fuck.' You have to give me money. You said it. You know you did. Everyone heard."

Vicki nods vigorously.

"Okay," I say, digging in my pockets, "I never said I didn't." I hand her a dollar in quarters.

"I don't accept coins."

I fix her with such a look. "Make do." She thinks about crying but can't be bothered. So she makes herself busy with the ice cream collection, a sweet little kit I slipped passed Holly, eye shadows in the shape of scoops on cones. I turned them upside down and told Holly they were erect dicks. Montana dips a brush in the Pistachio (or Syphilis, I had to tell Holly).

"A range for preteens is kind of a great idea." I pause. "I just don't know how we can justify it morally."

"Justify makeup morally." Ivy snickers. "It's all lies." Her emphasis on the word *lies* tells me again that I must get her alone for a chat before the week is out.

"If we can find a way to justify it," I continue, "I know exactly what we should call it."

"What?" says Holly.

I take a deep breath. "Are You There, God? It's Me, Makeup." Everyone exhales. "Wow."

"Done deal." Holly, who between the ages of ten and twelve jerked off exclusively to Judy Blume books, hugs me. Vicki looks very interested in her shoes.

We order in lunch, and Montana, in the same tone in which she requested her plum, sliced, says: "Ah, yes, I would like a Coca-Cola and a tuna melt." Seeing my raised eyebrows, she adds, "I am allowed soda twice a year."

"Only twice a year?" screeches Ivy. "That's so stink!"

"I don't mind." Montana shrugs. "I don't really like sugary things."

23 IT'S A POSE

AFTER OUR DAY OF MAKEUP I take Montana out for an early-evening ice cream. I am surprised she wants one, but after her Coca-Cola, she has been talking about it nonstop. I think she got the idea from the eye shadows.

"An ice cream on the way home might be nice?" She says it as a question. Then she says it three more times before we leave the office, as though the thought has just occurred to her. We take two stools at the counter of the corner diner and she orders vanilla with hot fudge sauce.

Passing a newsstand on Broadway, she asks if we can share a Tootsie Roll. Then, when I stop in the deli for water, she wants to try a Ding Dong and I let her because she has never even heard of them before, which I find shocking. After that she wants a milk shake from McDonald's. Everywhere we pass seems to hold a new delight, and I am so delighted by her delight that I keep caving. Then we have bubblegum from the vending machine at the subway station. And on the train is when she starts throwing up.

"Oh, Jesus Christ!" Marley screams as I carry her to his door. "What did you give her?"

"Bad food, Daddy, bad food," she murmurs.

"I didn't give her anything I didn't eat too."

"The shit you eat could kill a horse."

My face flushes and my internal edit hits a snag. "Take your wheatgrass and shove it up your arse."

Montana, weak, her face covered in puke, says, "You owe me another dollar."

"You too, you little crybaby. You can't hold a chocolate shake, then don't come out with me."

Her hair is sticky with puke. In my head I can't help thinking, Bet you don't love your long blond hair so much now.

Marley looks at me. "You should leave, Sadie, before you make this worse."

By the time I get home my internal edit is back on track and I have apologized so many times in my head that it hardly stings at all when I call him up and beg for forgiveness.

"I can't really talk right now. I have to hose down my daughter and get her to sleep before her mother comes for her tomorrow afternoon."

"Well, assuming you do get her to sleep," I say meekly, "do you think I could bring you breakfast?"

So now he watches me eat my almond croissant at the kitchen table where we used to fuck before Montana rolled into town.

"I can't look at food. So much puke last night. You better just pray her mother never finds out."

"Are you going to tell on me?"

"I'm not, because I don't want to get myself in trouble. But I gotta tell you something about eight-year-olds: they're tattle-tales. Oh yes, 'Jemma did this, Cynthia did that.'"

"I'm screwed."

"No, but are you sure you want this?"

"What?"

His shoulders slump. "I just feel like damaged goods. I have an eight-year-old daughter, who I love and have to protect and who will tattle on you if you feed her food her mother doesn't approve of."

My heart feels crushed at the sight of his incredible, broad shoulders in a sad little hunch. I want to run away. Really. I try to will myself out of my seat and out of my love for him and out of the relationship. I try to run away, but I can't. So, wiping crumbs off my shirt, I resort to dark humor.

"You call that vomit? I used to projectile-vomit like you wouldn't believe."

"I'd believe it," he says. There's a sweetness to his tone that makes me wonder if he'd be proud of my projectile puke, like, "You're so strong. Of course my baby pukes harder than the other kids."

I put my hand on his, which is still a little shaky.

"I'd like to apologize to Montana. Do you think she'll forgive me?"

"Maybe. You never know."

I go up to Marley's bedroom, where she is watching TV. She peeks up at me over the covers, a guilty look on her face.

"You're not allowed to eat chocolate, but you can watch *Jerry Springer*? That doesn't sound right."

"Don't tell on me!"

"Okay, then don't tell on me to your mum. Do we have a deal?"

"I'm sorry you made me puke," she whispers.

"Thank you?"

Later that morning she comes downstairs and decides she's ready to eat again, so her father goes into the kitchen to rustle something up.

"You were very brave yesterday, Montana."

"I'm sorry you got in trouble, Sadie."

"That's okay. I deserved it."

By that point I hate Montana's mother, Jolene, so much, she exasperates me like a roommate. I see Jolene's stupid organic food in the fridge. Her organic scuzz in a ring around the bathtub.

Montana makes a point of saying "Hmmm yum yum" as she eats the spinach with soy protein her dad brings in.

Finally Montana leaves. The doorbell rings while I'm hiding in the bedroom. I look out the window and see a black limo pull away, two blond heads visible in the darkness like flashlights.

24 PILE 'EM HIGH

THE BIG NEWS AT WORK ON MONDAY is that Cameron Diaz has said in an interview that Grrrl is her favorite line of cosmetics. The gals want to give her a preview of next season's colors so that she will say it again, but louder.

"Oh, please let me take it to her. Oh, please?" I hop up and down for emphasis.

"You're a spaz," says Holly.

"I don't think that's the politically correct term. I think the word you're looking for is *starfucker*."

"Dude, you have a filthy mouth," says Holly.

"I do not," I answer, genuinely shocked. "I don't. Do I?"

The gals put together a selection of glittery eyeliners, nail polishes, lip stains, and a spray for your hair with pink glitter in it. It's really like the stuff you buy for ninety-nine cents at the drugstore on Halloween. Except ours costs sixteen dollars.

"Do you really think Cameron Diaz would spray glitter in her hair?" says Vicki doubtfully.

"Oh, yeah, I think so for sure." How little Vicki knows of

Cameron Diaz. I am so good at convincing everyone that she would love it that they decide I can hand-deliver it to the photo shoot she is doing over at Chelsea Piers. I ride the rickety elevator up to the fifth floor and the doors open straight into the studio. The receptionist is a skinny gay boy painting his nails.

I slip past him, the stylist, and the caterer and stand behind a rack of clothes watching her strike poses. When she takes a break to have her lipstick retouched, I approach her as noisily as I can because I don't want her to think I am creeping up on her. Still, she looks kind of startled when I thrust the package into her hands.

"These are the Grrrl cosmetics you asked for. I like your broken nose. My mum does too." And then I walk out.

My mother notices the most peculiar things about celebrities. "I really love the shape of Cher's head, don't you?"

"It's all right."

"No, it's really fabulous. It comes to a point. It makes her hair always look like it's been back-combed."

"Maybe her hair always has been back-combed."

"Sadie, you're spoiling it."

Like I was spoiling a cake she'd been baking or a legal case she'd spent months researching. "I think Cher wears wigs, anyway."

"That's Raquel Welch," Mum corrected.

"Raquel Welch was so beautiful."

"Yes," agreed Mum.

"And now she sells wigs. Like a used-car salesman."

She sighed and was so disconsolate she had to hang up.

My dad called me back. "Why have you been upsetting your mother?"

"Raquel Welch upset her."

"Oh," said my dad darkly, "I see."

When I get back to the office, Holly is curling her eyelashes with the back of a spoon. She sighs and pulls off her Clash City Rockers T-shirt, flopping onto the sofa in her shorts and blue bra.

"So," she says, "how's it going with you and Marley?"

"Oh, God, Holly, I really like Marley. But what is a twenty-eight-year-old doing with a kid?"

"Here's the thing: You're used to older men, you're used to celebrities. They *are* kids. Isn't this a better deal?"

"I don't fucking know. I don't know anything."

"Nothing?"

I sigh. Then I sigh again.

"How're the names coming along?"

"Oh, they're coming, they're coming. I think you're going to be really happy. By the way, what's going on with Ivy?"

"Oh, she's such a misery guts."

"Don't you love her anymore?"

"She's a pain in the ass."

"But a good pain in the ass, right?"

"I don't know anymore."

"She seems kind of sad lately, don't you think?"

"She does? I haven't noticed."

You haven't noticed anything, you selfish bitch.

25 FIRST LOVE MIX TAPE

MARLEY AND I HAVE BREAKFAST AT GORKY'S. As I read the papers, my eyes well with tears. "A child lost an arm in a shark accident and then got up and surfed again."

Gorky's is playing a mix tape that sounds suspiciously like one I made Marley when I first met him. It's embarrassing. I'm worried he might think I ripped it off from a coffeeshop tape or, worse, made the same tape for the owner. I look at Marley. He is singing along loudly and poorly to Sly Stone. Thanks to Gorky's and my continued attempts to write there, I have been having a croissant for every breakfast, a cupcake every evening, and not writing at all. I have gained five pounds in the process.

"I've gained five pounds, Marley," I tell him as I polish off my croissant.

"I noticed. I love it. But you haven't gained weight, you've gained curves."

I tell my mother this in our next conversation and she practically shrieks, "But you had enough curves already!"

"I love the curves," coos Marley later that night, "I want to draw you."

One time in a London park, when I was still young enough to think I was the most beautiful girl in the world, a caricaturist drew my picture. He charcoaled me with a huge nose and tombstone teeth. I didn't understand what caricature was. I thought it was his name. When we got home, I cried and cried and my father burned the picture. I stood holding his leg and watched it burn. I still shiver when I pass caricaturists and artists.

"No thanks, Marley." The mural was quite enough. "Are we gonna shag, then, or what?"

"Not shagging. Making love."

"Oh, Jesus," I groan. It sounds like arts and crafts. We are making a papier-mâché bunny and then we are making love. But deep down I know just what he means. We have been making something that doesn't disappear with orgasm.

"I used to ejaculate," he said. "With you I have an orgasm. I've never had such great sex."

Marley and I are lost in a quicksand of sex that weekend. I get up to make breakfast then come back in and he's ready to go again—I forget, he's a young man, that's what they do. It always pinched a little with the others, like there was something up there hibernating that didn't want to be disturbed. With Marley all I want is "disturb me," shake me up. It is like nothing I have ever felt before. It is love. It is lust, longing not when he is with me as I felt with others, losing Christmas before it's over, but contentment. It is a secret language. I never thought I'd have one. One I know the alphabet of instinctively. No learning required.

Before we fall asleep on Sunday night I give him a blow job that is a transcendent experience. I am crying while I'm doing it, because I'm not doing it to prove anything. I'm doing it be-

cause I want him in me as much as possible. I love the taste of
him, the feel and shape. My heart is full, or is it my . . . I can't
say the word he says, but there. They seem interchangeable,
both are beating so slow but so loud. I could fake death. I put
my hand on his chest and feel for his heart. The same thing.
Our heartbeats are fucking too.

With my permission he reaches across to the dresser table
and picks up his camera phone. Barred from drawing me, he
takes pictures—snap, snap, snap—and my face starts to burn.

"I've never done this before," he says.

"How ugly are they?"

"I don't know."

He shows them to me. They are beautiful. I look religious,
the colors and shapes not quite clear; the lighting and radiance
take away the obscenity, although they are as obscene as they
could be. And then he erases them.

"Why did you do that?"

"I show people photos of Montana on my camera phone all
the time."

"I understand."

"And . . . it might work between us. Or it might not. I don't
want you to worry about them."

Suddenly, I want desperately for him to keep the pictures.

26 ANGEL'S HAIR AND BABY'S BREATH

MARLEY HAS A BIG MEETING with a design firm on Monday. They want a mural in their conference room (word, I guess, has spread about ours). How amazing to coopt the underground to that extent. They are paying him big money to deface their property.

"I used to get arrested for this," he marvels.

"What are you going to paint?"

"I'd like to do a mural about corporate greed"—he grins—"but they're paying me, so I'll do whatever they want!"

Montana's around and her mother is busy, so I take her to work with me again, quite sure that this is not a good idea. Take your boyfriend's daughter who mostly hates you to work day. I pick her up from his house and he gives me a quick kiss while she's playing with her hair in the mirror. A sixth sense makes her whip around, but she isn't fast enough to catch us.

He gives her a big hug, which she wriggles out of, then Marley walks us to the subway. Montana is not happy about riding the subway, but she makes this known only once her father has left.

"Dumb, dumb, smelly, dumb."

"Do you want to hold your card?"

"Why?"

"I don't know."

So she can be in charge, have something of her own, although to suggest that she is not in charge and does not own everything in the world is not something her parents have allowed to cross her mind. She clings to me, tight, inching so close to me that her hair is in my mouth. Blond tastes different. Real blond. It tastes like wheat. She has a bunny rabbit hat on and a pink velour tracksuit. People keep saying she is cute and I can see what a drag it is. "Little girl, you are just too darling." Which makes no sense. Too rich, too thin, too darling. Not possible. It is making her crosser and crosser.

"Take off that damn bunny rabbit hat."

A loon comes over and sings in our faces. He has no front teeth. "The Martians took my teeth! The Martians took my teeth!"

"Yeah? What'd you get for them?"

Montana smacks me. "Don't talk to him."

He looms in front of her.

"No smacking your sister, little girl."

"She's not my sister." She says, "Smelly no tooth!" as he exits at the next stop, and I turn to her.

"That's not nice. Think of all you have and how little he has."

"I know." She clings to me. "I'm sad for the man with no teeth. Can we find him?"

"No. He'll be okay. You just have to be kind in New York, every day, all the time. California is bigger. You don't have to see humans so often, humans who have nothing and humans who are frightening or make you sad."

"I see them, but we drive past them."

"Yeah."

"My daddy helps them. My daddy helps everyone."

I have a drawerful or Reese's Pieces in my desk, waiting as patiently as geishas to be consumed. But in deference to Marley's rule that no refined sugar be allowed to enter the holy temple of his child's body, and after the last disaster, Vicki has gone to the health-food store on Broadway to buy organic animal crackers. Vicki is the most unorganic person I know. Every single thing she does is planned, everything is a fucking concept. Today she is wearing red Victorian lace-up boots, with hundreds of hooks and eyes on the sides. How a person could think their way into that concept, I don't know. It would take hours. But she has managed it and keeps prancing around the room and resting her feet on her desk so that we can all celebrate her achievement.

Holly and Ivy go home early because they have a White Stripes show to attend. Holly was sent VIP tickets and I wonder if Jack White knows that. A CEO of a makeup company asked for and received free tickets. Was that his big plan back in Detroit?

I yearn to be in the office alone—although Montana is being so well behaved that she doesn't impinge on my concentration in any way. I keep trying to get Vicki to leave, but she keeps waving dolls at Montana, insisting on being "good with children" the way men insist on being "good in bed." Oh, Jesus, I used to think with Isaac, I guess he's planning on being good in bed tonight. He'd ostentatiously go down on me, dribbling all over my thighs until I thought I was going to be sick, the worst part being when he'd pause to look up at me, eyes hooded in faux lust as though to say, "Look at me. I am going down on you." It was like Lifetime TV movies, where mothers whose children have been killed in a bike accident scream, as they survey the carnage, "Whyyy? Why did my baby have to be killed in a bike accident?"

Yes, I know, you're going down on me, you big spastic. I'll get the medal ready.

Vicki continues to skip around the office while I am trying to think, but now, when I look up, I see she has finger puppets on both her hands and is using the tiny felt jaws of a miniature alligator to feed herself animal crackers. It is appalling to see the alligator drop the organic rhinoceros into her pink mouth. Cannibalism, I think, my stomach turning.

"Yummy yum yum. I yuv deeze cookies," she coos.

Montana has on a hell of a scowl, her lips curled inside out as though preparing for a war dance, and eventually Vicki gets the message and leaves. I can tell that Vicki is devastated, and will be pondering for days her failure to delight a child.

Once Vicki is gone, Montana feeds me animal crackers while I work, not saying a word, just peering over my shoulder. At one point she leans on me—I think she is tired—and wraps her arms around my neck. It makes me gasp the same way I did when her father first touched me and I hide it the same way too, swallowing my delight like an oyster. She is a hell of a good kid and I am a stunted, jealous freak, an affront to feminism. As I ponder my hostility to a younger woman, I wonder how people would feel if I named the next line of lipsticks after feminists. Friedan. Greer. Steinem. I could write to them, ask them to collaborate on colors for International Women's Day, and we could sell them for charity. As I am hatching my plan, Montana plops herself in my lap and surveys the makeup samples spread across my desk.

"Can I touch this one?" she asks, pointing at a concealer-combination pencil I have named White Lies.

"Sure."

"Can I touch this one?" she says, picking up a peach blush from the last collection.

"Absolutely."

"These?" she asks, eyeing the batch Holly deposited with me before she hurried off to watch Jack White masturbate with his guitar.

"Ah, no. Those are the ones we need to present to the client on Monday."

She sniffs, reverting from her real voice to the Miss Manners tone she had affected when I first met her. "Those. I want to play with those."

"But those are the only ones I can't let you . . . you can have all of these, any of these you like."

She removes herself from my lap and begins to sob for her father, as though I were a department-store Santa who had gotten an erection.

"I want to go home! I want to go home!"

"Okay. Okay, we'll go home." I shut down the computer. I am ready to leave. I am tired.

"WHY DO YOU CRY ALL THE TIME?"

She dries her eyes on the sleeve of her pink velour tracksuit. It is amazing: Her eyes dry instantly, the same way Superman is able to heal his own wounds. "Why do *you* cry all the time?"

Ignoring her query, I put on my coat and zip her into hers. She lets me but turns her head away from me as I do it.

I am too tired to ride the subway, so we hail a cab on Lafayette. Montana buckles herself in, which is good because I would have forgotten to. Instinctively, I check our driver's name on his license. "Samuel Jean." I like it when I get a Hai-

tian cabdriver because usually they are listening to the BBC
World Service and I can practice my French. I started learning
French when I was four, although it's almost all gone now. I
understand every word they say but can speak very little. I feel
that's the tragedy of my life: I understand everything and can
communicate nothing.

But Samuel Jean, instead of being tuned to the BBC World
Service, is listening to Fox News. The topic is George Bush's
surprise visit to Iraq. The caller currently on the line to talk
radio says he hasn't felt so proud to be an American since
the days of Ronald Reagan. Instantly, I begin to cry. Montana
was right.

The cab pulls up at Marley's front door and, wiping my face
with the back of my hand, I take her dejectedly back to him.
"Hi, baby." He beams. He is covered in paint. She goes straight
up to her room.

"What happened?"

"I'm not sure. I wouldn't let her play with some of the makeup
we needed. It wasn't her shade anyway. She got really upset."

"Ah, no big deal, that's kids. Contrary."

"That's kids? That's what they're like?"

"That's what humans are like. Adults just have better volume control."

"Really."

"Well, not you."

"I don't?"

"No. You have no volume control at all. I love it."

"How could you love it?"

"Because it's truthful."

I love him so much I want to bite his eyelashes—velvet
black and long, asking for it really—but instead I say, "Let's
run away to Hawaii."

I could lie out in the sun and just be as much of a jerk as I want and it would all be telling the truth.

"If I didn't have a daughter, we'd run away tonight. But this is my life."

The velvet imagining of his lashes catch in my throat.

"These are your lives. They don't touch."

I remember, when I was eight or nine, having a phobia about my food touching. The mashed potatoes couldn't touch the peas. I loved them both, but I had to eat them separately. I wonder if I am potatoes or peas to him. Mashed potatoes, I hope, chewing the inside of my cheek as though it were gum, at least let him find me comforting. And in his comfort he won't realize how fattening I am, and soon enough no other woman will want him.

His smile is as weak as diner coffee. "Sometimes I feel like I'm a conduit for you to grow and change, and then you'll grow and change and be gone."

"We could get married."

"That's so childish."

"Why? We could. Anyway, you just said—"

"Hey." He pulls me to him and I let him, but as he holds me I lean into his chest and think about my father dying one day, my mother too, me all alone with my lipsticks. As if he hears me, Marley says, "Listen, I've been thinking about something. You need to get an accountant, okay? You've got to get your finances in order. You'll feel a lot better, a lot calmer. You don't have to want to make mad cash. But you should want to be on top of what you do have."

"You're so responsible."

He taps a framed photo of Montana.

"But I don't have one of those," I say.

He taps my chest.

"Okay, I get it. I'll call an accountant, I promise. I'm tired. I'm gonna head home."

"You okay?"

"Yeah."

But I don't want to leave. I don't want to have sex. I just want to crawl into Montana's bed with the stars on the ceiling and go to sleep. Montana is leaving the next day, so I decide to let them be alone. "Let me pee and I'll head out."

Montana's pink toothbrush is by the sink. The herbal non-fluoride toothpaste that I know will leave her with cavities by the time she is twenty sits, oozing uselessness, beside it. Marley's wash bag is open, so I riffle through it. Chapstick. Tea tree oil. A razor. And samples of Cool Yoga bath products from Jolene: little squares of soap wrapped in paper and labeled Joy, Inspiration, and Karma. What stupid things to wish for via bath products. Who uses facial scrub as a messenger? Jolene is probably one of those Buddhists who prays for a new dishwasher. The Karma smells of grapefruit, so I take it.

That night I wash with Jolene's Karma. To wash with stolen Karma seems, on reflection, not the greatest idea. The grapefruit smell, instead of soothing me into sleep, has me wide awake. I listen to CDs. I look at my bills, thinking it would be a good time to get through them. Then I look at my computer, thinking I might get some work done on my novel. Then I try on my hats, which I have hung on the wall above my bed. I put on a different song for each hat. A fedora is the appropriate thing to wear when listening to David Bowie. Then I read old issues of *Rolling Stone* I have saved from high school. I don't know why I keep them because they make me unbearably sad: seeing artists hailed on the cover as the next big thing and knowing that their second album flopped. I have seen the future and it does not include Neneh Cherry. I cry for a while, then I write her a letter:

Dear Neneh,

You were so beautiful and so awesome. I remember you dancing on *Top of the Pops* when you were eight months pregnant. Why did you go away? You're half Swedish, right? My mum is Swedish, but not like you. I figure if you have Swedish blood, it only works if you have something at the other end of the ethnic scale to dilute it. That's why Isabella Rossellini is prettier than Ingrid Bergman; at least Isabella has some Italian. But I digress. I am dating a man who has a child. You're a single mother, I believe. Do you feed your baby organic? I know you were a punk, so I can't figure it out, whether or not organic food is rebellious. The child's mother is probably everything bland you were fighting. I know he loves me and it's not independent or cool for me to waste my thoughts on someone else, so sorry in advance for disappointing you. I learned self-respect and big gold hoop earrings from you. Should I stay in this relationship or not? I would appreciate your thoughts on my dilemma.
Yours,
Sadie Steinberg

P.S. I know you named your baby Tyson before Mike Tyson was convicted of rape. If you haven't yet renamed her, here are some suggestions: Butterfly. Ramona. Eloise. Tuesday. Tatiana.

I decide to find the fan club address but then become worried she may no longer have a fan club.

27 KARMA CHAMELEON

WHEN I WAKE UP, I mistake the cocktail hats on my wall for African masks and feel very frightened. I pull the blankets over my head and overheat and shake until I am able to think rational thoughts and remember about my hats. When I look again, I congratulate myself on my newfound ability to reason with my imagination.

Proud, I decide to continue my adventures in adulthood and arrange for an accountant to come over the next day. It is time to knock my ten-grand tax bill on the head. Knock it and bite it and kill it. Like cleaning for the cleaner, I go through my financial records as best I can. I have saved the receipt for every hamburger, hotel, and high heel of the last three years. This is the main reason my apartment is such a mess. Shoe boxes bursting with little yellow slips of paper, a thousand different numbers printed on these slivers of consumerism, but the same name signed over and over again. Mainly I now use them to blot my lipstick. Finding the shoe boxes hugely pregnant, several giving sloppy birth, I have stuffed fistfuls of besmirched receipts into the silverware drawer, my underwear drawer, the cat-food cupboard. Receipts fill the pots and pans I don't use to cook the food I never open. Packages of pasta and bottles of sauce, unopened, next to unopened bills.

I generally pay bills when the creditors call for them. I take the checkbook from my underwear drawer and clear my good name. Most take my checking-account details and hang up. One nice lady from American Express said, on successfully clearing check 34, "Ma'am, may I ask why it was that you didn't pay until now?" I answered cheerily, "Oh, I'm a novelist. We're very spacey, you know." Then I got off the phone and into bed, stared at the ceiling, and dreamed about slitting my wrists because my life would never be in order. One day my parents will die and I will be alone with my debt and I will go to prison and, hopefully, at least I will be able to keep my cell tidy. I thought long and hard about it, but I couldn't bring myself to slit my wrists, so I drew red lines on them with a felt-tip pen instead.

THE UNOPENED DEMANDS have somehow, in my attempt to ready myself for the accountant, migrated to the bottom tier of the cat tree. Sidney Katz helpfully sits on them.

"Good. Stay there. I don't want to look at them."

I have come to loathe the moment when, withdrawing money from a machine, you are asked in green digital letters whether or not you want your receipt. "No!" I yell at the ATM. "Don't tell me!"

Why I prefer to find out what my available balance is by having my card declined, I don't know. Yes, I do: Fear, fear, and more fear. Fear like the dimly lit door in a horror film, the door you should never open. And so I don't. Final reminders remain sealed for months. I become afraid, as I try to organize, that there might be living breathing things inside those sealed reminders, baby animals that I've let suffocate slow painful deaths by not releasing them from envelopes stamped with red, tiny, tiny kittens and puppies that MasterCard has sent me as a gift. Prying them open, my eyes popping, waves of relief wash over me to see that all they contain are final cutoff warnings.

My dad is fuck all help when I call him on his lunch break.

"Um, I think I have to fill in a bunch of B-52s. Does that sound right?"

"I dunno," he says, and smackingly chews gum.

He hates talking about work, especially with me. Dejected, I ring off and get on my hands and knees, moving piles of receipts into subpiles. The numbers are unreadable to me.

Soon enough I have such a bad headache that I have to knock myself out with migraine medicine. When the accountant turns up, I am wasted. He is like an accountant from central casting, not like my dad at all. He has mousy blond hair and glasses and a suit. If he had a twistedness to him he could be James Spader, but he doesn't, so he is just a blond man in a suit. Pulling his face into focus, I see his expression of horror and, looking around me, remember that there are lipstick stains on every single receipt and the receipts are in piles on the kitchen floor being held down with an array of forks. Electricity, phone, rent, and AMEX: lipsticked and cutleryed.

I've seen my dad do this since I was little. Not with lipstick stains but with mess. Everywhere. Food spread around him. Sandwiches made with crushed salt and vinegar chips and mayonnaise. We'd crush the chips together. I hated them, but he liked them, so I liked them. Then I'd put my head on his stomach and listen to him digest. I thought it was the most fun in the world. Sometimes he'd let me look in his ears with a flashlight at the hair and wax, and that was also a great joy. I wanted to know how he worked, what he was made out of, what produced those glorious intestinal gurgling noises, not to mention the rapturous farts and burps.

"I need to get my finances in order," I tell untwisted James Spader.

On his knees poring through my defaced receipts, he looks up curiously. "What finances?"

I sit down at the kitchen table, deflated. "Good point."

His voice is high and makes me feel higher. "Two years ago your account shows you had a balance of thirty thousand dollars. Now you're in overdraft to the tune of ten grand. What, if I may ask, did you spend it on?"

"Um . . . chewing gum? Bits of string? Gym membership," I say triumphantly.

"How was it?"

"I don't know. I haven't been."

"You've spent five thousand dollars on clothes this year."

"Wow. I wonder where they are." I desperately rack my brain, as last time I looked there was not a single thing in my closet I could wear. "Bras! I have lots and lots of bras!" I pull aside the sleeve of my T-shirt as though to explain through sign language what a bra is. Sounds like "car."

"Well, good for you," he says, looking away.

He is blushing, or I would offer to show some of the more expensive ones to him: the really beautiful Moschino one with the pink lace trim, the Aubade demicup in butter yellow.

He changes the subject. "You're earning again, I see. Quite nicely for a girl your age. You're going to need to put money aside if we're to do anything about this tax bill. I want you to take whatever you have left in your checking account and open a certificate of deposit. Today."

Untwisted James Spader leaves my apartment and heads back to his midtown office, possibly pausing to have sex in the back of a burned-out car, but probably not. My high continues on the subway and ends as soon as I walk through the doors of Citibank.

My teller is a very pretty Spanish girl with pale green eyes and her hair pulled back in a ponytail and parted on the side. I know men probably jostle other customers to be seen by her. She is a ray of sunlight in the funereal head office. Ines Rivera.

"Hi. I have money?" I add the question mark at the end of a sentence that was not a question. I wait for Ines to answer, but she just looks at me. "Can you please move everything I have in my checking account into a certificate of deposit. Please," I add again.

"Swipe your card and type in your PIN." She has the same Long Island whine as Mariah Carey, but none of the instability. Boy, I would like to have this woman around if I ever spilled red wine on a carpet. She'd know what to do. What a great quality: to exude an ability to cope with a crisis major or minor.

I swipe my card and, on the third try, get my PIN number right.

"You don't have enough to open a certificate of deposit. You have ninety-eight dollars."

She looks at me for an answer, but there is really no response to ninety-eight dollars, so I leave. It is a disaster. I feel like shit; really, the most depressed I have been in a long time. As soon as I get home, I call Marley and say, "I just had the greatest day. I had a great meeting with an accountant and the people at the bank were so helpful. I'm so glad you told me to do this. It's so easy."

"That's fantastic! I just got back from the airport. Do you want me to cook you dinner?"

So I choose a dress and lipstick, but I get rained on, and when I get to Brooklyn, I have to go straight to the bathroom and wash it off.

"I love seeing you without makeup," he says, gasping. "You look so beautiful."

That's always a warning sign. When men say they prefer women without makeup. No, they don't. They prefer women who look like they haven't got any on, but those women use concealer, brown mascara, eye-bag diffuser, tinted lip balm, peach blusher, and eyebrow gel. It's like when men say they love women who eat a lot. Those same women starve themselves when they're not out at dinner with a guy. I work at a makeup company and Marley prefers me without makeup? I love makeup. It's my favorite form of procrastination, and now I get paid to help other women procrastinate, freeze them in the aisles with my mascara stun gun. But something in his voice seems sincere. He kisses me and I feel my clitoris blush.

"I'll get you something to change into."

Coming back downstairs with an oversize T-shirt and a towel, he dries my hair and wraps it expertly in a chignon. He is a macho man who knows all the most useful gay things.

"Now watch this."

And I do watch, as he debones fish and steams broccoli and it is so wonderful to watch, but no way am I eating it, and I guess I should have said that I don't like fish or broccoli in the first place. He looks at it, untouched on the white plate in front of me. I am scared he will be mad. He goes to the kitchen and as time passes I fear he might be crying. Then he comes back with a smile, along with a peanut-butter-and-jelly sandwich and a glass of milk. And he eats my dinner. The peanut butter is almond butter, the bread wheat-free, and the milk soy, but it is a nice gesture. He is one big, nicely toned nice gesture and I can't understand how someone so nice can be so muscular. Isaac was so mean and so weedy. He once made me carry a champagne bottle for him. He couldn't do it himself. I look at Marley and feel so lucky. Luck. Rhymes with *fuck*. So we do.

"Everyone's happy," he whispers, slumped in a chair as I lie breathless on the kitchen table. I climb onto his lap and we sit there for a while just looking at each other. I remember that Andy Warhol once said that if you have beauty flaws you should point them out at the beginning of a relationship so they don't get held against you later on. I pause and say: "I was born with bags under my eyes."

"I see them."

"Once when I was seventeen I was bored, so I plucked the hair around my mouth and it grew back thicker. Now I have to wax."

"Okay, I get it, because sometimes it's bald and sometimes there are little hairs." He strokes the little hairs, and had it been any other man I would have died and then killed myself and then thrown up. But with him it's okay.

He pets my hair and smells it. "You smell of something."

"Karma."

"What?"

"Nothing. Grapefruit."

"It's nice. But I prefer your real smell."

"Be inside me," I say in the tiniest little-girl voice, so lusty and enticing, and he blanches until I realize he thought I had said "Pee inside me." We figure things out and make love again, and as usual it is amazing. When I am amazed, I go quiet, so I am quiet with Marley a lot. My volume control swings wildly pre- and postfucking. Before I have no muffler. Afterward I am speechless, without speech, without defense. I hated it at first, but now I love it. It is relief. After sex with Isaac I would talk and talk and talk, even when he turned away from me, even when he turned onto me and crushed me into his chest. I couldn't really breathe, but I'd keep talking.

28 CABBAGE PATCH KID

WE ARE LYING IN BED when I ask the question I have been wondering about since I saw her photo. "Why is your baby blond? Are you sure she's your baby?" I catch myself. "That's a very rude question, isn't it?"

"Pretty rude, but I would expect nothing less of you. I like your rude."

"My rude?"

"Yes." He pulls me close.

"But she is yours?"

"Yes. Her mother's very blond."

"Oh. Do you like blondes?"

"I like women. I told you that. What's with the blond?"

"You're blond when you're a kid."

"I never was."

We laugh.

"Maybe we were never young."

"Born old."

"You were. Sort of. I look at you and I see too young and too old."

"Two toos. That can't be good."

"It shouldn't be. But somehow it is."

He holds my face in his paint-stained hands. "I've tried to talk myself out of you. My life is complicated. I don't need this. I've tried and tried to talk myself into being a loner. That's what I want. I remember hanging up over bridges, painting, alone. My friends would be on lookout, but really it was just me. I loved the lonerness of heroin. That was my favorite part. But I can't talk myself out of you."

"Hey. Guess what? I've taken up knitting." A half-finished scarf sits on the bedside table. "Do you want me to knit you something?"

"No thanks. Makes me think of my mother. Itchy things. She tried to knit to prove she could be a domestic housewife if she felt like it. But she couldn't. They were all misshapen and scratchy. Come to think of it, so were her chocolate-chip cookies."

"Oh no, I use only merino wool. Here, feel."

He rubs it on my cheek.

"It feels good," I admit.

"What do you want?"

You you you. You alone. No one else. No one else to take your focus from me. No one else to knit for.

"Knickers. Knit me some knickers."

On the subway home, I read over the shoulder of a fellow straphanger the latest column by Isaac Bennett. It is about the iconicism in American pop culture of younger women with older men.

"As beautiful and talented as she undoubtedly is, we would rather have a younger version of Kim Basinger than have Kim

Basinger. Right or wrong, this is the male instinct. While men age like fine wine, women seem to wilt. You can tell a man who is seeing a younger woman by the vibrancy in his step. Older women for companionship is all well and good, but for inspiration it's a young girl every time. Great minds require this."

The straphanger flips the page and I am so grateful to have that vile column physically removed from my sight that I actually breathe a sigh of relief. Isaac Bennett. What an asshole!

29 YO! BUM RUSH THE GLOW!

ISAAC'S COLUMN PISSES ME OFF. It really gets under my skin. But I think the trouble starts because I have been watching *Bright Eyes* for a couple of days straight. I am trying to learn Shirley Temple's tap-dance routine to "The Good Ship Lollipop," but I can't do it. I keep stubbing my toe, clanking my heel against my calf. I am rewinding the tape and pausing it on each and every step. I have been doing this for hours—pause, play, and trip—and my eyes are starting to swim.

She's four! I think. Shirley Temple's fucking four, and she can do it.

I have a long interior dialogue with myself, attempting to reason, reminding the other voice that I have other talents, that it isn't the end of the world if I can't learn Shirley Temple's tap routine.

I tap and tap and tap, my toes starting to bleed. I have no neighbors beneath me, just the derelict office of a lawyer who has been sent to jail for tax evasion.

I turn up the volume. *Tappa tappa tappa.* Look at those

shiny ringlets, bouncing with every perfectly executed move. The more I try to reason with myself, the more it becomes crystal clear that my main failing in life is not being able to master this routine, and that if I could, everything else would fall into place. Exhausted and bloody, I realize I can no longer live in a world where tap dance is a prerequisite for social success. I drink four beers and then call people, but no one's home. I call the cell number David Consuela Cohen gave me.

"Turns out I'm coming to L.A. in a few days."

"Oh, my God, you have to call me!"

"I will."

"You'd better, girl!"

I wonder what he will do to me if I don't call.

I ring Marley again, but his cell phone is off. Frustrated, I pull a sweater on over my dress and head over to his house.

"Hey. You had your cell phone off."

"Yes. I was reading to Montana."

"I know I'm not really invited tonight. But I missed you."

I can smell the alcohol on my own breath.

"Right. Well, I just got Montana to sleep, so maybe you should go upstairs and lie down."

When I go to sleep, the room is spinning, and when I wake up, it is still spinning but slower, like a hula hoop about to hit the ground. I crawl out of bed wearing the fuschia dress I had tap-danced in, sweat stains under my arms. As my feet hit the floor, I melt into the ground like a pathetic pink puddle. I sit there for a while, feeling like something someone else's suitor would cover with his coat so they could step over me.

I start to inch my way down the staircase of Marley's house. Really, a staircase? Who has a staircase in New York? Right then I hate him for having a healthy bank balance.

"Marley?" I call, although it sounds like "Marwee?" because

I am feeling so sorry for myself. I hoist myself into the kitchen and put the kettle on. Then I take a tea bag from the special Sadie shelf he has made me in the cupboard and make myself a piece of marmite on toast. I carry the tea and toast forlornly to the living room and turn on the TV. As soon as I eat I start to feel better, but I keep sniffling and sighing anyway, just in case Marley walks in. Every few minutes I moan his name pathetically like a baby still hoping for Mama to pick her up out of her crib even though she's already pooped her pants.

Between episodes of *The Powerpuff Girls,* I hear a car pull up at the house. I peer through the curtain and see Marley, Montana, and, in the driver's seat, obscured by Marley's big head, a lady. I stay glued to the sofa, desperately wanting to get up and have a look at her, but I suddenly fixate on the Zovirax commercial. It combats cold sores really fast. It has twice the healing power of rival brands. I try to memorize all the claims and all the dangers as though I am preparing for a final exam. I am so afraid of seing this woman. I close my eyes and repeat the words coming from the TV: ". . . may cause dizziness or dry mouth. Side effects include loss of appetite, headaches, insomnia."

"What's insomnia?"

I open my eyes and Montana is standing in front of me wearing a pink leotard and a white tutu. "It's when you can't—"

She cuts me off. "I just came from ballet. I can do an arabesque and a plié."

"So can I," I say quickly. I catch my breath and ask, "Where's your dad?"

"He's outside talking to my mom."

The word stings me like an offensive word from the fifties, as though she has said, "He's outside talking to my coon."

She watches me as I try to compose myself and adds: "My

mom's name is Jolene." She beams and then says it phoneti-
cally: "Joe-Lean."

"What a pretty name."

Just alert enough to be sneaky, I venture, "I bet your mom is
very pretty."

"Oh, about average," says a tall blond woman with an ear-
to-ear grin. She is an Amazon, with endless legs and muscular
arms. Her mouth is obscenely huge, her scooped nose clearly a
slightly crooked rhinoplasty, but her eyes are gigantic and
green, two spinning orbs anchored in place by lush lashes. She
is almost gorgeous, a beauty who has been dragged through the
hedge backward and then gone back for more.

"Mommy!" squeals Montana, and hugs her leg. "Are you
staying for lunch?"

"Jolene," I say lamely.

"I know, right?" The strapping blonde laughs. "Stupid fuckin'
Dolly Parton fans as parents." She has a husky voice and punc-
tuates each sentence with laughter.

"*Mommy!*"

"Sorry, baby." Jolene looks at me and shrugs her shoulders
like it's me and her against Montana. "Now I owe her a dollar."

"Yep. I've been feeling the pinch myself ever since Montana
came into my life."

"And what a happy day I bet that was," jokes Jolene, and I
laugh. "Hur-hur-hur."

"I have two hundred and seventy dollars in Mommy's
curse box."

"I'm saving to send her to college," booms Jolene. "Fuckin'
Harvard."

"*Mommy!*" squeals Montana, and collapses onto the sofa in
delight.

Jolene sits down beside her. "I went to Harvard."

"Gracious," I say, still waiting to be introduced.

"For a little while I dropped out to become a stripper. Toured the country. Never strip in Alaska." She points a manicured finger at me and lets her legs flop apart as her skirt rides up her thighs.

"Uh, okay." Jolene is not exactly what I have been led to expect. This is not some lentil-eating do-gooder. This woman is, how do you say it? . . . bonkers. Bonkers, and wearing very *expensive* stockings.

"We were all saving money for college or medical school. I made good money stripping, but not as much as the other girls. I haven't got that much up front, not like you. Wow, what are you, like a double D?"

"Just a D," I stutter.

"They look bigger." She squints at me. "Maybe 'cuz you're so short."

"Thank you." I press myself as far back into the sofa as it will allow, wondering where the hell Marley is.

Jolene fixes me with her green stare and says, "He's gone to the corner to buy eggs. I'm cooking my specialty."

"Eggs!" exclaims Montana. "Eggs! Eggs! Eggs!"

"Bonky eggs!" says Jolene.

"Oh, God," I say, and then try to soften it by adding, "I'd better get dressed and get out of here."

"Oh, no, honey," says Jolene, "you're invited. This is all in honor of you. Marley doesn't know that, of course. This is my way of meeting the new girlfriend without causing a scene and getting you all stressed. Gotta make sure the woman who's hanging around my daughter all week isn't a crack dealer! Man, do you look stressed! C'mere!"

"No," I whisper.

"Don't worry, I'm coming there."

She straddles me and starts kneading my shoulders with her huge hands. "I'm a licensed massage therapist."

Montana changes her singsong from "Eggs! Eggs! Eggs!" to "Girlfriend! New girlfriend!"

"That's right," says Jolene as she karate-chops my spine, "this is Daddy's new girlfriend and he likes her very much, so let's be extra nice to her."

"Nice!" screams Montana, "Nice! Nice! Nice!" and throws herself into my lap, face squashed against my bosom as her mother presses my neck with her thumbs.

Just then Marley walks through the door. He looks like he's going to be sick. My eyes are ablaze with terror, like a cat with a thermometer up its ass. Seeing Marley clicks Jolene into a different mode and she unhands me so fast I feel like I am being dropped. Montana melts out of my lap like a clock in a Dalí painting.

"I see you and Jolene have met, then" is the best he can manage.

"Man, is this one a doll," says Jolene, which is true in the sense that I sat there absolutely silent while she molested me. "Okay, let's get this show on the road," she barks, clapping her hands. "Who wants a bonky egg?"

"Me!" shrieks Montana.

"What's a bonky egg?" I ask, praying it isn't a type of massage.

"Follow me to the kitchen."

Jolene makes her way through the cupboards as if she has never left. Her fingers mold to the handle of the pan, the lid of the bread bin, as though she might never let go again. She takes out the almond rice bread. "First, you cut a hole in the bread with a cookie cutter. You wanna do it, honey?"

Montana reaches up and presses her little hand hard over the circle, and when she lifts it, the bread is marked, like the face of a lover on the pillow.

"Then you heat up the frying pan, add a little butter—just a very little, we don't want to get fat like Aunt Tula, do we?—and wait for it to melt."

We wait. Marley clears his throat.

"Then you crack the egg and pour it into the hole."

"Mommy, you said 'hole,' you owe me money."

"Bullshit!" gasps Jolene. "Who told you *hole* was a rude word?"

"Tom McEwan."

"Tom McEwan? He's five! What does he know?"

Montana accepts this argument and falls silent. Jolene carefully flips the egg-and-bread concoction over. The smell of burning butter begins to make my beer-soaked stomach queasy.

"You eat eggs?"

"Yeah, sure. Why wouldn't I?"

"Oh, it's just that I had it in my head from Marley and Montana that you're a really healthy eater."

"I am a healthy eater and that's why I get fried eggs once a week as a treat." Marley looks very embarrassed. He is standing at the other end of the kitchen from me, but I see his cheeks pinken.

"Now hum to yourselves, kids!" Jolene demands.

I begin to croakily hum "On the Good Ship Lollipop" because humming helps me control nausea. I'm starting to feel a little bit better until Jolene booms, "I like it! Great tits *and* she can sing!"

I hum louder and Marley looks at the eggs as though they contain the key to the universe.

"You owe me more money, Mommy."

"For what?"

"Tits. You said she had 'great tits.' "

"We count that as a bad word? I don't think we should,

honey. Tits are beautiful, all shapes and sizes and colors. Big nipples, little nipples, perky ones, pointy ones. Nope, I don't think 'tits' is gonna cut it."

"Mommy, you said 'cunt.' "

"No, I didn't, I said 'cut.' "

"Oh." Montana sighs. "Well, usually you say 'cunt.' "

To reiterate: Jolene is not what I expected. And she smells quite strongly to me of surreptitious cigarettes. Speaking of which, I wonder what Marley was smoking when he described her to me. Is this the right woman? Was there a case of mistaken identity? How the hell does he describe me to other people? "Oh, you'd love my girlfriend, Sadie, she's a deaf-mute who travels the world rescuing orphans from war-torn areas." I'm as good at the sell as anyone—I invent countless different names for cosmetics that are all exactly the same color. But this, this is something else. He's taken her color—Obnoxious Blonde—and listed her as Spun Gold, Marigold, Dewdrops in the Garden, Chelsea Morning. Well, now at least I know where an eight-year-old heard the word *fuckhead*. And smelling the cigs on the organically pampered skin of a health freak, I also see how an eight-year-old who says "fuckhead" has a swear box.

The bonky eggs are better than they smell, and as I eat them I realize I need them. I have a real live hangover. Just as my focus is starting to return, Jolene says to Montana, "You were so much better than the other girls in ballet today. Why don't you do a dance for us!" and it all goes blurry again.

We all sit on the sofa and watch Montana dance. Marley sits next to me and that tiny little gesture brings me such relief. Of course, it's not like he would really go over and have Jolene sit on his knee—or, more likely, hop onto hers—but I'm feeling a little crazy. He squeezes my thigh from time to time and it's good to know his touch can be as comforting as it is exciting. "Plié!" cries Montana. "Jeter!" she booms, accidentally invoking the baseball player rather than the ballet pose she hops into. No one corrects her. She isn't very good, but she enjoys herself. What a waste of a great tutu, I think.

"Now listen, sexy Sadie," says Jolene, "I have to get out of here in a minute, but before I go, I have to tell you, I love Grrrl."

"You do?"

"Well, not for me, obviously, but what a great idea!"

"What's the idea?"

"You know. Ugly. Back in the day I would have rocked it for sure. How rad would it have been to wear that shit when I was stripping? Fuck those assholes, right?"

"Shit. Fuck," notes Montana, reaching into her bag for a diary and writing the words down.

Marley squeezes me a bit too hard. Jolene continues, "Honey, the obsession with beauty is so intense in this culture that it's bound to go full circle. Of course women are going to want to know where they might be able to go with ugly instead."

"I guess," I answer limply. Here was a woman to talk Poe and politics with. I want to. But I can't get a conversational hard-on in front of her. She is too intimidating. Intimidate . . . that's a good name for a true red lipstick.

"Hello!" She snaps her fingers in front of me. "Are you there? Honey, are you hung over?"

"No," I say too loud, giving the room a start and myself a headache.

She's smart. I like what she's saying. I get it. But I'd be lying if I didn't admit that it bums me out too. I don't want to be known as the girl who works for the ugly makeup company.

"Well, listen, I've looked at the names you've been putting on those little tubes and I think they're fabulous. That's the first thing I do when I shop for makeup—look at the names."

"But you don't buy any of it?"

"Honey, I really don't buy anything. I get *sent it all.*"

"Sounds like a good life."

"It's all right," says Marley sharply, and the two of them exchange looks.

"Okay, I gotta go. I'll see you later, baby girl." She kisses Montana on the mouth, kisses Marley on the cheek, and then comes toward me. I try not to screw up my eyes. Phew. A brief peck on the cheek, closer to the ear than to the mouth. Montana follows her to the door and waves and waves at the black limo as it pulls away. Marley gently nudges her back inside. He wants her to bathe, but she is reluctant to take off her tutu. As he washes her, she makes me stand in the doorway holding the damn thing so that she can admire it the whole time she bathes.

"Make it look like it's dancing," she instructs, and I twirl the skirt from side to side while she grins. "I love this tutu, Papa. It is the best present ever."

"You got it for her?" I ask.

"Yeah," he replies, looking at me strangely, because what's the big deal? And I look into my strange heart because what *is* the big deal?

"I'm going to hang this in your room, okay?" I tell Montana as he dries her.

"Be careful with it!" she warns. I hang it lovingly on a wall hook opposite her bed. Hanging there with nothing inside it, it looks like the final remains of a dancer who died of anorexia. As I look at it, I understand what's bugging me and I feel terribly ashamed. He gave it to *her* and not to me. And because he gave it to her, I want it.

That night after Marley and I have sex I can't sleep. I flick through *The New Yorker* at his bedside but soon find myself compelled to creep out of bed and down the hall into Montana's room. She is fast asleep, tiny snores hopping in and out of the perfect O of her pink mouth. The tutu is still hanging on her wall. Sliding past her like a cat burglar, I first touch the leotard, then I touch the lacy ruffle of the skirt. I ever so gently pick it up off the hook and carry it down to the living room. Shrugging off my pajamas, I unzip the back and before I know what I'm doing, I step into it. Somewhat big on Montana, it stretches generously to make it almost halfway up my thighs. There the generosity expires. It stops on my thighs, refusing to budge. I am tugging at it in front of the mirror when I hear a terrible rip. I am trying to struggle out of the leotard when, like a bloodhound, Montana appears at the door. She starts to scream and Marley comes rushing down.

"What's wrong, baby, what's wrong?"

"Daddy! Daddy, she ripped my tutu! Daddy!" and she falls upon her father, who clutches her in his arms. They look like bear and bear cub. Bear protecting his young from a predator. The tutu is a ring around my thigh.

"I'm sure she wasn't trying on your tutu," says Marley, although anyone with the gift of sight can see that I was. "That's ridiculous. Um, Sadie?"

"I was really good at ballet when I was her age," I say lamely.

"Right."

"I still am. Watch." I do a little hop. It rips some more.

Montana screams, a guttural scream.

I excuse myself, go to the bathroom, step out of the tutu, and hand it back through the crack in the door. Marley takes it from me. I get my clothes, dress, and start out the door, without another word, for my apartment. He leaves her crying for a second and follows me out.

"Sadie . . . are you, um, okay?"

Montana is howling. I zip my jacket up to my nose, turn around, and under my breath mutter, "Sheesh, what a crybaby."

"What did you say?" he says furiously.

I look at him a moment. "I was talking about myself."

On cue, a tear slides down my cheek. He searches my face but decides to let me go. As soon as I get home, I start to absolutely bawl. I think I'm halfway through a panic attack when I get enough breath to realize why it is I'm crying so hard. It's because I've been caught out. A kid using tears to distract from the fact that she's done something wrong. But there's no one here to distract. Sidney Katz looks right up close in my face. But Sidney Katz, though I don't like to admit it, is, after all, a cat. I laugh out loud, a hollow stage laugh that, like the tears, finds no audience. Then, tearless and laughless and, most damningly for a woman still stretching for girlhood, applause-less, I realize the other reason I had hysterics. It's a good reason: I am certain I have lost my love.

I know he is going to break up with me. I am loopy, unlovable, how could he not? And almost instantly pride kicks in, slapping heartache to the sidewalk and kicking cocky in its face. I cannot allow some twenty-eight-year-old graffiti artist to dump me. I decide I have to break up with him first. I do a Jedi mind-trick, turning on my computer, for the first time in days, and send him an e-mail.

Dear Marley,

I have been meaning to say something for a long time but have been unable to find the right moment. I like you tremendously and have nothing but good memories of our time together. However, I don't think this is working out between us. Please do stay in touch. My best to you and your delightful daughter.

None of this is true. I have not been meaning to say anything other than that he makes me feel beautiful and I am in love with him. I do not send my best to his delightful daughter. I hit send and go to bed, taking a couple of migraine pills to get through the night.

The next day I am woken by the ringing of my phone, which I locate under a pile of shopping bags.

I know it will be Marley, chastened by my e-mail, desperate for my love back. Ha. Power trick. I lie on my back on the bed, wait as many rings as I can, and then pick up. "Hello, you."

But it's the wrong "you." It isn't Marley. It's my dad. At the sound of his voice, for the very first time in my life, I feel not comfort but panic. He hasn't much to say and I ring off as soon as I can. I don't want to keep the line tied up. Marley doesn't call. And doesn't call. And after not calling, he doesn't even call. For several days, almost on the hour, I pick up the receiver, hover my fingers over the keypad, and then hang up. Vicki shoots me knowing looks from her desk and Ivy shoots me sympathetic looks and Holly, well, she's in and out of the office so much, I'm not sure she looks directly at any of us all week long.

I begin to feel exquisite pain, a snowflake of pain, an antique lace slip of misery, immaculate, admirable handiwork whose interwoven pattern has to it a delicate beauty.

"I guarantee you," says Ivy, "that he is feeling just as bad as you, if not more so."

We go out for coffee. I sob my eyes out.

"You do realize, don't you, that you're taking on his pain too. Because men can't deal with it, they give it to women."

"You know a lot about men and women."

"I'm essentially with a man, aren't I?"

"Yeah. I guess."

"Look, every feeling and thought exists and if its owner doesn't absorb it and drink it, then it's floating around in the hemisphere until it gets breathed in somewhere. It has to be breathed in and exhaled as something different. If the owner doesn't do it, then whoever's close to the owner does."

Ivy has become this very wise woman. She's stopped wearing all the fuck-you glitter and her skin is so pretty. I don't think Holly is so much more beautiful than her anymore. Not really. It is nice to hang out with Ivy. She is . . . nice. I try to pay the check, but Ivy insists on getting it.

"I do technically own the company."

I forget that most of the time. We go back to work where all of Ivy's good advice goes out the window and I check my e-mail every five minutes. Literally.

"You should just hack into his account," says Vicki, looking up from her *In Style*.

"That's awful! I would never do that."

"It's a woman's inalienable right to read her lover's or ex-lover's or future lover's personal e-mails."

"You spend way too much time online."

I hear her e-mail ping. As she reads her latest message she says, "I bet his password is his daughter's name."

"That's too stupid."

But it is. That's his password. My heart lurches as his web-mail appears on my screen. All there is are e-mails from me. He has arranged them in a file. "The Jewess." I have my own file! This keeps me going for the rest of the day. He cares. He really cares. I log off and my heart rate falls back to normal. But when I get into bed and try to sleep that night, it starts thumping away again. Just as I am about to pop a headache pill, Ivy rings my doorbell. It looks like she's been crying.

"Where's Holly?"

"I don't know. She hasn't been home. I'm used to her dallying. But this one, this one is becoming more serious, I can tell."

"Do you want to stay the night?"

"No. I'm good. I'm okay. It is what it is."

I give her a hug and she goes home. Her lack of control over her romantic situation shows me how much control I do have over mine. If I want it. When she leaves, I dial the number and this time I don't hang up. He answers sleepily. I pray he is alone.

"Marley?"

"Sadie!" He is pleased. He sounds happy to hear my voice!

"I missed you, Marley. I missed you so much."

"If you missed me, then why didn't you just call? I would have loved to have heard from you."

"Because that's not what girls are supposed to do."

"You're not a girl. You're a woman. And that's what women do."

"Why didn't you call me?"

"You told me not to. That's how men are. We do what we're told."

"I'm sorry I sent an e-mail breaking up with you."

"I was devastated."

"Oh, Marley. My Marley. I was scared you were going to break up with me."

"Sadie, it's not a contest."

"I know. I'm so hard to handle, I'm selfish, and I'm sad."

"Now I've gone and lost the best baby I ever had."

"You like Joni Mitchell. A guy who loves Joni Mitchell. What was I thinking, how could I lose you?"

"You haven't lost me. I'm here, aren't I? I'm confused, but I'm here."

"I'm confused. Life is confusing, right? I mean, take Jolene." He inhales. "What about her?"

"Marley, the woman I met last week is not the woman you've

been describing. Not at all. It kind of freaked me out, Marley. She's really scary. You made her sound like a wood nymph."

"I think, Sadie, I think that all it is, is that I like to look for the good in people instead of the bad."

I am silent, chastened.

"She's my present because we have a child together. She's my present because she got me clean and was there when I became the man I am. Otherwise she's my past. Come on, can you really see me riding in limos and handing her the packages of free shit she never has to pay for?"

"No. Not at all."

"Well, then. Why do you think we broke up?"

I breathe a sigh of relief. But when I take the air back in, I bring with it a new fear: He doesn't want to be with her because her life is so shallow. What the hell is mine? And isn't it just getting more so? I stare at the list of lipsticks tacked above my desk. If I succeed, then I am still just a success in cosmetics, the ultimate fakery. If I fail, then I can't even succeed at the shallowest job in the world. Suddenly I don't just want to think of the next Cherries in the Snow. I want whatever it is that would get me nominated for a Pulitzer Prize.

"Marley, I have to pack for L.A. We're opening a Grrrl counter at Fred Segal and Holly wants me to check on it. I'm glad I called. I wouldn't want to fly without making things okay. Can you come over?"

"I'll be right there."

When he gets here, I open the door and start crying too hard to look at him. It is really unattractive, snot and red eyes.

"I just really love you. I really do. It hurts. I don't like it."

"Who wants to live a life with the edges taken off? Not a writer."

"Oh, God." I throw my arms around his neck and he carries me into the bedroom. And he makes it all go away. And I make it go away too. There is no job, no selling out; there is even, he confesses later, no Montana.

"You should call Jolene when you're in L.A. Really you should. She'd be very offended if you didn't."

Of course I have absolutely no intention of doing any such thing.

30 BRATTISH

MARLEY DROPS ME AT THE AIRPORT, waving at me as I wheel in and out of people with my green luggage. Then I am buckled into my seat, flicking through *Elle* to see where Grrrl is featured this month, when I come across an article about L.A.'s top breast-implant specialist, Dr. Ron Kitchen. I keep coming back to it, and when I am eventually able to put it down, I pick up the *Star*. The cover trails a new look. The new look is apparently pedophilia because all of the celebrities they feature are under twenty. Apparently one of the Olsen twins is anorexic. They seem to have picked a sister at random because they both look hella-skinny to me. On the next page I discover that teen sensation Lindsay Lohan may have had implants. I look at the photo. Real or fake, they are quite marvelous, jutting from her halter top like round scoops of ice cream. She is seventeen. I am twenty-four, which is almost twenty-seven, which is ten years older than her. When I'm not feeling competitive with eight-year-olds, I'm being competitive with Hollywood box-office behemoths.

A car picks me up at LAX and I feel very little in the backseat. My legs don't touch the floor. It's funny to fly business and then get picked up by a limo. It makes me think: Oh, yeah, our company makes money. It's easy to forget that when you're in the office. Marley told me on the way to the airport that he had a huge commission he would be working on while I was gone, so he might be hard to reach. Against my better judgment I call David Consuela Cohen and he insists we have dinner that night.

"Oh, my God! We'll go to Les Deux! It's fabulous on a Friday night."

I go straight to Fred Segal, meet the manager, make nice, admire our makeup, bitch about the counter having less space than Stila and Benefit. After she goes back to her office, I move the products around so that ours are in front of Stila's. A security guard comes up to me.

"Miss. Is everything okay?"

"Great. Great. Grand."

"All right then."

He keeps his eye on me. I zoom in on it with my makeover mind and psychically curl his lashes and put purple powder on him to bring out the green in his irises. As he goes about his business, my makeup is still on him although none of the other shoppers seems to notice.

Before I leave, I stop to look at the clothes, rail after rail of jewellike beauties. Delicate, spaghetti straps, strapless, chiffon, satin, silk. But when I try on the tops and dresses that I'm drawn to, none of them look right. All of them have something in the way: my bra straps. So I take off my bra and, whoomp, the outfits fall flat, to say the least. "Oh, Christ, no," I say to my reflection. I go to the lingerie department and pick out a flesh-colored strapless bra.

"Can I have this in a thirty-four D?"

"Sorry. It doesn't come above a C cup."

"Okay, okay, no worries."

I leave depressed and empty-handed and return to my room to brood. I pick up the phone and call Dad.

"Did you save the wash bag from the plane?" he asks. I can hear how excited he is for me that I have a job that sends me traveling, pays for me to fly business class, no less.

"Yeah, Daddy. It's pretty good. I'll send it to you."

"What's in it?"

"Uh, toothbrush, toothpaste. Comb. Nice comb made of balsa wood, not plastic."

"Sweet."

"A moisturizer and face wash."

"What brand?"

"Aveda. What's it to you?"

"Oh, I've heard that stuff's good."

"From who? Who's been talking skin products with you?"

"I know stuff. So, anyway, how's your room?"

"It's huge, Dad. But I feel a little lonely."

"You do, baby lamb? Why so?"

"I dunno, Daddy. I just do. I wish you were here. You know how it is."

"Yeah, I do. Can you call someone?"

"Well, I'm seeing this gay guy I know tonight for dinner. But he's kind of silly."

"Well, that won't help, will it? Anyone else?"

"Uh, this is weird, I suppose, but Jolene, Marley's ex, said I should call her."

"Is she kind of silly?"

"Yes, but a different kind. A more interesting kind."

"So call her. I don't see why that's weird. They're exes, after all. You don't have any suspicions about them, do you?"

"No. But she's crazy."

"And you're lonely."

I hang up with Dad and try to psyche myself up to call Jolene, but I can't do it. The intimidation factor is still too high. After I met her at Marley's, I Googled Jolene on my laptop and came up with this:

Jolene MacCall, forty-two, is the inventor of Cool Yoga, a kind of yoga in which participants perform intense poses in freezing temperatures. She claims that the cool focuses the mind. The success of Cool Yoga led, of course, to Angry Yoga, which integrates yoga and Tae Bo and Yoga Defense, which featured the invaluable input of the Israeli secret service.

Forty-two, my ass. Her body is better than mine, technically. But it has a lot of vanity to it. The vanity of being forty-six and wanting to beat a twenty-two-year-old at her own game. Twenty-two, note, not twenty-four. My body's way too downhill for Jolene. She's like a successful version of my mother. In her head my mum's beating all of the twenty-two-year-olds at their own game, her body sinewy and taut, but in reality it's soft and sad and can't move off the sofa. There's such a thing as soft and happy, don't get me wrong; why do you think the whole world loves Drew Barrymore? There's something incredibly erotic about a body that looks like it doesn't have a single muscle in it. It made Marilyn Monroe a star too.

I demanded the whole weekend in L.A. and now I don't know what to do with myself. Worst of all, I am missing the Saturday-night launch party for our Are You There, God? It's Me Makeup line. I try to change my flight to go home the next morning, but it would cost five hundred dollars to do it and I left the company credit card at the office and Vicki refuses to tell me the numbers.

"Oh, no, Sadie. It's not really my place."

I try to reach Holly, but she and Ivy are in meetings all day long.

"What the hell are you meeting about all day that you can't answer my calls?" I IM Holly. I get no answer so I try Ivy. "Yo, lady. Where you guys at? I need you to call me back!!!" No reply. Bitches. Useless bitches and their dumb ugly makeup.

By the late afternoon, I realize that though I have done nothing but lie in bed, my deodorant isn't working. It's troubling to me that a deodorant can just stop working like that and you are a person with body odor issues. And it's awful to smell yourself, alone, where there is no one to offend and so it is only a smell, without social context. The soft water that flows from Angeleno taps is making my hair straight instead of curly. Straight hair, b.o., what does that collectively mean to the outside world? I'm not sure, so I stay in my room, which is vast and hideous. Vicki did the booking. I call the office again.

"Vicki, when are they coming out of there?"

"Never."

"Vicki, go and bang on the door."

"I tried that. Holly yelled at me to fuck off."

"What did you do?"

"I fucked off." She is in a snit. "Really, this is ridiculous. We have a huge launch party tomorrow night. They're making me nervous."

"Really, it's ridiculous. That's my makeup line and I should be there. Just give me the fucking credit-card numbers."

"I told you, Sadie, I can't okay the fare change without getting the word from Holly."

"But Holly's in a meeting!"

"See, exactly. So anyway, how's the hotel?"

"Vicki, have you stayed here?"

"No, but I heard it was fabulous. Is it?"

I hang up on her as I gaze at the terrible paintings on the wall. Terrible. I can't stop looking at them. One is quasi-Cubist. The other is of the Hollywood hills at night. They don't go together. They are like two desperate people having bad sex, trying to fit big things into small things and soft things into the wrong holes. It gives me a headache.

I call David and arrange to meet him at Les Deux at nine. To pass the time I keep ordering room service and the food keeps getting worse. It isn't fun at all. The french fries have cheese on them and no matter how many times I ask for them without they come back cheesed. I line up the inedible portions in the bathroom annex so I won't have to look at them. The shower is good and strong. I try to shower away my headache, aiming the nozzle at my forehead, and it works while I am in there, or at least the sensation distracts me, but once I towel off it is back.

My room smells of chemicals, broken dreams, but how many could there be in a new hotel? It opened last week. It must be the workers who built it. I drop my bobby pin in the multicolored carpet, and when I bend down to look for it, the smell almost knocks me out. I lie on my back and look at the ceiling.

A taxi picks me up and takes me to Les Deux, where David is waiting.

"Woo hoo!" He waves. "Woo hoo!" He is wearing a button-down T-shirt with rainbows on it. I steel myself for a long night. "My bitch!"

"David, have you noticed that all the clothes nowadays are cut for women who don't have to wear bras?"

"What are you complaining about, you're only twenty-four, you don't need a bra."

"Any woman with real D-cup breasts needs a bra!"

"You mean yours are real?"

"Of course!"

"Oh, fabulous. I never would have known." Isn't that what you're supposed to say about fake breasts?

"That's because I'm wearing a bra."

I have a glass of Merlot, then I reckon: He's gay, I'll show him my breasts. He'll tell me the truth. Gay men love breasts.

"Come to the loo with me, David."

"Ooh, are we going to do coke? Because the last time I did that was with Robert Downey at the *Vanity Fair* party at Morton's. Or was it the *Vanity Fair* party at Cannes?"

"I get it. You've been to a *Vanity Fair* party."

"They're very hard to get into. Most publicists don't manage it. Anyway, that wasn't the point. The point was that I was with Robert Downey. Note, I don't bother with the 'junior.' That's how well I know him."

In the bathroom I unhook my bra and lift my shirt. I did that once in a toilet with Isaac. Man, was that a letdown.

Not sexy at all. Of course, I faked up a storm. He was all proud of himself for a week and he wrote a blazing column that ended up winning him a Columnist of the Year award.

"Oh, yes," says David, "I see the problem. You can buy the natura bra and keep your clothes on when you fuck. Or you can go to Dr. Ron Kitchen. All the top porn stars go to him."

"David, I haven't really seen much porn—actually I haven't seen any—so can you tell me what they look like?"

"Tall, blond, they look fabulous. . . ."

"No, I mean the breasts."

"Oh, perky, but not overdone. You don't make real cash with the big bazonkas anymore."

I have not heard the word *bazonkas* since grade school and I'm not sure that I needed to.

"I don't want them to be bigger. I just want them to be higher."

"Call him tomorrow! I'm so excited for you!"

He lets me pick up the check. I go back to my room feeling more hollow and depressed than I can remember. I can't get ahold of Marley. His cell phone is turned off.

The sprinkler has a sign warning not to put a coat hanger on it in case of flooding. The hotel staff keeps telling me they are delighted to assist and then they don't. I call down five hours after I have asked for the number of the nearest pharmacy and they answer me like I am someone they have slept with and can't place.

"This is Jared, delighted to assist."

"Remember, I called down before for the pharmacy number?"

"Uh . . ."

"Sadie Steinberg?"

"Uh . . ."

I hate it when my name sounds like a question mark.

I call my father again. "Daddy, my head hurts. I hate it here. Come and get me. Please get me out of here." I know it is like asking to be taken off a plane to Australia. But it helps to ask.

"What's wrong with it?"

"It smells funny. The carpet smells weird."

"Why were you smelling the carpet? You can check into a new hotel."

"I don't want to be here. *Here.*" I gesture around my head. It could mean Hollywood or California or the Earth. All feel true.

I call Marley. "Would Jolene really have me?"

"Of course she would. Jolene is one of the kindest people in the world. She would never let you sit there crying."

"I'm not crying."

"Yeah, but you were. You still have her number?"

I had secreted it in a tampon case as though it were illegal drugs. I had smuggled it past the sniffer dogs, this number of the ex, which sounds like the number of the beast. I call her with trembling hands and she answers with a booming voice.

"Man!"

I'm a lady, I want to interject.

"Man! I'm so psyched you called! What's doing? We gonna hang out? How's the hotel?"

"Jolene, I think . . . it's a little depressing here."

"Would you like me to come pick you up tomorrow?"

"Maybe."

"You could spend the day with me, then I'll drive you to the airport Sunday."

I don't bother to vacillate. "Okay."

31 SECOND BASE

JOLENE PICKS ME UP from La Poubelle in her red truck. I was waiting half an hour, not because she is late, but because I wanted to be out of my room and I was so excited to be leaving. She comes from having her nails done exactly the same color as the truck. I was killing time, hanging around the hotel shop looking at fifty-dollar bubble bath. I think that's why I know nothing. Every time I went on a school field trip to a museum, I just wanted to go to the gift store. If there was a dinosaur skeleton in front of me, I only wanted a postcard of the dinosaur skeleton.

She calls me on my cell and I run outside before the valets can move her on, which they do at a rapacious speed. She is parked in front of two limos. "Sorry I'm late, I had to get a manicure." The idea that a person has to get a manicure. Need is odd. But who am I to judge? I scan her truck for more things to judge. There is dry cleaning in the front seat and empty packs of American Spirit cigarettes. She sees me clock them.

"My only vice!" she cries. "Two a day! And never, never in front of the kid."

She is wearing a white tank top, a cut-off denim miniskirt, and Ugg boots. "I've had these bastards for five years, long before Sarah Jessica Parker picked up on them. She's a client of mine. Sweet woman."

I climb in and she thrusts the dry cleaning onto my lap. I buckle up.

"Fuckety fuck," she says, "I smudged my nails." When you become a parent, your curse words become Seussian. "Had my hair done too, then saw that I was running late for you and didn't have it blown out. What do you think?" Her wavy blond hair is being dried by the California sun through the open side windows.

"Is that an expensive dye job or is it from working outdoors?"

"Expensive dye job, honey, which is why it looks like I've been working outdoors. My coloring lasts longer because I spend so much time in my cool room doing Cool Yoga. Hair color's come a long way since I was bleaching my teenage mop with lemon juice. I mean Stevie Nicks had great hair in the seventies and they didn't have colorists then. What an amazing woman."

I have always liked Stevie Nicks's songwriting but have never thought her an amazing woman, definitely not for her hair color. If I had lived in another time, I could be an amazing woman for getting out of bed. I can't figure out what decade that was. I imagine a year in the Middle Ages when women couldn't get out of bed and the country was threatened with ruin and I am the first one to get out and I am made queen. Maybe I'll use that scenario in my novel. Which I plan to work on this weekend.

I notice Jolene's left arm is tanner than her right, from hanging out the window making obscene gestures at motorists who piss her off (all of them).

"Oh, suck my left one, you moron!" she screams at a car with two children.

"We had a nipple rouge called that."

She ignores me. "I fucking hate kids."

"But you—"

"I love my own because she is the most brilliant and talented and gorgeous creature ever. Jesus, I don't know what I would have done if I'd had an ugly child." She shivers. "You should see some of her friends. She loved this girl in her class, this little drowned rat who was picking on her. You know, best friends forever at five. She worshipped her and this girl was a shit to her. I went up to her in the playground. 'Don't you pick on Montana just because she's pretty and you're ugly.' "

"You said that to a child?"

"Don't fuck with me. Don't fuck with me if you're five. Don't fuck with me if you're five hundred."

I look at her muscles and resolve not to fuck with her.

"So we're having apple bobbing tonight."

"In summer?"

"Yep." She eyes me for enthusiasm.

"Oh, how fun."

"Yeah, it was my favorite as a kid. Montana forgets she likes kid stuff and then I trick her into it and she has the best time. She cries when I drop her at a kid's party. She has a really hard time with kids her own age, you know. She's too smart. But on the other hand she wants to be my little baby. The other day I got separated from her in the grocery store and by the time I found her, two minutes later, she was just inconsolable with fear. Don't tell her father."

"Marley won't mind."

"You don't know Marley."

I thought I did. It has been only four months, so maybe I don't. What better way to find out than a weekend with the ex?

"Love at first sight, right?" Jolene looks at me expectantly.

"Yeah. It was."

She checks her skin in the rearview mirror. I notice she has small traces of adult acne.

"Not for me. He followed me around, poor kid, for six months before I noticed him, stretching away in the back of my Pilates class. He was skinnier than a minnow, had just moved out of his crazy family's apartment. I was still working in New York then, hadn't had my brainstorm yet. I have an office there now, of course, but it's so great to work out of my home."

I see this woman as everything my mother had wanted to be. Not the success (I wonder if it had ever crossed her mind that a woman could have success like Jolene) but the just-so hair color and the way it dries as though it has been in high rollers, the nail shade the same as the truck, even if it is smudged. My mother would admire this woman. And hate her for it. I make an executive decision not to judge the brand of cigarettes she smokes or the dry cleaning draped in my lap.

"Is Montana okay with me coming?"

"Why wouldn't she be?"

"I don't think she likes me."

"If Montana didn't like you, you'd know about it."

I know about it. I fish in my bag for my lip gloss. She peers over.

"Thank you so much for the package of makeup you gave Montana. We loved it."

"You did?" She nicked her daughter's makeup.

"Yeah. Sexy Rabbi. That's a good one. I had a friend whose

dad was a rabbi. I have such a vivid memory of crawling into his lap in a bikini."

"Was that a fantasy or a real memory?"

"In my life, honey, one and the same."

Her "honey" feels a lot like marmite, salty as hell.

She must have made an unhinged teenager, given the mad hormones floating around, the ones she seems to have by nature. Or maybe they never left, maybe she is still a teenager and *that*, not Cool Yoga, would explain her toned arms and stomach. Everything is about sex or rooted in sex or tied-around-its-ankle sex, to drown out who she really is.

We reach traffic.

"Wanna see my breast implant?"

"Implant singular?"

"I just have one. Tit dropped when I breast-fed. She'd only take it from the one. Ignored the other completely. My fabulous, fabulous plastic surgeon put a tiny egg-shaped implant in the right one, evened them out. See." She lifts her top. Underneath is a blue crochet bikini, and I realize she is a woman ever ready to jump in a pool. Although a woman like Jolene would be happy jumping into a pool in all her clothes too. Or naked. I believe the world is divided into people who enjoy being shoved into pools and those it enrages. Those who like people stopping by unannounced and those it makes feel violent.

"I never wear bikinis. One-pieces are more flattering on me."

"Aw," she replies, patting my arm without looking at me, "it's just puppy fat."

What? Thank God she isn't looking at me or she would see my eyes water. "Puppy fat"? What is she talking about? Who asked her, anyway? Hell, I was just making conversation. I know how good I look in a bikini, better than her, skinny one-implant yoga bitch. I stare straight ahead, my arms burning, praying for something terrible to cry about on the radio, but it is still just soft rock. God, let there be a mudslide. Please, please, let there be a disaster so I can have a reason to cry. And then it comes.

We take a turn off the main road and start winding up. Up and up and up. The incline becomes steeper, the road narrower. At first it is just unpleasant and then it is nerve-racking and then I am terrified. I don't want to die with the insane ex-girlfriend of a man I've known only four months. In a truck with laundry on my lap. At least let it be my own dry cleaning. God, there has to be a thousand dollars' worth of sweaters and dresses. I feel the fabric under the plastic, trying to distract myself. Cashmere. Silk. Satin. Oh, God, I'm going to die!

I watch the cell phone range get smaller and smaller on my phone until it vanishes altogether. Englishness takes over, steepening with the road.

"Um . . ."

"Yes?"

"Um, Jolene?"

"Yes?"

"Uh . . ."

We start driving up a winding mountain path akin to a black run. I put my hands over my eyes and say in a very soft voice, "I'd like to get out now, please."

"What are you saying?"

She smells of coriander—or is it patchouli? Name the scent, save your life. If I can guess it, I will be okay. If not, then I'm doomed.

"What is your perfume, Jolene?" I ask much too loud. She looks disturbed.

"Chanel Number 5."

"Aaargh!" I scream.

"It's not that bad!"

"No, no, let me out, let me out."

"I can't let you out at the side of the road."

"Please! Please! I must get out!" I wrestle with my seat belt.

"What are you doing, crazy girl?"

"I'm allergic to . . ."

"What? What are you allergic to? Do you need a shot?" Her eyes are crazed, her arms ready to spring into Amazonian action.

"I don't like heights."

"Why didn't you tell me?"

"I didn't know. Until right now."

"Let's just get up there."

"I don't like this."

"I heard ya."

"I DON'T LIKE THIS!"

"I HEARD YA!"

Finally the road levels out and dust swirls up around us. We come to a gate and then a red dirt driveway. We drive in silence, tears streaming down my face.

When I get out, my face is red from crying. Montana sees me emerge from the truck wiping my eyes and shaking. She runs up to her mother and into her arms. She peers over Jolene's shoulder at me. Jolene makes a gee-whiz face.

"What are you doing?" demands Montana.

"Oh, God. Oh, God, I need to lie down."

Jolene drops Montana gently to the ground and puts her arm around me. "Of course, honey."

Montana sits close to me and looks intently at the tracks of my tears, which was not at all what Smokey was imagining when he requested that we take a good look at his face. Montana's nose seems to turn even higher in the air as she peers, so she looks like thing one and thing two combined.

"Would you like to see my snake?"

"No!" I start to sob again. Montana backs out of the room, facing me, moving with small, slow steps. I sink onto the bed. I try to get control of myself. Breathe breathe breathe.

"You should shake the sheets out for spiders," she says from the doorway.

My sobs start again. "I can't. I'm too frightened."

She shrugs and closes the door.

The air is stiflingly hot. A millionaire and no A/C? It has to be ninety degrees today. I lie very still so no spider can get to me. I cover my ears so one can't go in there. If spiders are to crawl on me, I just don't want to know, like a cuckolded husband. Just let them get on with it. I dream about a ballet performance with my cat and Montana. She is holding him as her dance partner in outrageous positions. He bends his back around over her head. They are beautiful. Then she flings him at me. I catch him and we both curl up, breathing hard. That's how I wake up. But no Sidney Katz. I pray the automatic cat feeder isn't malfunctioning and that none of the neighbors complains about the TV I left on for him. All shopping network, all the time.

When I get up and creep out of the bedroom, no one is there. The house is perfectly round. There are strange religious images: gay monks, stucco walls with wrought-iron crucifixes, a weeping Jesus, a Buddhist temple set up in one corner.

In the kitchen Jolene has little cherubs lined up on the shelf beside the salt and pepper, three of them. They are Japanese cutesy, with slit eyes and round bellies. I glimpse myself in the reflective window of the microwave and think I look like them. It was a long trip. And I don't want her to see me looking bad, just as much as I wouldn't want a lover to. It's bizarre. I am trying to comb my hair with my fingers when I hear her come back in.

"Montana and I are swimming. You okay?"

"Yeah, yeah. Sorry about that. I like your doll babies."

"One for every abortion," she says boastfully.

"With Marley?"

"One with him. So you gonna take a dip?"

"I left my bathing suit behind."

"Swim naked. Nobody's looking."

Uh, apart from my boyfriend's ex-girlfriend and his peering snub-nosed child.

"No, thanks."

"Borrow one of my bikinis."

"Do you have any one-pieces?"

"Oh, right, you prefer one-pieces. See, I was listening. Yes!"

After rummaging in her closet, she returns with something a spider might have woven if it wasn't taking its Ritalin. I retreat to my room to try it on. Technically, yes, it's a one-piece. But it's black crochet with huge cutouts at the sides. It just skims the breasts and there is boob galore out the sides. I've seen Christina Aguilera wearing it in red on a "what was she think-ing?" page of the *Star*. I adjust and adjust, but there is no ad-justing to be done. It is like a philosophical catch-22. Boobage or ass crack?

Gasping for air in the devil-powered heat, I decide to just run and jump. I run through my room, the living room, the garden, and into the pool with a splash worthy of a girl twice my size. As I hit the water, the costume rips off me in one swift movement. I come to the surface for a gulp of air and start bobbing for my swimsuit, my white arse gleaming on the sur-face of the water, Montana's shrieks of delight audible under-water. I finally grab it and scoop myself back in, not easy when you're in the deep end, and taking the steps so as not to have to haul me and my booty out by my arms, I lie down on the empty recliner and close my eyes, hoping they won't talk to me. Fat chance.

"Damn, girl, you got some jelly going on," Jolene says.

"Boobies boobies boobies," sings Montana, "big bum big bum big bum."

"Thank you." I don't open my eyes.

"Hell," hollers Jolene, "Marley's a lucky man."

I think I am going to be sick. Thankfully her cell phone rings.

"I gotta go take this inside. Can you watch Montana for a minute?"

I open one eye and watch her, peer at her as hard as she does me. "Thanks for having me, Montana."

"You're welcome."

"We apple bobbing tonight?"

"She wants to. I think it's stupid."

"It's pretty stupid."

"Let's say we want to watch TV instead."

"Okay."

"If you say it, she'll have to do it. You're the guest."

"Is that what you want?"

"Uh-huh."

"Then it's a deal."

Jolene comes back out and flops on the recliner in her blue bikini and deep tan. We are all turned on our tummies, tanning our backs, when a guy comes through the garden and Jolene sits up, beaming. He looks about twenty-four and kisses Jolene on the mouth but with no tongue, then looks at me.

"Oh, hey." He is disinterested. He has that Swedish tattooy thing with punk hair. He is gross.

"Marc is my publicist," says Jolene, waving as though he is something she has purchased real cheap on eBay.

Publicist is a degrading job for a woman, but for a man? Sheesh.

He frowns at me. "Do you do Cool Yoga?"

"Not yet."

"I can tell. Your aura is a little overheated."

It is the rudest thing anyone has ever said to me in my life and I have no idea what it means. I know this shallow queen has no business talking about aura. Jolene sends him to work in her office and I excuse myself to go look at my tan lines. I can gain or lose weight in a day and I can get tan or pale in an hour. Sure enough, there are peachy markings above my pubic bone and weird round patches where the swimsuit has gone Aguilera on my ass. I shower and moisturize, keen to get home and let Marley enjoy my tan, and that makes me remember where the hell I am and with whom. The ex, the de-virginizer, the baby mama knocks on my door. Even her knock is too loud.

"So you wanna do some yoga?"

I pull on a sundress and open the door.

Montana and Jolene are standing on the other side wearing matching Juicy Couture jogging suits, Juicy monster versions of the fifties housewife and her spawn.

"Not massively."

"C'mon, you have two plane rides in one weekend. You should stretch out. The cool room is set to minus five."

Although the heat is oppressive, the idea of doing yoga with Montana and Jolene is more so. "I'm going to work on my novel."

"Awesome."

"Tell her what else you want to do," says Montana.

"Watch a video."

"After apple bobbing?"

"She doesn't want to apple bob."

"Oh. That's a pity. Well, sure. What video?"

I look to Montana for my cue.

"The Little Mermaid."

I can't make out what she is saying as she mimes waves. *"The Poseidon Adventure?"*

Montana shakes her head and re-mouths, *"The Little Mermaid."*

"All right, my little mermaid." Jolene's maternalness outshines her hard body. She is a good person.

Once they get back from the Cool Yoga room, their cheeks all flushed, we all get on the bed. It is remote-control reclinable.

"This bed is for old people," I joke.

"I'm an old person, honey." She leans over and whispers, "Pussy like a newborn baby, though. Kegels. You should start doing them now."

Oh, Christ. The word *pussy* gives me shivers worse than Marley's use of *cunt*.

Ursula the sea witch fills the screen. I find her terrifying even though she's animated. Montana just watches with a tight little smile.

"Oh. I like this part."

"Do you like when all the people get turned into worms and trapped in cages?" I ask.

"Ha ha, yes," she says with a shrug as though to say "Crazy, I know, but that's just me."

"But they're really very sad."

"Uh-huh."

She gets bored with *The Little Mermaid* and puts on *Finding Nemo*. Almost instantly I start to sob and Montana gets a good look at my face, the tracks of my tears.

"How many times, Jolene, how many times can he lose his fucking son?"

"I guess a lot of times is the answer."

Suddenly a spider nips across the bed, shiny and ugly.

"Fuuuck!"

"Ten dollars."

"Fuuuuuck! A fucking spider!"

"Yes, there're lots of them around here."

I scream and scream. "I have to go home!"

"I can't take you till the morning."

I lock myself in the bathroom to get my composure. I want to go home then and there. She is twenty years older and so much thinner than me. But all she eats is raw food and cigarettes. In the morning she makes me toast and tea, just like Marley.

I pack my bag and pull on my jeans.

"You can't go in jeans," protests Jolene, "you won't be comfortable. Here, hang on."

I follow her to her walk-in closet, where she has hundreds of shoes and hundreds of tracksuits. She holds a few colors against me then settles on a pale blue. "Take it. Have it. Give it back next time I'm in New York."

The car idles outside the airport, Montana sitting in the back in her pink tracksuit. I long to leap into the arms of the skycap. Jolene is being uncharacteristically tentative. "So I hope you had a good time."

"She didn't," pipes up Montana. "She had a bad time."

"I had a great time."

I look in the back of my compact mirror for an answer, an illegal exam result. There is none, so I hug her tight as I can, feeling her Amazon bones.

She kisses both cheeks. "Good luck, kid."

I turn to Montana. "Good luck, kid."

Montana laughs and blows me a kiss.

"She'll be back with you guys next week," says Jolene.

"Great," I say under my breath. Then I trundle to my gate in the tracksuit Jolene has given me to wear.

32 GOT ANY GOSSIP?

AT THE TERMINAL I pick up a *New York Post,* which has the
following report on Page Six:

> Seen over the weekend: Vicki Arden with Marley, ex of
> Cool Yoga inventor Jolene MacCall. They were dancing
> close at the opening of Grrrl's fall line, the runaway pre-
> teen hit Are You There, God? It's Me, Makeup.

I have to fly back via Dallas and get downgraded instead of
up. As a surprise, Marley is there to pick me up at the airport
and I am royally grumpy. I want to throw the newspaper in the
trash with my heart.

"What is this?" I shove it in his lap as he drives.

"It's bullshit. She squeezed up next to me when the photog-
raphers were nearby, otherwise she didn't give a damn. She was
over by some movie star. She gives me the creeps."

"Why didn't you warn me?"

"I wouldn't have known except you told me. No one else I know reads that."

Bet Jolene has read it. He has no idea. Like Marley would ever even dream of reading a tabloid. I hate surprises. As angry as I am, I hate his seeing me without makeup fresh off a plane, no White Lies, the prototype deep in the debris of my handbag. I can't even muster a smile, let alone a kiss.

"Your cell phone was switched off."

"It was?"

"It was."

"Why are you being like this?"

"Because I'm used to men."

"I'm not men. I'm Marley."

"Jolene is a little loopy."

"She is?"

"But she's a good mother."

"She is?"

"What did you see in her?"

"I was impressed."

"I bet she was amazing in bed."

"No. She wasn't. She was distracted."

"Plastic surgery is so gross."

"What do you mean? What's that got to do with Jolene?"

"Nose job, collagen, implant."

"Implant?"

"Implant."

"Really?"

"Uh. Yeah."

"I never realized. Maybe I'm very naive."

"Maybe you are."

"Are you sure?"

"Yep."

"Wow. You think you know a person . . ."

The office is very subdued on Monday. Nowadays Holly seems to be out all the time, on a barrage of errands and meetings, none of which we are invited to. Vicki acts like nothing has happened. She never mentions it. But one day, on my way to the ladies' room, I notice she that has the Page Six item clipped and placed in her datebook.

33 SAY HELLO
(WAVE GOOD-BYE)

MONTANA HAS BEEN IN TOWN for a whole week and she has not hurt my feelings once, largely because I have yet to see her. She and Marley are spending quality time together and I am too desperately on deadline to conjure up new and unusual offenses she might commit, as has been my wont of late. I lie in bed and drift off thinking of all the different ways in which she might express her dislike for me. It knocks me out every time, as effective as counting sheep . . . sheep circling in my mind like some kind of malevolent conga line.

I am dreading the big Friday-night dinner Marley has planned for his two girls (*his two girls* is my phrase, not his, bursting as it does with a breeziness that does not exist between the three of us). He is taking us to Balthazar, Montana's favorite restaurant, which shows you right there the difference between her and a regular eight-year-old kid contentedly drawing on the paper tablecloth at Olive Garden. Montana isn't eight, she is a miniature adult—at her worst, a poison dwarf.

She loves to eat mussels and dip strips of steak in French mustard so unbearably strong it makes my lips curl just to look at it.

We went to Balthazar on our second date. It is our restaurant. I don't know how I feel about it being her restaurant too.

She says she craves olives, but I doubt her on that, catching her nose wrinkle as she pops the cocktail stick into her small pink mouth. She professes, even, to enjoy capers, which riles me irrationally as I have never known if capers are supposed to be a vegetable. They taste of day-old wee and their name is a joke: They are the most unamusing of garnishes.

Funny the things we believe make us adult. For years now I've thought it was being able to swallow, whereas Montana thinks it is being able to swallow olives, both arbitrary and superfluous show-off moves that make your tummy feel sour.

Heart as heavy as a Sunday *New York Times,* I turn up at Marley's house wearing army trousers and a little cropped satin top. The tuxedo trousers I wanted to wear are buried in the depths of my closet and I hadn't had time to venture into its soul-shaking recesses.

"I've missed you," says Marley, kissing my mouth, eyes, and forehead, then: "Is it really appropriate to wear army pants in a time of war?"

It is going to be a long night. My tummy does things in the night like other people's hair. Rumpled or flat, popping out with no rhyme or reason. I feel like I have a cowlick in my stomach that no brushing can control. Although I had woken up at midnight and gone out for a slice, it is flat.

Montana, skipping down the stairs, takes an instant dislike to my cream satin top. Ooh, the look she gives me as she eyes my exposed stomach, an expression that encompasses both the bold-faced stares of the Latin boys on the 6 train and the scowls of their girlfriends. Magazines talk about actresses who "men want to be with and women want to be," but I'm the girl whose sex appeal, such as it is, is rooted in making everyone feel angry.

That lunchtime I had gone off to get a Tasti D-lite and had my teeth bleached on a whim at a beauty salon advertising one-hour whitening. The effect is the same as a cup of icy soft scoop: I have a headache, my teeth hurt, and I feel a very mild self-loathing like a perfume transmitted through osmosis from someone else's cardigan.

The self-loathing belonged to the dentist, on whose own clothes the odor smelled more like sour defeat. They say the same perfume is different on different people. In truth I don't think he was a dentist, as he visibly blanched when I asked him if he felt my gum line might be receding. In further truth it wasn't a beauty salon but a hairdresser's. Hair was being swept up from around my feet as he placed the rubber trays in my mouth. The worst truth of all is that my teeth weren't even especially discolored, no more so than anyone else's.

But the neon sign said "Whiter Teeth in an Hour" and I just felt that if I could have that so instantly gratified, then anything was possible. One-hour offers are almost always my downfall. I left the hairdresser's two hundred bucks lighter and my teeth looked a little whiter if I tilted my head in certain ways, which I kept doing, much to the confusion of the girls at work.

"Grrrl girls don't get tooth bleaching," blasted Holly.

What Grrrl girls do and don't do is beginning to feel increasingly oppressive, a punk rock version of a 1950s etiquette guide. I have known since I joined the company that Ivy wants to develop a line of lipsticks that would make teeth look grayer and eyeliners that highlight bloodshot eyes, so I wasn't really surprised.

Holly is often a little crotchety, just usually not with me. "You ding-dong," she said when she saw my teeth, and it stung.

The inanity of "ding-dong" highlighted, like the lipstick Ivy dreamed up, that what she really meant was "dumb cunt." When Marley first used the word *cunt* to describe my vagina, I was shocked. In England it is a word both terrible and banal, like afternoon tea spiked with arsenic. It was only ever used, back home, as a curse word, never ever to describe the female genitalia. "Oooh, you fucking cunt!" we'd scream at one another in the playground. Or "What a cunt," my dad yelled at the TV newscaster. My mum said it on occasion, with her accent stretching it out beyond all decency.

Mum has started doing yoga and I had to hear about it over Dad's shoulder when he called me last Sunday morning. "Your mother wants you to know that she's started doing yoga."

It seemed an aggressive boast, like she was clawing her way back and would soon be younger than me, thin and beautiful again. She could never get over having gotten fat and she has been that way for three decades now. From being a Swedish model of the sixties to elasticized waistbands. She spent much of my childhood wearing a stunned expression, and that was before the face-lift. She told me the weight was from her pregnancy with me. Dad confessed recently that that wasn't true and that she was already well on her way to borrowing clothes from Aretha Franklin by the time they got married. She spent her twenties fucking celebrities, all hundred pounds of her. Then she found my dad and let go. Started eating. Stopped taking dexies. She keeps up the little things from the olden days, the false eyelashes, the fake nails . . . all, to my mind, procrastination.

She did not want to breast-feed. I had a bottle. Jolene says that children should do it till they decide not to. She even went to a support group for breast-feeders. I distinctly remember being horrified by the idea of her tits shoved in Montana's face. Get them the fuck away from me. I have the same memory of first blow jobs. If I suck and suck, this will be over. My mum makes up for her shallowness in the oddest ways. She breast-fed me for a week. I clawed and tugged because I was trying to get away. I wanted to suck my father's nipples. Lie on his chest in bear cub pose.

My mother doesn't like Grrrl cosmetics, preferring old-movie Max Factor theatrical makeup, thick pancake to cover her freckles. She never even lets me see them: It's like being naked to her. I think of her sometimes as a little girl in the Swedish countryside, swimming in the sun, drying out on the jetty, freckles popping up one after the other as she wiggled her toes in circles. When did she realize she didn't like them? When do any of us realize we hate that one thing about our appearance, and why that one thing? Why the freckles? Why the straight or curly hair? Why the bump on the nose, the width of the shoulders?

As Montana fixes her pigtails in the bathroom mirror, Marley kisses me in the kitchen. I peer over his shoulder, on Montana watch, as her catching us at it in even the mildest form guarantees a bad night. He runs his tongue across my teeth, but they are too sensitive from the bleach and I yelp. We both jump back, two cats with arched backs, wanting to be petted and left alone at the same time. Over the course of the last few months I noticed that we had been our best selves in that kitchen. We'd had our best sex there, our best conversations, our most useful arguments. Feelings in proximity to the fridge get frozen, crystallized. I never thought we would have our first bad kiss there.

Montana comes out of the bathroom, pigtails as high as a rent hike. I have laid out on the kitchen table a bag of sample products not available until the spring.

"I got you these."

She sniffs. "I don't like makeup."

"You don't? You liked it last time we played together."

She tightens a ribbon. "I was just trying to be kind."

The misjudged kiss on my mind, I decide to ignore the comment, try as best as I can to make things work tonight.

"Well, Montana, you've done such a great job with your hair. Would you possibly do mine for me?"

She can't help but brighten. "Okay!" she yelps, and runs back to the bathroom for a bag of bobby pins.

"Come on, though," says Marley, "the reservation is for seven."

"Okay, okay," she says, and proceeds to put my hair up in scores of messy clips. I know she means to sabotage, or maybe it's just that her fingers are too little, but it is an absolute wreck. And it looks kind of hot.

"Thank you, Montana. I love it!"

"Wow!" says Marley. "So do I!"

This disgruntles her no end and that is just the start. She is wearing a little red dress and carrying a matching velvet handbag. Sitting to her right in the taxi, I ask, "What's in your handbag?"

She snatches it away from me and spends dinner jealously guarding it, as though I were attempting to copy her math homework. As soon as we are led to our seats, she lays her head on the table.

"Hello?" coos Marley, patting her hair, but she shakes him off.

"I am dead," she hisses.

"What did you die of?" I ask. Expensive French cuisine? She doesn't answer.

Marley touches my foot under the table, but I kick it away a little harder than I mean to. She is made out of him—he must have a remote control. Why can't he guide her, battery-powered, to better behavior? I know it isn't his fault. But I put aside my knowledge to sulk with her, my archnemesis and my compadre. Marley is the only grown-up at the table, trying valiantly to hold it together, saying "Yum, yum" as he eats his steak and french fries, like a nervous party guest.

He looks so handsome. And so tired. Tired of us. We are both losing him a little tonight. Bags under his eyes, pale skin. Even his fingernails look tired, curled up and taking naps at the tips of his fingers, pulling french-fry fat around them like a duvet.

I am facing the painstakingly aged Balthazar mirror, flecked at its edges with fake rust stains. In its expensive artifice it somehow makes all who gaze into it look naturally thrown together. My cheeks look healthy, not be-blushed, my lashes generous, not mascaraed, my lips wine-stained from sips taken between elegant discourse on the history of art. This mirror I face goes against every tenet of the Grrrl cosmetics ethos. Holly and Ivy insist that if you are going to fake the funk you should flaunt it, big spidery eye makeup, no all-American-girl look for them. They want the Grrrl buyer to be the chick whose outlandish liquid liner causes cheerleaders to throw spit balls at her in the locker room and the math professor to have troubled dreams. "Liquid liner melting down her face as she unzips his tweed pants and rides him like a little bitch." That was Holly's advertising pitch for the fall line.

"That sucks," I hissed in the marketing meeting. "You're too fierce a dyke to celebrate the sexual fantasies of middle-aged men. It's like when the pre-out-of-the-closet George Michael kept recording songs like 'I Want Your Sex' and other come-ons that made no grammatical sense."

We settled on "I fake it so real I am beyond fake," which Ivy thought of and which touched me so deeply that I actually woke in the middle of the night crying about it.

I keep looking at myself in the mirror, trying on natural

expressions to go with my natural look. So Marley has one child with her head on the table and another pulling faces.

"Sadie, what the hell are you—"

"Laurence Olivier looked at himself in the mirror for two hours every single day."

"You choose names for makeup and you're the premier theater actor of your generation?"

"No, but . . . I might be and just not know it yet."

"When are you planning on knowing it?"

"Soon." Under my breath I add, "Fuckhead."

I pull out my compact mirror and slide it down my body like a lecher. The crop top was a mistake. I look like a Britney Spears fan who has never actually seen her idol live and thus is basing her emulation on a doll version of the singer. Montana looks like a Victorian doll come to life to terrorize the Britney doll, flinging its sparkles in her face, battling on the top shelf above Marley, who, unaware of the tumult around him, is fast, fast asleep in the spinning poltergeist room.

"Do you have to keep looking at your reflection?" he asks. "Would you like all the knives and spoons so you can also check yourself out in them?"

I want to snap the compact shut like a castanet, but I can't. I am trapped in mirror world. It feels like the dreams you wake from urging yourself to breathe. Speak speak speak. Anything.

"You know my absolute favorite dessert in the world, Montana?"

She raises her head wearily. "Buttmonkey pie?"

"No."

Her blue eyes blaze. "Poo-poo diarrhea vomit puke?"

"Montana!" Marley snaps.

"No," I say, "not poo-poo diarrhea vomit puke. Although that's an excellent name for our new eye shadow, so thanks for that."

I watch my lips move in the aged mirror. "Profiteroles." I point to them on the menu, like she is retarded as well as rude.

"Those are Montana's favorite too. She's allowed them very occasionally as a special treat."

"They absolutely are not my favorite." She sits bolt upright, affronted, as though he has misrepresented her views on abortion.

"Yes, they are. Remember the last time we came here and you said that it was your favorite dessert in the whole world and you could eat it forever and ever." He watches her intently. "Let's get two orders, baby girl."

"I don't want anything."

"You sure?" he asks softly.

She grabs the volume from his control. "YES!"

She folds her arms and goes back to the dead-kid position, yogic in her anger. The waiter comes by, French and pleased about it. World's stupidest idea: opening a Disneyland in Paris. I've traveled around the world and I'll tell you this: the French— not so big on kids. As a child in Morocco, I was tipped upside down endlessly. In Italy, my chubby cheeks were grabbed on the hour. Running through the gates to hug Mickey at Paris Disneyland, I was greeted by a Mickey who was smoking a fag, saying, *"Non, non, finit!"*

"I'd like two orders of profiteroles, please," Marley tells the waiter.

"Dad!" howls Montana.

"Just in case," he says.

In case of fire? In case of meltdown? It's true, I try when possible to eat dessert before the main course just in case there's a fire and I have to run out without pudding. I was born a few weeks early and at first Mum ignored her labor pains, convinced I was too much Christmas cake. Maybe that's why I'm addicted to sugar.

The ice cream pastry arrives and Montana watches me eat. It is taking everything I have not to rub her little face in the chocolate syrup. I plow through my portion, licking the plate clean with the same studied vim and vigor I once used to give blow jobs.

"That's rude," she spits, and I wonder if she has heard my secret memory.

"You should know," I answer.

Marley looks like he wants to be eaten by French waiters and left for dead.

"Coffee, anyone?" I ask with the forced brightness genetic to the British middle class.

"Mmmplrdl," she answers, talking into her elbow.

"I can't hear you."

"Children don't drink coffee."

"I did." My mum also gave me Valium to get to sleep when I'd wake her with terrors late at night.

"Ugh! Coffee? Repuggo!"

"Really?" Repuggo sounds like an antidepressant my mother used to be on around the time she'd hand out Valium.

"Even the smell of coffee makes me puke."

"Even the smell? Wow."

I think of the Steve Martin movie *Dead Men Don't Wear Plaid* and add: Dead children can't puke.

Merrily, I start to eat the profiteroles from the other plate. A thought crosses her mind. I see it happen. As I lift the spoon to my mouth she whispers, "Careful, Sadie. There might be spiders in it."

"What?" asks Marley, who has been sitting there barely drawing breath.

"Sadie's afraid of spiders. When she left Topanga Canyon, me and Mommy laughed at her."

"Mummy and I," I correct her.

"That's enough!" says Marley. "Get up!"

"Whyyyy? I hate you!"

"So hate me!"

"I hate her!"

"But I'm not hateful," I object.

"You're stupid!" she screams at me. "You stink!"

"Of what?" I ask, unable to mask my curiosity. Everyone has a distinct smell, but none of us can ever smell our own.

"Of bitchy!"

I start taking out my hair clips and laying them on the table one by one.

"Don't take those out. Don't you dare take those out!" She focuses on me like a bloodhound. "I put those in there. I worked hard on those."

She starts to cry hot, angry tears. With the removal of the clips, I have somehow removed the need to care.

"Is there anything that doesn't make you cry, Montana?"

"You can talk, spider bitch!"

"What's that about?" Marley asks.

"Sadie's afraid of spiders," she bawls, shoulders heaving. "I told you."

"No, what is that behavior about? Sadie is my special friend."

"And you schtup her." That is a Jolene word if ever I heard one.

He nods his head. "And that too."

And, I want to add, but I don't, it was *good*!

"You are causing me to see a red mist!" she shrieks.

All of a sudden Marley puts down his credit card, pushes back his chair, and says, "I can't take this." Then he shouts it and everyone at the tables next to us and even those across the room turn around to stare. "I CANNOT TAKE THIS!"

"No, Papa!" she wails. "Don't leave!"

"I am going to take a piss."

"You said piss!" she says, recovering from her weeping as the possibility of cash for her swear box presents itself.

"You said spider bitch and buttmonkey pie and poo-poo diarrhea. . . ." He struggles to remember, so I help him by adding, "Vomit puke."

Montana laughs nervously.

"And you are going to sort it out," he says. "You are going to stop being mean to me. You are making Daddy cry. Both of you."

"She started it!" I point at Montana, because who else had started it?

"You are twenty-four years old!"

"That's nothing! I'm a kid."

"That's *everything*, Sadie! Grow up!"

He walks off and I start to cry and cry. I lay my head on the table in the dead-kid pose. Soon enough I feel a little hand on my back as I gasp for air, making a scene I hadn't planned on. Most of my scenes are planned.

"Don't cry, Sadie. Please don't cry. My daddy loves you"— and this she adds in a whisper so soft it sounds like a butterfly burp—"and I don't hate you."

We look at each other; maybe we look better through the blur of tears. Her sharp edges seem to be gone, her blond a little faded. I can look at her without feeling blinded. Or blindsided. She is just a kid. And right now she looks tiny. She sits there dejected, but I tap her lightly and hold out my hand. Then I lead her to the banquettes between the two main doors where cool air blows on us and we can hear each other speak.

"What else don't you like? I know about the subway."

She wipes the last of her tears away. "Group singing. I don't like people singing 'Happy Birthday,' just one at a time."

"I don't like the flames on birthday cakes. Or clowns."

"Me either."

"I thought there'd be a fire and the clown's nose would catch fire."

She laughs.

Encouraged, I add, "Uncles."

"Uncles?"

"They're all creepy. Tourists stopping to talk in the street taking up the whole sidewalk. I'm scared I'm going to kill them. I wouldn't go to their country and talk on the sidewalk."

"Chewing gum. I know you're not supposed to swallow it so I don't, but then I get scared it's somehow going to jump down my throat anyway. I don't really like it. Laura—"

"Your friend from school?"

"Yeah, she likes it, so I pretend. But really it scares me."

"Listen. Life is scary. Let's talk about the things that make it better. The little things."

"A rubber ducky in the bath?"

"Pomegranate seeds spat on the sidewalk."

"Spilling berry juice on a white shirt."

"Really?"

"I love it!"

"*The National Enquirer* on a Friday."

"My mommy says that's the devil."

"It is. The devil has all the best shots of movie stars looking fat."

"Your tummy is flat."

"So?"

"And mine is fat."

"Montana, what the hell are you talking about?"

"It sticks out."

"Your tummy sticks out because you're a little girl." I am really shocked. I knew she had a self-esteem problem, but I thought she had *too much* self-esteem. "When I was a little girl, I was ugly and gawky and had a beautiful mother and my daddy thought I was beautiful. Your daddy loves you so much."

"I know."

Marley comes out with the boxed-up profiteroles, which I have forgotten all about. I feel awkward with them.

"We'll have these later."

She eats them in bed. She lets me lie with her over the covers. "You're cozy. I'll bring you your toothbrush."

"I'd like to stay the night. Is that okay?"

"Yes."

"See you in the morning. And we'll have a lovely time."

"Hmmm. We'll have an okay time."

I shrug. "Good enough."

Then I get into bed with Marley.

"I love you, Sadie."

I exhale a long breath, long enough to wear as a wraparound silk scarf, flapper-girl style. I love him too.

34 TAINTED LOVE

LOVE IN MY HEART, puffing it up like lips kissed red and full, I am sent back to Los Angeles to oversee the placement of the first ever Grrrl billboard on the West Coast, right on the Sunset Strip.

"Give her the corporate credit card this time," says Ivy, "so she can do what she likes."

Something about flying back to the scene of my last neurotic breakdown causes me to slip backward in my trust. As soon as we land at LAX, the full heart of love starts to lose air and all I can think about is that Page Six story on Marley and Vicki and Marley being so very handsome and so very alone in New York City without me. I believe him that nothing happened with him and Vicki, I do. I have to believe him. But it's unleashed a new crazy in me. I want to check his e-mail. I need to check his e-mail. I need to know I'm right to trust him, to put all of my trust in him. I need to know I'm right to have real orgasms instead of fake ones and to give him all my heart. I think about it the whole cab ride from the airport to the hotel and as soon as I get there I plug in my laptop. This is wrong wrong wrong. Don't do it, Sadie, don't do it. I go to AOL. I look at it and look at it. Then I type in her name: MON-TANA. And Marley's in-box comes up. There are no unread messages. But there are three sent messages. Two to me, both professing love and lust. And one . . . one to someone else.

> Dear Portia, how awesome was last night? Sadie is only out of town until Monday. Let's get together again tonight.

Oh, my God. I don't know who Portia is, but I know that her breasts don't sag. I want to call my father, but I can't collapse on him the way I want to over the phone. He can't help me. I am already crying. His voice will just make me lose it completely. Instinctively, I call Holly. I dial the number and then I hang up. She is too preoccupied. She won't care.

I grab my diary and search desperately for the number I need. The only one that can help. I find it, where I made a note in my diary, and punch in the numbers like I'm in a fight with the phone.

"Hello, my name is Sadie Steinberg, and I need to see Dr. Ron Kitchen as soon as possible." I have the corporate credit card in my trembling hand.

"He has a two-year waiting list."

"I don't care, this is an emergency."

"Hold on, let me get the other line."

She clicks away and I try not to sob. Then she clicks back.

"I guess it's your lucky day. That was a cancellation. Can you make it here by eleven?"

"Where are you?"

She gives me the address and I jump into a taxi. Looking

out the window at the ice-blue L.A. sky, I am sure I see a witch on a broom point at me and cackle as she writes the words *Surrender Dorothy!* I look behind me until the words begin to vaporize. There's too much traffic, so I run the last block. I get there, panting, at one minute past eleven. My chest is still rising up and down when the doctor examines it.

"What I would do," he says, taking out a pen, "is lift here and here"—he marks my skin with swift stripes—"and fill you out on the top half of the breast." His skin, at once deeply tan and completely unlined, has a painted-on sheen to it. His short brown hair and chiseled cheekbones suggest that this man who carves soap stars was once one himself. The walls of his office, like his waiting room, are painted blue with hovering clouds and pert-titted Greek goddesses. Or given their blond pubic hair, Nordic goddesses. "This needs to be raised," he continues, the word *need* making a mockery of all the times Marley kissed them. "I would pull the muscle back and reattach it behind your neck, almost like a bra, but one underneath your skin. . . ." His phone line buzzes, and as he answers, he continues to mark me with his free hand. "Uh-huh, uh-huh," he says into the phone, then turning to me, "Excuse me, Saucy." "It's *Sadie.*" "Excuse me, Sadie. I'll be back in a minute."

"Saucy"? This guy has done one too many porn stars. I look up at the Nordic goddesses and suddenly Marley is in the mural too, entwined in their oil-painted arms, his fingers wrapped in their hair. Oh, my God, I am going insane. Ten minutes pass and the doctor does not return. I start to hyperventilate. I look up at the mural where Marley is now energetically fucking one Nordic goddess from behind and then I look down at the markings on my breasts. They rearrange themselves to form the word *ugly.* This is it. I have lost my mind. I scramble for my cell phone and flick through the list of numbers.

I don't know who to call. I don't know who to call. I don't know who to call.

So I call Jolene.

"Please help me, I'm in a plastic surgeon's office, Dr. Ron Kitchen, I've made a terrible mistake, I wanted to have my boobs done, but . . . I gotta get out of here. Wait, he's coming back."

I close the phone and sit up rigidly, trying to ignore Marley's sex show as the doctor draws more lines.

"While we're at it, you could also use some lipo here. . . ." He moves his hand to my hip, and cold as it is, it gives me a flash to Marley's warmth, his hands around my waist. The doctor is at it another ten minutes, me biting my lip not to cry, he never once asking what it is I want as he moves his pen down my body.

All of a sudden I hear a commotion. Then they burst into the room. Jolene and Montana, a receptionist chasing them, like Batman and Robin trying to lose the Joker.

"What are you doing?" Jolene asks me. "What are you doing?" She barks at the doctor. "Get away from her." Montana stares him down.

"This girl has two of the most beautiful breasts I have ever seen in my life. You people are sick fucks. You take a perfect twenty-four-year-old girl and tell her she needs work? Look to your souls, you bastards!"

"Put your clothes on, Sadie." Jolene points to my sundress on the chair. Montana hands it to me, helps pull it over my head. Jolene stays eye-to-eye with the doctor. Then she takes Montana's hand and my hand, and leads us out of the office and through the waiting area, where the receptionist is still flailing and the doctor follows us right to the door.

Montana turns as we walk through it and hisses to the receptionist, the doctor, and the assembled *Playboy* hopefuls: "Fuckers!"

In the truck we drive at breakneck speed back to their house.

"What were you thinking? What on earth were you thinking?" screeches Jolene.

"But, Jolene, you've had surgery."

There are tears streaming down her face as she answers, "And I am not proud of it."

"Mommy, don't cry," says Montana, and pats her hair.

"I got my nose job when I was nineteen years old with money I saved from stripping. Crappy doctor that was. I got the corrective surgery when I was thirty-nine and a millionaire. I got lipo when I became the poster girl for my own corporation. You think I would give a shit otherwise? I am stuck, I am stuck in this hall of mirrors because of all the money I got under the mattress."

"Is that really how you feel?"

"Yeah. It is."

Montana takes a tissue and delicately wipes her mother's eyes. There are some mascara stains, so I fish in my purse and find a sachet of Walk of Shame. I tidy her up. As I do so, I sneak a peek at Montana and whisper urgently, when I think her attention is distracted, "He's cheating."

Jolene's eyes widen. "Bullshit."

"No. I know that he is."

"No. I know that boy and he may be many things, but he is not a cheater. Whatever you think you know, you're wrong."

I want to show her the e-mail, but then I would have to admit I hacked in. Even though she's just rescued me from one of the most humiliating situations I've ever been in, telling her I've hacked into the account of her child's father just seems too awful. Maybe it's because it involves the written word and somewhere in my rotting heart I still think of myself as a writer. I file it away to break down over when I return to New York.

When we get back to the house, we all climb into the reclining bed, Montana in between us, and watch *The Little Mermaid*. Jolene looks past Montana's head and smiles at me as the little mermaid sings a song with a Jamaican crab.

"Now she," says Jolene, "has a rockin' body." We laugh. Different laughs—hers throaty and rude, mine high and needy— same joke.

35 ANGER MANAGEMENT

I DON'T READ ANY magazines on the flight home. I make notes for lipsticks the whole way. It's hard to think of the new Cherries in the Snow in California, where all the women are so tan and wearing pale lip gloss. Although I have sent him an e-mail to say that I will be fine on my own, Marley is there to collect me at the terminal. He stinks of paint. It has been such a long weekend and my eyes are on fire enough without that paint stinging them.

"Fuck off!" I shout, the other arrivals staring at us. "Get the fuck away from me!"

"What's going on?" He blanches. "What happened?"

"You know what happened. I don't love you anymore. I don't think I ever did. I don't love you and I sure as hell don't love your freakin' daughter. We have no future together and I never want to see you again."

"Oh," he says, and, "oh." I can see that it takes the wind right out of his sails. His big brown eyes are holding back the floodgates, I can see that, and he turns and leaves before I can

watch them burst. I take a cab home. I cry all the way. Inside
the apartment, I collapse onto Sidney Katz, weeping into his
fur, and he lets me, taking the tears stoically, until I am spent.
I feed him, pet him, and head to work. Stopping at the door,
I say, "Thank you, Sidney," and I think he nods like "It's
nothing."

The office feels like a ghost town. Holly and Ivy are out to
lunch, though *not,* notes Vicki dramatically, with each other.
She asks me if I want to go to Sephora with her. I hate her too,
but I am feeling so low I say yes. I scoop up a hand basket at the
entrance and start dropping things in it faster than you can say
"Alpha-hydroxy exfoliating beads." We traipse up and down the
aisles, first the Benefit counter, where I pick up two wands of
their Bad Girl mascara, then Nars, where I choose a green eye
shadow they called Sea Foam, but I would have named Cabbage
Patch Kid. Then we cut across to Paula Dorf (the great thing
about shopping at Sephora with Vicki is that it shuts her up),
where I grab their mattifying oil and a nifty little product that
converts eye shadow to liquid liner. I pay for my loot before
Vicki has finished in the Hard Candy aisle. The Spanish girls
who work at the register have been ordered, I think, to look
French, their hair slicked down into severe chignons.

I stand near the exit and spray a perfume on myself while I
wait for Vicki to pay. Maybe if I smelled of my real smell instead of Versace vanilla, things wouldn't turn out like they do.
Because that's when I see him, walking toward the exit, a little
black Sephora bag in his hand. The girls in Sephora don't
watch CNN. The middle-aged women do and they eye him,
flashing menopausal at the Dr. Perricone eye-cream counter.

Isaac sees me. "Sadie Steinberg!" He laughs. I laugh too. I
know who I am.

"Isaac."

Immediately his hand is in mine, presumptuous. And warm.

Vicki backs away. She is already on her way back to the office to tell. She will tattle tales until it becomes appropriate again, an old lady with nothing better to do than peering through her window, the voice of the twitching net curtains that populated the London suburb I left so long ago.

Isaac does not let go of my hand and I look at his hand before I look up at him. Long fingers, slim; he's usually on a diet, like my mother, but it only ever seems to affect his extremities, his fingers and toes. I remember instantly what he looks like naked. I do not let go of his hand as I look up. The hair more salty, less peppery; still a good-looking Jew.

"What are you doing here?" he asks, gesturing around Sephora.

"I live in New York City and I'm a girl. And you?"

I have embarrassed him, which I regret straightaway. I want him to be an arrogant dick like he always was. I want him to be the opposite of Marley. Or the way Marley was before I knew he was screwing around. Fuck, they're all the same in the end, so you might as well go home with the obvious bastard instead of the one who throws yoga in your face before he breaks your heart.

What the hell do Isaac and I say to each other? He is searching my face for the cue. "Your toe healed then?"

I do a little pirouette, French for *twirling*. And I know I am going to ditch work, just like I ditched my car the first time I met Isaac Bennett.

So we get into his limo, and I flash back to that time I left my car behind in a Springsteen concert parking lot. Only now I am leaving my love, my Marley, my savior; back into the mess and mire I go. The day after I met Isaac I went back to retrieve my car. I shall not be retrieving my love. Isaac makes a grand gesture of switching his cell phone off. A huge gesture but not a huge deal as the calls will divert to either one of his secretaries.

I resent that my chin hurts from months of Marley's stubble; angry spots have broken out during the last week. Or maybe it's not his stubble but my hurt feelings poking through my skin. I always wanted to be perfect if I ever saw Isaac again. The way he looks at me, he doesn't seem to notice. "Am I still beautiful?"

"More so than ever."

"Wow. You got ripped off then, Isaac."

He kisses me. I kiss him back. Nothing. I feel nothing for this man. So it's easy to keep kissing. We get back to his hotel room and he undresses real fast before he even touches a button on my shirt. He runs the shower in his all-chrome bathroom. He is in there a couple of minutes before he exits, a white towel around his waist, showcasing newly defined abs. How Isaac to take a shower *before* he has sex.

"I just got back from L.A.," I say. "Do I smell of airplane?"

He comes close and breathes in at the side of my neck. "No. Take your shirt off."

It strikes me that I do not like being told what to do. Love in the afternoon, like meeting your lover at a Springsteen concert, is all very well. But this isn't love. It's time filled in.

"Excuse me a moment," I murmur.

I lock myself in the bathroom. Next to his toothbrush is a Clinique antiaging moisturizer. And next to that is a Dr. Perricone antiaging eye cream. I look in the mirror. I cannot do this. He is not him. I write on the mirror with my finger: MARLEY. Then I rub it out with my hand, trying to hold it together. I have to get out of here.

Unlocking the bathroom door, I leave without buttoning my shirt and without saying good-bye.

"Hey! Hey, Sadie!" He follows me down the hall. I keep walking until I get to the elevator. And he stops following.

36 DIVALICIOUS

AS I'M IN A CAB heading back to work, my cell phone rings. It's Holly. I hear something in her voice I can't quite place.

"Am I in trouble for not being at work?"

"I've gone home. Just come here now."

When I get there, she answers the door then pads back to bed, where, from the rumpled sheets, I can see she has been lying down. There is a bottle of Baileys on the nightstand.

"Have some," she says.

"Okay," I say with a laugh, "for old times' sake."

"Vicki told me. That you left with Isaac."

"Oh. Are you disappointed in me?"

"What about Marley?"

"He's been cheating. I read an e-mail of his."

She snorts. "Cheating, cheating, cheating. Fuck! What a day. What a day."

She pulls me into the bed and we lie, looking up at the ceiling, drinking Baileys, as physically close and as emotionally far apart as I can remember.

"It sounded like it was something important on the phone. I'm working on the names. They're almost done."

"I don't give a fuck about the names."

"You don't?"

"No."

"Oh." I try to think. "I'm stumped, Holly."

"Sadie"—she takes a deep breath—"Ivy left me."

I don't hear her because I am looking at her face. She is crying.

"Why are you crying?"

"I just told you!" she screams.

"I didn't hear you. I was watching you cry."

"Ivy left me!"

"Oh."

"She caught me with"—she studies me—"some guy. What am I going to do?" she wails. "What will I do without my baby?" She is choking on her sobs.

"Holly . . . I never realized you cared so much."

"What do you mean you never realized I cared? You're my best friend!"

Was I her best friend? Or her handmaiden? Come to think of it, which was Ivy?

"Holly, it's just . . . I wouldn't have known you cared so much because . . . you weren't very nice to her."

"What are you talking about? I stayed with her all these years when I could have left her for anyone."

"Okay, so you didn't leave her. But you also cheated on her left, right, and center."

"That's just dyke politics. You don't understand."

"Look. First of all, I don't think you are a dyke. She caught you having sex with a man. And second, that isn't gay politics. They do have committed relationships. If you wanted a free pass to fuck anyone you want, you picked the wrong orientation.

"So who have you been fucking? Who did she catch you with?"

"Oh, that . . ."

"Yeah."

"Well, it's funny you should say that because it's someone you know."

"It is? Who?"

"Oh, Isaac. Isaac, who you used to . . . Isaac, who you were with this afternoon. How funny is that? Who would have thought when we were ten years old that we would end up more than a decade later sharing the same guy? Isaac who—"

"Yes, thank you, Holly. I know only one Isaac."

"I'm surprised Vicki didn't tell you. Or Ivy. I know the fat bitch has suspected for months."

"Months you've been seeing him? And calling the love of your life a fat bitch doesn't exactly paint you as devoted."

"Look, you were with Marley, so who cares?"

"Why didn't you tell me?"

"Because I knew you'd get funny. I don't have to ask your permission."

"No, but if you had told me while it was happening, I wouldn't feel funny right now."

It makes sense, her and Isaac, two people who fake an interest in sex. She is not a lesbian. Not if she chooses to be with someone who gives such crappy oral sex.

"How did you meet him?"

"That time he called looking for you. I guess he had his people track you down. Anyway, you weren't in. And we ended up having phone sex."

That column. It wasn't about me. It was about her. I jump out of the bed.

"Where are you going?"

"I'm going to see Ivy."

I hail a cab back to the office. Ivy is slumped at her desk. Rather than comforting her, Vicki has her chair swung around the other way and is jabbering on the phone. I put my finger on the receiver.

"Go home. Now."

I wrap my arms around Ivy. "How are you, Ive?"

"A wreck. But a good wreck."

"Yeah."

"I wanted to tell you . . ."

"It really doesn't matter, Ivy. I don't love him. I'm in love with Marley. Only thing wounded is my pride."

"Yeah, I know that one."

"But you loved her."

"Yeah. I did. I do."

"Why? You're so kind and so good and so interesting."

"I guess I just . . ."

"I've been having a bit of a time of it too, Ivy. Marley's been cheating on me."

I don't want to bogart her tears, so I strain and strain to hold it all in.

"What?"

"I went into his e-mail account and I saw a note to some girl I've never heard of. I know it off by heart. 'Dear Portia, how awesome was last night? Sadie is only out of town until Monday. Let's get together again tonight.'

"I have no fucking clue who Portia is." I sigh.

"I do, you idiot. Portia is the girl who assists him when he's working on a graffiti project. Not an office project. A real project. She looks out for the cops. Sadie, he was working on something for you this weekend. It was supposed to be a secret."

"What are you talking about?"

"I highly recommend that you take the train to his house. And that you be ready to apologize. Profusely."

She kisses me ever so gently on the lips. "Go see that good man who loves you so."

37 BABY DOLL

I DECIDE TO WALK THE BRIDGE, better to think through the conversation about to take place. Something, something cosmic, something as silly and as serious as lipstick makes me turn around. There is my name, right next to Montana's, a huge mural in purple, peach, butter yellow . . . colors I didn't even know you could buy in spray cans. I am a name in the city like Montana, next to Montana, the same size as her. I belong to New York. And to Marley. I have come here from this stupid tiny island in the sea, looking to find something, maybe a new kind of shampoo, or a pair of green shoes, or my name on the gossip page of the paper. And I have found love. Or it has found me, stalking me, *tappy tap tap,* making me catch my breath and cross the street zigzag to see if it is really following me or whether I am imagining it. I am not imagining it.

He opens the door, sleepily beautiful, his eyes red and puffy from crying. I hug him and we sink to the floor, where I cradle him in my arms like a baby.

"Sadie, what happened this morning at the airport? I don't understand what happened."

I sob. "I hate myself. I hate myself!"

"No. No, my darling."

Then he rocks me back and forth in his arms on the floor. "Oh, my darling. What's wrong with my baby?"

I choke on my tears. "Don't call me that."

He is quiet, leaning his chin into my shoulder. He just keeps rocking me back and forth. Finally I get enough of a grip to talk. "Marley. I've done a terrible thing."

"You've done several terrible things. You yelled at me at the airport to fuck off and told me you never wanted to see me again in front of a terminal full of strangers, but you wouldn't tell me why. You ripped my daughter's tutu. I suppose that it was less terrible than it was just really bizarre."

"I thought you were cheating on me. I read your e-mail. It said 'Portia . . . Sadie . . . out of town . . . let's get together tonight.'"

"But that's because—"

"I know now."

"You went into my e-mail?"

"I'm so sorry."

"I went into your phone messages."

"You did? Oh, thank you, thank you." I smother him in kisses. "So we're two paranoid jerks in love."

"I don't know why I did it, Sadie. I didn't want to. But I had to. Love is the drug, man."

Then I remember what I've done. "I kissed Isaac. I saw him at Sephora and I went back to his hotel and then we kissed."

He starts to loosen his grip on me.

"Please don't let go. Oh, God, please, I beg you, Marley, you can leave me in ten minutes, but if you let go of me right now, I swear to God I'll die."

"A lot of God in this room for someone who doesn't believe."

"I believe in you." I slump back on the floor like a snow angel in Montana's toy debris. Marley is just watching me. I see the lashes and I remember a time in the shower when water was on them. Surrealist Man Ray droplets on his eyelashes with the sun bursting through them. The droplets now are from his own eyes and they are imperfect. I beckon to him and he leans forward and one of them drops onto me. It's as though these were my last words on a hospital bed, on a beach, on a life raft. Even then I know: "One day I will die. One day I will die for real and this will haunt me, my bourgeois slut heartbreak version of what it is to die." Still, bourgeois slut heartbreak can feel real. And that's what matters.

"I kissed him and nothing else happened. That's the truth. I tried to be with him, but I couldn't. Because he wasn't you."

"I believe you."

"You do?"

"I do."

I clasp him tight as a crucifix. "Please take me to the bathroom. Wash me. Fix me."

He bathes me in the water, dips my head down, and I am being cleansed. I am being anointed. "I think I might be one of those crazy girls."

He laughs. I don't know where he found that laugh, where he could have been keeping it for a time like this.

He is crying and cleaning me up at the same time.

"You're making me tidy."

"That's what dads do."

"Am I your little girl?"

"No. You're my lover."

He kisses me. I kiss him back.

"Can you taste him?"

"No. I can't."

"Marley?"

"Yes, my baby?"

"There is no novel."

"I know."

"You knew?"

"Yeah. But you didn't want me to say. So I didn't say. I don't care. I only care that you wasted that energy pretending to write a novel when you could have been, say, writing a novel."

"Marley."

"Yes, my baby."

"I haven't had cystitis in a long time."

"I noticed that. Clever girl."

"I love you."

We go to sleep together curled up on the bed. I wake up and watch him for a while. He smells of paint. The whole room does. An eye on the time difference, I creep out of bed and pick up the phone.

"Dad, can you come see me?"

"We could make it out at Christmas. It would be nice to have Christmas in New York. And I'd like to meet your man."

"I'd like you to meet him too."

I don't tell him that they have already met, two young fathers, in the playground in my head.

EPILOGUE

"Color is its own reward."
—Crowded House, "Fingers of Love"

MARLEY PAINTED A NEW MURAL for **Montana** in her New York bedroom. Using a special glow-in-the-dark paint, he put stars on the ceiling and clouds on the walls. The paint was still drying the first night she got here, so she slept in our bed between us. In the night I felt her warm body against mine and remembered being between my parents on a Sunday as my dad read the papers and my mum snoozed. Hell, I wasn't her mum. But I felt I could be someone's mum one day. It didn't seem so far from me, so much like another breed, a different version of woman.

"You would look amazing pregnant!" Marley said one morning and then blushed. "But really . . . you would look like a fertility goddess. Sometimes I have to shake myself not to think about it."

"Gross," I said. But it didn't seem that gross.

For Christmas Montana and Jolene got me a tutu, in honor of my crime.

"I thought that was the funniest shit ever," said Jolene. "Actually, I have one too. Every girl should have one." Because it was from Jolene, it was the most expensive she could find, pink netting folded over and filled with fake rose petals.

Marley taught me how to vacuum and I vacuum in my tutu. I found I kind of liked the satisfaction of making something clean so fast. Sidney Katz followed me between my two rooms, pointing out fur balls with his paw.

Jolene's line of bath products was as successful as her Cool Yoga videos.

I spend most weekends at Marley's and often Montana and I collide. She sits on my lap, straddling me. Her father, with whom we are both deeply in love, fixes wheat-free pancakes in the kitchen as she leans in close as a lap dancer, her flaxen locks tickling my nose, and whispers, "Oh, Sadie, you're pretty, I'm *sorry* you have dark hair."

"I like it. I think it suits me."

"Yes, well, I suppose. But I could never have it because I want to be a ballerina."

Montana has never been to the ballet, just the ballet in her head. We've all been to the ballet in our heads. And it's always us dancing. And it's always our daddies, or men who look like our daddies, twirling us over their shoulders. On cue Marley walks in and she leaps into his arms. "Papa! Papa!" she cries, smothering him in kisses. He squeezes her tight. "One day," I want to tell her, "one day you're gonna say"—and I feel I should warn him too—"you're gonna scream 'Put me down!' " But I keep that to myself.

I never said "sorry" before I met Marley, never. He made me want to take responsibility for my actions. He didn't make me. He never made me do anything. And that made me want to.

I began apologizing sooner and sooner, the space between the crime and the apology shrinking like a Gobstopper in my mouth.

I HADN'T SEEN MY DAD in so long and yet we talk on the phone so often that it was almost awkward the extent to which we just picked up where we left off. I wondered what he would make of Marley. They were both loud. Loud in their love of their families and of their lives. "Exhibitionists," tutted my mother, although really, neither of them was in the slightest.

My mother insisted they fly business class, which I knew Dad could not afford, but somehow he did it. She was happy, ecstatically so, in Manhattan, because she could see celebrities in restaurants—some she had even slept with, one who even remembered her. We all went to brunch at Balthazar, and halfway through her eggs Benedict, my mother, whose head was darting around the room looking for famous people, suddenly stopped dead still. She began to blush. Striding toward us came Albert Finney, jowly, older, but still every inch the star.

"Oh," said Albert Finney, "Mia." She quaked that he recalled her name. "It's been decades, but you look just as beautiful as you ever were." She left with a smile and kissed my father, and he kissed her back. Odd to see that instance where interest in someone else could make you love your partner more, your flesh and blood lover made more beautiful to you by the recognition of a hologram love.

Out on the icy sidewalk after our Christmas brunch, Montana took an almighty *klonk* to the head. Everyone gathered around her and waited for her to cry, but she twisted and twisted her face almost inside out, and when it twisted back into place, there were no tears and we all went on our way.

Just then Montana snaked her hand into mine. I couldn't decide whether to put my free hand in my father's or in Marley's. So I did neither. I held my own hand.

With the end of Holly and Ivy, so came the end of Grrrl. There was no official disbanding, just a call from Ivy that I needn't come to work Monday and would I perhaps like to see the new Richard Avedon exhibition with her instead. Although I had worked hard on finding the name that would move Grrrl to the next level, I was philosophical. One day after I got my final check, our makeup simply wasn't on the shelves anymore, like a lover who just stops calling. In a human, that's cruel and unforgivable. In a lipstick, it has a tender poetry, like the phrase "Cherries in the Snow." Our fans didn't have a chance to stock up on their favorite products because they didn't know what was about to happen. And that is how we got to the next level: They will miss us. They will have, while cooking meat loaf for their two kids in a Long Island suburb, from time to time memory flashes of the cleavage-tipped lipstick that they felt awkward and excited about putting on their mouth when they were twenty-one years old.

It was sad that an all-girl company had to fall apart. But we were all just a bunch of little girls, bossy, needy, attention-seeking, and easily hurt. If we had been an all-woman company, we might still be going right now. Sometimes I miss the chatter across phone lines and the eyebrows raised above computer screens. But I enjoy having my days to myself. And though money will soon be a worry, it isn't yet: Ivy, who it came down to in the end, gave me a very generous severance. She gave herself a good one too, taking off to Costa Rica for a month and returning brown, slim, and squeezed dry of tears. Just as Holly had to confront the truth that she really wasn't a lesbian, Ivy had to confront the truth that she really was.

Ivy and I don't talk about it, so I'm not sure if Holly's still with Isaac. I don't see her anymore. Wait. I saw her once, in the aisle of Sephora where our counter used to be. I looked into the mirror angled above the Fresh counter as I was trying on lotus eye gel and saw in the reflection Holly, tiny, standing alone in the space now occupied by Hard Candy, looking dazed. I was going to ask her if she needed help. But I didn't.

I'm not angry at her and I don't hate her. It's just that some of the things you loved when you were thirteen you still love when you're twenty-five. And some of them don't make sense anymore. I do hang out with Ivy. Marley likes her a lot, and now that she's lost weight, Montana finds her less objectionable. I sometimes see a supersheer lip-gloss ghost of Holly. And then she vanishes, and Marley appears next to me, a real flesh-and-blood man with his rough hands resting softly on my waist. When I was a little girl, I chose Holly. But she never chose me back. It's important to feel chosen by the person you love. I've hung on to her mother's Kanebo lipstick. I've wanted to give it to her, explain what it meant to me. But I don't think Holly's ready to go to those deep places. Not yet. One day.

My breasts are still falling, you know, but it doesn't make my heart lurch the way it used to. I have a very good bra, sensible, white, sturdy, and when I take it off, the only people who see them are me and Marley. And he loves them. And I, lying back in the bath, seeing my breasts float in the water above me like shopgirls taking the weight off their feet, can deal with them.

One day as the water drained, I sat at my desk, writing a birthday card to my father, a yellow towel knotted across my wayward chest, bright red mouth because even in the bath I've always said you need your Cherries. I looked at my lipstick short list pinned to the corkboard, unused, never to be seen by Holly, let alone the cosmetic-hungry public:

Pig Butt Called
Red Mist
Harvard Stripper
Surrender Dorothy
The Ripped Tutu
Love Is the Drug

And I kind of had an idea for a novel. I wiped off my lipstick and turned on the computer.

About the Author

EMMA FORREST is a novelist, screenwriter, and columnist. She lives in New York City.